FORBIDDEN DAUGHTER OF KASTEEL VREDERIC:

VOWS FROM THE BEYOND

BOOK SIX OF THE *KASTEEL VREDERIC* SERIES

"Forbidden daughter returns as the blessed daughter by crossing the door of death and entering through the door of life."

Ann Marie Ruby

Disclaimer:

This book ("*Forbidden Daughter Of Kasteel Vrederic: Vows From The Beyond*") in no way represents or endorses any religious, philosophical, political, or scientific view. It has been written in good faith for people of all cultures and beliefs. This book has been written in American English. There may be minor variations in the spelling of names and dates due to translations from Dutch or Indian provincial dialects, regional languages, or minor discrepancies in historical records.

This is a work of fiction. Names, characters, places, and incidents are the product of the author's imagination or are used fictitiously. Any resemblance to actual persons, living or dead, is purely coincidental. While the cities, towns, and villages are real, references to historical events, real people, or real locations are used fictitiously.

Published in the United States of America, 2022.

ISBN-13: 979-8-218-03718-5

DEDICATION

"Forbidden by the unforgiving mouth of the blistering toughened soul, yet as time passes by, remorse takes over the actions committed. It is then we recite our vows from the beyond as, 'I shall never let you go, if only you were mine.' Yet remember all actions of life must meet up with the wagon of karma."

"If only you were mine," is recited by the twin flames looking for one another throughout time. Yet this line is also recited by the children longing for their parents who have abandoned them. Life is a journey where we make mistakes and try to live with our committed mistakes. Misunderstood events of life take our journey of life through the dark alleys we can't forgo, forgive, or forget. Forgiving oneself takes the effort of rectifying the wrong done by oneself. Yet the wagon of time only moves forward not backward.

The question we live with is how we rectify the past that has moved on to the future. It is then we know we must get acquainted with the wagon of karma. For facing karma and knowing it is our own boomerang that comes back at us will ease the pain and sufferings of the mind, body, and soul.

The wagon of karma follows us throughout our life. Yet what happens when life is no more? Does karma follow us through rebirth? Does karma come and haunt down our future generations? Can we find forgiveness for our actions and maybe escape being captured within the hands of karma? I wonder if karma could follow us even beyond reincarnation. I know the memories of karma remain intact, even when our memories fail us. So, I do believe forgiveness is given throughout time if we can accept the gifts or punishments of karma.

FORBIDDEN DAUGHTER OF KASTEEL VREDERIC: VOWS FROM THE BEYOND

One small mistake committed intentionally or unintentionally takes us upon the wagon of karma. The rejected children of this world suffer all their lifetime by being called names. Yet remember the wagon of karma shall follow and not knock upon the child but the parents who had wronged the child and the people who had wronged the child.

Today I watch all the children around the globe who wait to find a home. A place where they can safely lay down in their own comfortable beds. A place they know their loving mother and father will feed them, so they don't go to bed hungry. A place where they are not rejected.

The term illegitimate child of the society has changed its name through time and tide. Yet the taboo behind this term still exists around the globe. Through the whispering winds of the ignored voices, I hear the children ask, seek, and knock upon doors screaming with their small unheard voices, "Why is it I am illegitimate, if I too am a creation of the Creator?" The answer too remains in this one line, "If only you were mine."

When a child is not accepted by the parents or the cruel society, the child then becomes the forbidden child. For throughout time, the child says, "If only you were mine." So, in my *Kasteel Vrederic* series, I have shown a forbidden daughter who never held any grudge against her family or home where she was not allowed to enter alive. Only upon her death was she able to enter her father's home, the home she waited all her life to be accepted within.

The beloved father who too waited to hold her at least once did not stay away. He had searched for her throughout her living life yet only in vain. She had finally met him but only after she closed her eyes and went to sleep. A father had brought his daughter back home. He refused to believe she was gone for he lived within her shadows all of his life. Yet life is not just or fair all the time. A small mistake committed by the arrogant objecting humans could lead to a lifelong regret.

The forbidden daughter became the protector of her predator. The daughter who never got recognition, became the family tree whose child had continued the family lineage. The forbidden daughter along with her twin flame never left the Vrederic household that had welcomed her only after her death.

The famous spirit of Kasteel Vrederic she had become to only protect her family that had never accepted her in life. Yet she protected her family even after death. So today in honor of the forbidden daughter of Kasteel Vrederic, I bring back the forbidden daughter and her parents. For I believe in forgiveness. Yet I also believe sometimes it takes not one lifetime but maybe more than one lifetime to bring back forgiveness to heal a family. Remember, we all must face the wagon of karma.

For life to be balanced into equal fairness, there we face the wagon of karma. People shout and call karma with profane words. Yet we all must remember we are the ones who have placed the wagon of karma on autopilot with our committed actions. As I personally believe in karma, I know the family members of the Vrederic household too will have to meet up with karma.

Karma will tell this world no child of the Creator is illegitimate. For I know karma will allow all the children of this world free rides in its wagon. The love and bond children have with karma's relatives who are truth, just, and honor are eternal. You the children of this world are never forbidden but are blessed by karma to enter the wagon of karma.

Let's enter Kasteel Vrederic once more and see how the inhabitants too must face up to the wagon of karma even though the wagon of time has brought them away from the seventeenth century to the twenty-first century. Time and tide pass by us yet karma follows our footsteps as we have created the path to our chosen destination.

This book was written with love. For where there is love, there is pain and forgiveness. So, I know Jacobus Vrederic van Phillip too waits with love and forgiveness in his heart, the heart that gives everyone without asking, yet keeps all of his emotions hidden within. As he awakens with forgiveness, let's see how the wagon of karma too comes and visits him.

In this book, as I keep love as the eternal nectar, twin flames are the eternal rising flames. Dreams, the path all dream scholars walk upon for guidance. Reincarnation, the ultimate blessing when twin flames unite. Yet here I have brought the ultimate path of life we all must walk upon and cannot avoid. If not in one life, then we will meet up with our twin flame in another life. I bring to you the wagon of karma.

I believe in karma, and its course is like a storm we all don't wait for, yet must meet up with. So, I have created another love story wrapped up in a family drama where the family members are at times magical, at times they travel time, they dream about one another, they have fought against witch burnings and the unjust wars, and they have solved murder mysteries too. Yet in this book as the eternally beloved twin flames Jacobus Vrederic van Phillip and

Margriete van Achthoven find one another, they too must meet up with the wagon of karma.

As Jacobus keeps on reminding himself and all of you through his diary, he committed one mistake, and that mistake turned his life into a nightmare. The love he waited for all of his life, their child, was lost through the waves of karma. So, I dedicate this book to the wagon of karma.

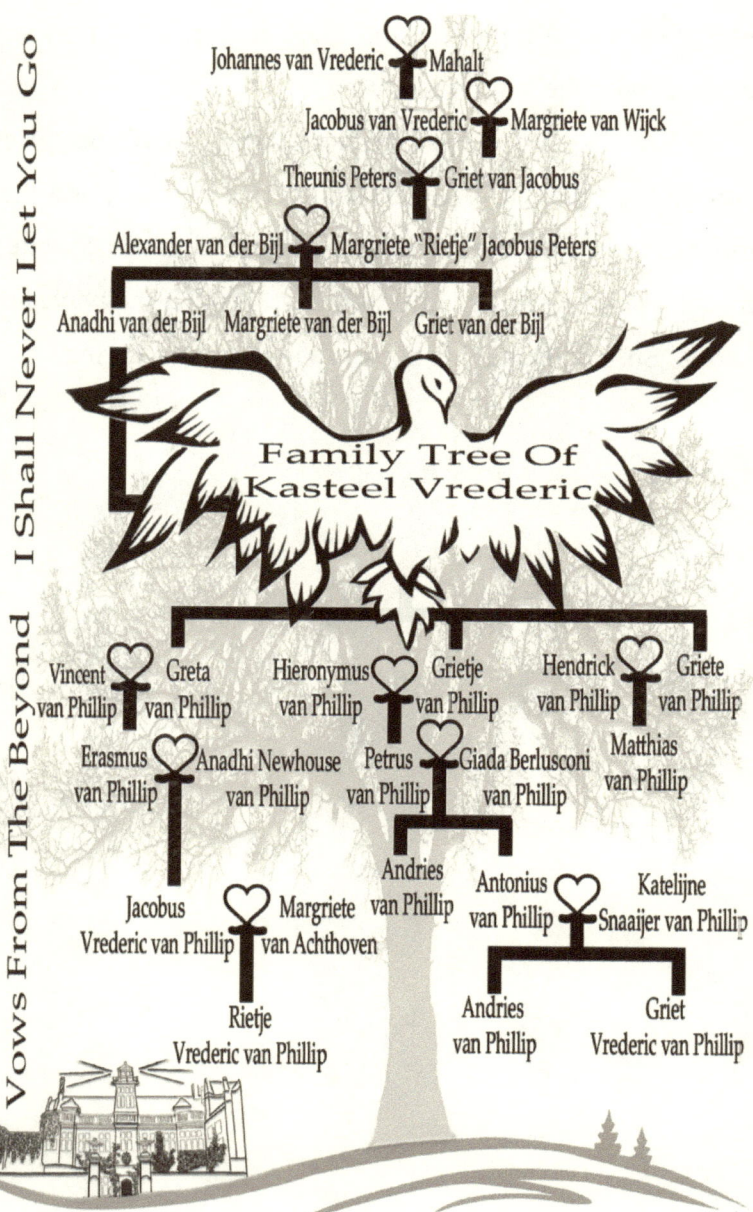

Vows From The Beyond — I Shall Never Let You Go

Johannes van Vrederic ❤ Mahalt

Jacobus van Vrederic ❤ Margriete van Wijck

Theunis Peters ❤ Griet van Jacobus

Alexander van der Bijl ❤ Margriete "Rietje" Jacobus Peters

Anadhi van der Bijl   Margriete van der Bijl   Griet van der Bijl

Family Tree Of
Kasteel Vrederic

Vincent van Phillip ❤ Greta van Phillip   Hieronymus van Phillip ❤ Grietje van Phillip   Hendrick van Phillip ❤ Griete van Phillip

Erasmus van Phillip ❤ Anadhi Newhouse van Phillip   Petrus van Phillip ❤ Giada Berlusconi van Phillip   Matthias van Phillip

Jacobus Vrederic van Phillip ❤ Margriete van Achthoven   Andries van Phillip   Antonius van Phillip ❤ Katelijne Snaaijer van Phillip

Rietje Vrederic van Phillip   Andries van Phillip   Griet Vrederic van Phillip

TABLE OF CONTENTS

PROLOGUE:

One Mistake

"Mistakes become memories, yet if both travel to the future with the beholder, what happens to the memories, the mistakes, and the beholder? Does life give him a second chance to rectify his one mistake?"

Dr. Jacobus Vrederic van Phillip treasures his past-life memories of his beloved within his chest, all wrapped up in dried tears.

FORBIDDEN DAUGHTER OF KASTEEL VREDERIC: VOWS FROM THE BEYOND

The foggy mist around our home has not lifted ever since we came back home. It's strange as we never left our home yet traveled time and back all within the walls of our home. I wonder is there a mist around the house, or us who have all awakened from our sleep like a jolt of electricity touched us? Or was it just my own feelings?

I want to run back to the *Evermore Beloved* garden, where all of my ancestors are sleeping ever so peacefully. I too am sleeping over there, yet here I am standing as I traveled through the door of reincarnation and am very much alive. I want to awaken one particular person. I wonder why she is sleeping so peacefully while I have a storm brewing inside of me. Time has separated me from the love of my life.

I am still standing in the same house, yet time has moved on. Then I ask my beloved Margriete, "Why can't I move on without you?"

For you I have written this love story. I know love stories need two halves to become one and complete. Yet who says love stories are only made through two halves? Have you not heard there are love stories solely written out of tears? Well, my love story is written with tears.

Memories and tears are my companions as I write and remember our love story. A love story where I had lost our only child, the last symbol of our love story. My one mistake gave her the name "Forbidden Daughter Of Kasteel Vrederic."

I hope in this life as I let the tears become dried roses for you, maybe you will follow the rose petals and come back into my life. Through your blessed hands, may our daughter too find her way back to our home. I will get the path made out of rose petals ready for you and our child, through my dried tears. Here is a poem for you, hidden within the pages of my diary.

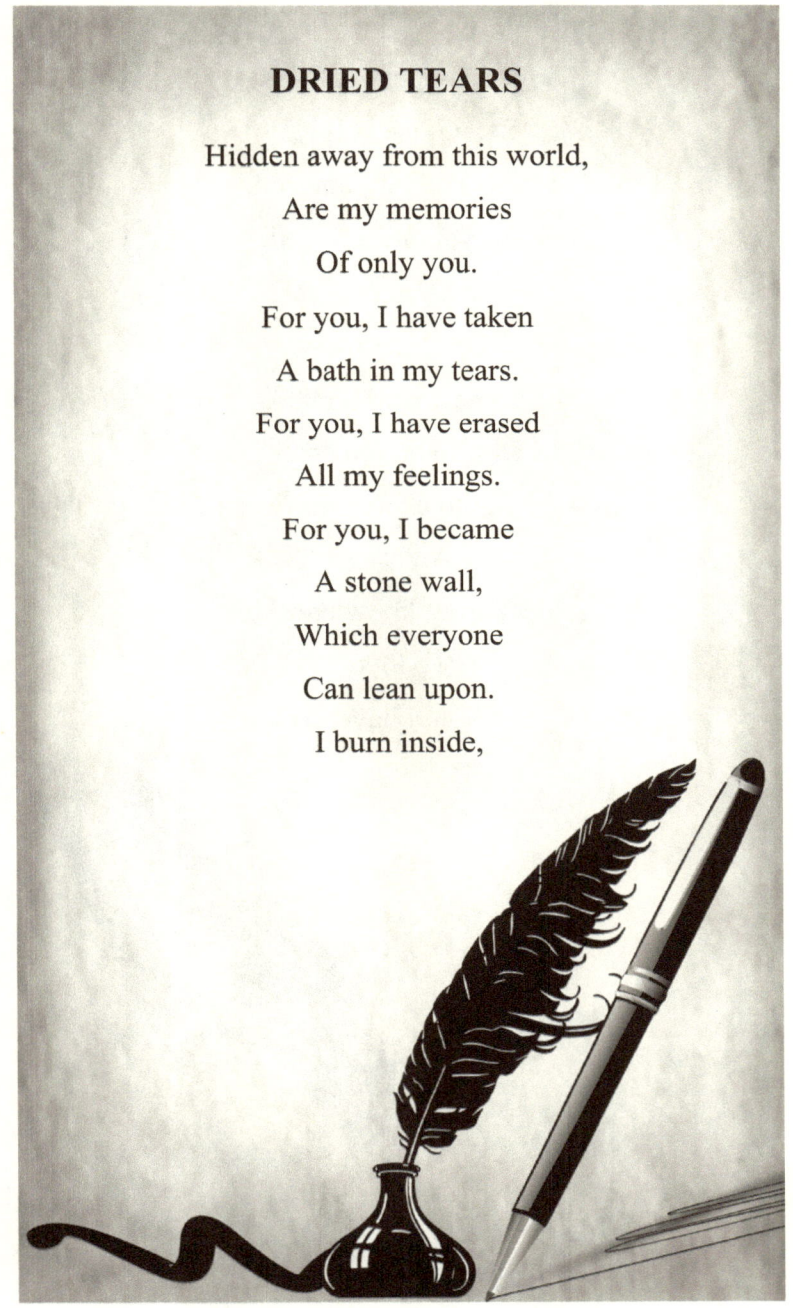

DRIED TEARS

Hidden away from this world,

Are my memories

Of only you.

For you, I have taken

A bath in my tears.

For you, I have erased

All my feelings.

For you, I became

A stone wall,

Which everyone

Can lean upon.

I burn inside,

So, I can pour out light,

So, no one gets lost

On their path.

For you my beloved,

I have become the

Dry river rock.

So now my beloved,

Don't you too come

And charge me

And say,

I don't know how

To love.

For you, I have made

Myself a soulless lover.

Remember my beloved,

For you, I chose

To become a stone.

I have no yearnings to

Recreate,

My love story,

With anyone else.

For my love story

Is made with only you.

As you are left in

My past,

My love story is also

Left with you,

In the past.

Today I write my love stories,

Not with anyone physically,

Yet through my memories

Of only you,

Which are eternally,

Printed upon my soulless chest,

With my,

DRIED TEARS.

FORBIDDEN DAUGHTER OF KASTEEL VREDERIC: VOWS FROM THE BEYOND

Wrapped in your memories, my beloved home, Kasteel Vrederic feels lonely and empty, even though our home is filled with my family members. Erasmus van Phillip, the famous painter, is my father. The dream psychic, Anadhi Newhouse van Phillip, is my mother. I am proud to be their son. My brother, the famous blind painter who was gifted sight through his biological twin brother, now through the door of miracles and reincarnation has his brother back as his son. Yet somehow everything feels different.

I have everything a man could want yet I feel empty inside. It's a thirst I want to quench yet nothing satisfies it. This diary is about my arrogant and ignorant heart which must learn to feel without touching. It's about my eyes that must learn to see without actually opening my eyes. It's about my cold heart which must hear the musical notes of my beloved, even though there are no musical notes playing. Yet how does a cold ruthless person do that? The person who had awakened my cold soul with her soft touch is nowhere near me. The only person in this world whom I could see, feel, or hear without seeing, touching, or hearing is missing. I don't know if she even exists in this lifetime.

My heart beats her name, yet I see her lying asleep on top of my lifeless body, not willing to let go of the promises we had made. All around are forget-me-nots growing yet my memories only remember her from my past life. I wish I could just rip the invisible wall that separates us and fall asleep with her in that world. I know I did fall asleep before her over there. Still my heart cries for her. I can't get a grip of myself. Sometimes I wonder if a cardiologist like myself who works with the heart could block my heart from feeling anything. I was known as the cold, heartless person of the sixteenth century, yet I wonder then why does my heart still call out for the love of my life from that century?

I must follow my mother's given lessons, my father's gentle strokes, and my brother's magical senses to awaken myself for the woman for whom my heart beats and is my destiny. Yet what if I don't recognize her for her? How could I even look at other women when I have only you in my mind, body, and soul? I wish I could rip my soul apart and erase your memories within. Yet I know I could never do that either as within my chest I have kept your memories alive. Your heart beats as my heart beats and within this rhythm I live my life for myself and for you too, my beloved Margriete.

A bang on the door had opened my bedroom door. I watched my very petite mother, with long black hair and beautiful grace walk into my room. She was still wearing her kaftan nightdress that I had brought back from my trips through India. She loves it as she reminds me, she is half-Indian and half-American. She is the only woman who would enter without even knocking or giving any notice.

The morning sun poured inside breaking the morning fog as I saw my mother did not look even a day over thirty years old. She had something on her mind as she was not all over the kitchen making all different breakfast items for us. I let her stand in the sunlight as I knew my heart also beats for this woman.

I reminded her every morning as I said, "Mama's heart beats Jacobus."

She laughed and said, "My heart had only your name as I searched for you my baby boy. Yet life was a blessing and now I have three boys, whom my heart beats for now equally. Strange but it's different from how my heart beats for your Papa. You will know as you find your twin flame once again."

She came and kissed my head, then she kissed my heart. I too kissed her head as I got up and sat next to her and let her talk. I placed my head on Mama's lap as she rubbed my forehead like she always did from childhood.

She said, "Jacobus, I hope you don't ignore Margriete. Even though you don't know her, maybe you should look beyond her face. I had a dream where you were young, and she was old. You were once again losing her as she was dying. I was young and so was Erasmus. It was strange and weird, yet you were crying as you did not recognize her and had lost too much time. Before you knew it, she was again lost to you. I worried all throughout my dream. I kept on saying to go back in time and change history. We might have changed ourselves and might lose more than we bargained for. Please try to see her from your inner soul not through your earthly eyes."

I would try to see through my heart and inner soul to find my Margriete. To read anything or write the prescription for my sister-in-law Katelijne Snaaijer van Phillip, I, however, needed my reading glasses. My sister-in-law Katelijne had changed her last name from her maiden name to van Phillip with Papa's blessings. She said she feels good carrying this name, as if it always belonged to her. I know Mama also accepts her and loves her as a daughter, not just a daughter-in-law. In my heart, I too have given her a sister's place.

I knew Katelijne would need her prescriptions refilled. Yet I didn't know where I left my reading glasses. I could only think of my mother.

I asked her, "Mama! Do you know where my reading glasses are? I need them. I have to order some prescriptions online for some of my patients. I need to go over the charts before I do anything."

Mama looked at me annoyed and said, "Jacobus, I can't find mine, so I took yours. We have the same vision, so I just borrowed them."

I wanted to say Mama, don't share glasses. It's not right. But I knew I could never say anything to my mother.

She kissed my head and said, "I will give them back after I can find mine."

I told her, "Don't worry, I have spares."

She said, "All right my child, I will keep them."

I watched Papa walk in and sit next to me. He said he too had a dream. He did not even wait for anything as I knew he already knew what Mama had seen.

He said, "My dream was weird, as everyone in the house was looking for the spirits of Kasteel Vrederic and the forbidden daughter. For some reason everyone had stopped aging and somehow Margriete was aging faster than normal as if she was getting older and dying. I cried and asked the forbidden daughter to forgive us. I told her she was never forbidden as we were the ones who should have been forbidden to have such an honorable child. It was my mistake, my arrogant mind that could only think of your mother and I forgot that we live in a family, a society. By opening my heart to one person, the beloved twin flame of my life, I actually had wronged my whole family. For then I had closed my heart to you and your beloved wife. My memories were wiped off by my physical and emotional illness. My grief had overwhelmed me with the memories of your mother. I know your mother would not have allowed this if she was alive in that life. This is why we have another chance to right what we had wronged."

I watched both my parents and knew something was wrong as I too saw the same dream. I did not want to share with them what I saw as I knew then it would only make them worry. For I saw Margriete was getting old and I was still young. I also thought we could not pick up Griet from the boat as she was a baby and floated away toward another boat. I watched my brother Antonius van Phillip swim after the boat and scream he would not give up. He never had a chance to fix the situation as he was not there in that lifetime. But he would not let my daughter just float away.

Then with a loud bang, my brother Antonius ran in and sat on the same bed next to Mama. I swear if he was younger and not a man of six feet and two inches in height, he would have jumped on top of Mama's lap. His bond with Mama is still the same as were all of our bonds. Even his son, the reincarnation of our brother Andries van Phillip, still

14

behaves as if he never died and actually is the same Andries of his last life. Only time moved on yet nothing else changed.

He said without trying to hide any emotion, "Big Mama, I saw I stopped aging and I saw Margriete was here and she was dying. I called the spirits of Kasteel Vrederic but they were missing. Big Mama, I walked back into the tunnel and I saw there was a child there who was crying in fear. She said she was the forbidden daughter of this home. She said she was lost as she was forbidden to enter this home and if she can't enter this home, then she would be lost. So, I told her no daughter of this home is ever forbidden but the blessed daughter of this home as I too am a son of this home. I then brought her through the tunnel on my shoulders just like I had brought Big Bro Jacobus back. Yet I placed her in my bed next to Katelijne as the child was terrified of being lost and alone in the tunnel all by herself. She said she was walking toward the lost and forbidden world. I told her never would I allow my niece or a daughter of this home to be lost. Then my dream broke."

I let everyone talk and stayed calm as that was my job as a physician. I must think and wait for scientific proof, not walk with just dreams. That day I had left my home and went to the hospital where I got busy with my patients. Yet I wondered, what if you do stop aging and your twin flame, your eternally evermore beloved, does not? What if time traveling caused us to stop aging? Would a person stop loving his twin flame if she was walking toward the door of death and he can't enter the door of death?

This diary is about an arrogant man who after hundreds of years had found his twin flame once again. Yet arrogance is not a virtue and ignorance is what made me a man I even dislike to see in the mirror. For in this diary, you will see how I refused to recognize her for her. Blinded by my love for her kept me from recognizing my twin flame as her. Yet as I do finally recognize her, I realize our time together is again to be only temporary. How do I hold on to her as for me time holds still yet for her time and tide just pass by leaving behind only memories?

Who could help us this time as the spirits of Kasteel Vrederic are missing? Where would we find someone who could guide us through this dark tunnel?

From the beyond again arrives like a fog the forbidden daughter of Kasteel Vrederic. This diary is my love story as this story began in the tunnel of light. A time traveling, reincarnated family now fights for time to not stand still for them as their loved ones would find time and tide never hold back for anyone. Another immortal love story where time and space are the enemy.

16

FORBIDDEN DAUGHTER OF KASTEEL VREDERIC:
VOWS FROM THE BEYOND

Traveling through the tunnel of light, I had journeyed through the doors of death, reincarnation, and birth. Finally, I had arrived in my parents' home through the door of rebirth as my mother's love and prayers broke down the skies above and Earth beneath to unite a mother and son in this lifetime. Through grace in this lifetime, I had united my parents, I had been able to unite my brother with his twin flame, and I had through the door of dreams united my granddaughter and her beloved twin flame.

Now I must not repeat what I, an arrogant introvert, had done ruining my previous life. I must find a way to unite with my twin flame in this lifetime. I want to raise our child, the forbidden daughter, as the blessed daughter, yet how when I don't even recognize her? I ask myself is she wearing a veil, or am I?

The one mistake I had committed in the sixteenth century as Jacobus van Vrederic still haunts the reincarnated form Jacobus Vrederic van Phillip in the twenty-first century. I had ignored my twin flame and our beloved daughter and gave her up. Searching for our daughter all my life could not unite a father, a mother, and a daughter. I could not bring my child back home while she was still breathing.

I, the unfortunate father, had brought back home the lifeless body of my daughter known to this world as the forbidden daughter of Kasteel Vrederic. Yes, it was my one mistake that had written the diaries of my family members for centuries. Who says everything ends as life ends? For my mistake had touched the lives of my ancestors and even now is haunting my current generation and will haunt even the future generations, if not liberated for in this lifetime. Yet how do I find my Margriete and our daughter and change the future even though the past still shall remain the same?

My dear child, my only daughter Griet, I have heard your words in my dreams for thousands of nights. I watch you cry and ask me why I had let you go. How could I tell you if I had one more chance, I would hold you within my inner chest and never let you go?

I can still hear your sweet little voice say, "If only you were mine Mama and Papa, I too would place my hand in yours. Yet like the forget-me-nots, I shall bloom and protect my home with a lantern in my hand as the forbidden daughter of Kasteel Vrederic."

I am Jacobus Vrederic van Phillip, the reincarnation of Jacobus van Vrederic, and this is my diary. I call this diary, *Forbidden Daughter Of Kasteel Vrederic: Vows From The Beyond.*

Dear Margriete, Griet, and Rietje,

FORBIDDEN DAUGHTER OF KASTEEL VREDERIC: VOWS FROM THE BEYOND

The three women who had taken away my heart. My wife, my daughter, and my granddaughter. I wish I could hold on to all of you and say I am sorry for the one mistake I had made. I let my daughter go in fear of losing you as I eventually lost you. I feared what was not there, yet my arrogance paid a huge price throughout time. I still am very arrogant and hope I don't commit the one mistake that had robbed me of my honor as I was an honorable man who only lived for honor and just. Here is a poem I had written for you three if maybe one day you would find this and know my heart still beats for all of you.

-Jacobus Vrederic van Phillip

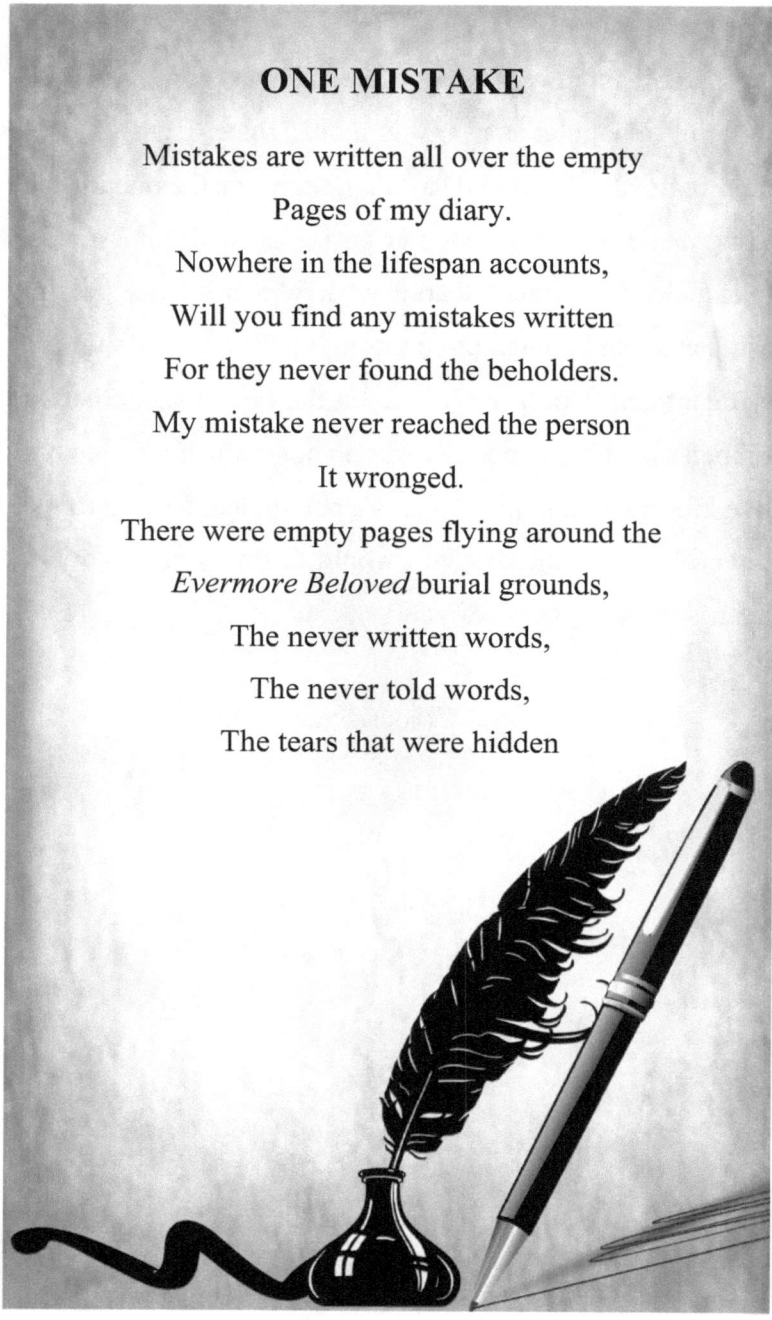

ONE MISTAKE

Mistakes are written all over the empty

Pages of my diary.

Nowhere in the lifespan accounts,

Will you find any mistakes written

For they never found the beholders.

My mistake never reached the person

It wronged.

There were empty pages flying around the

Evermore Beloved burial grounds,

The never written words,

The never told words,

The tears that were hidden

From the person I had wronged,

Were all planted near the burial grounds

As forget-me-nots.

For the blue flowers told my stories in the wind

As they danced and said I am sorry.

They cried under the rain

As their tears told a story,

Of a grumpy man who regretted,

Who lived with,

Who died with,

And who was reborn with,

All the memories

Of my,

ONE MISTAKE.

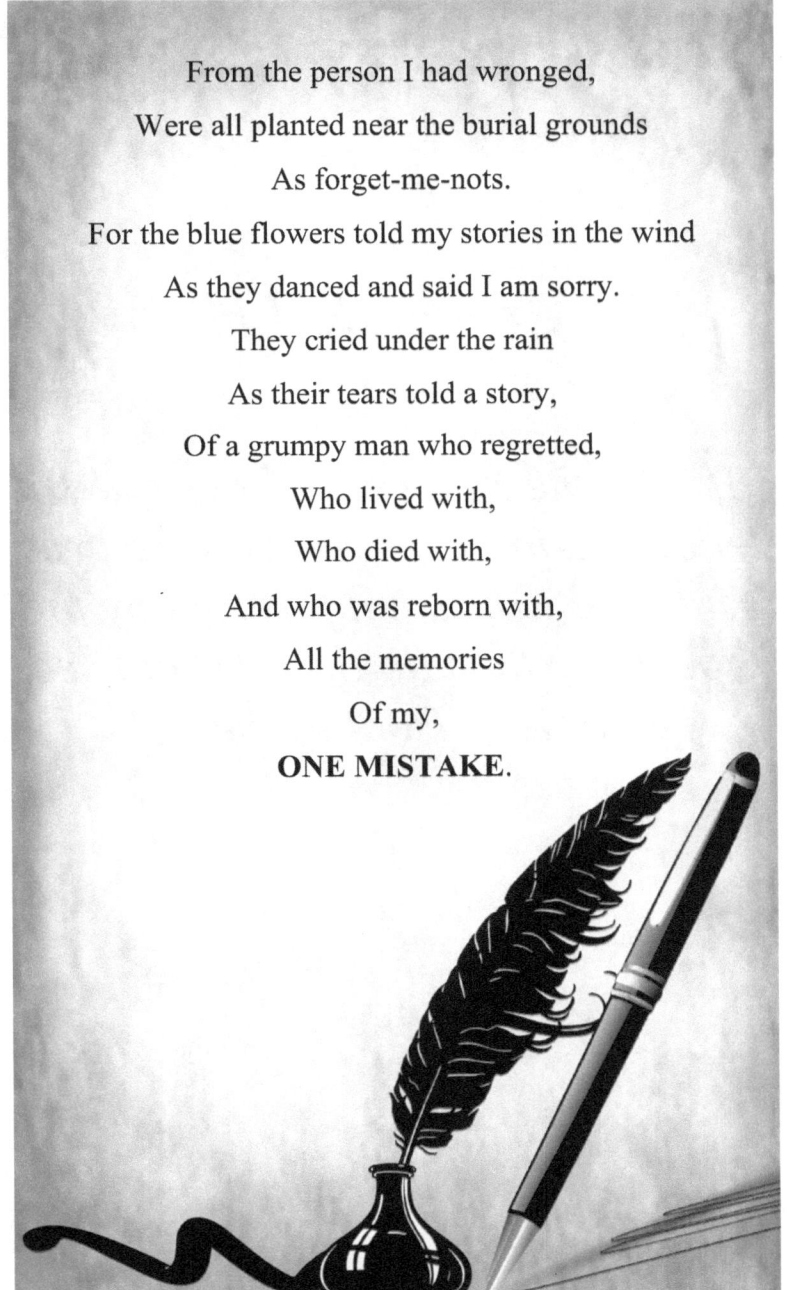

CHAPTER ONE:

The Concealed Heart

"If only the heart could see and not let our vision express. Yet, the eyes retell the words not foretold by the lips. How then do the eyes not see what is in front of them?"

Dr. Margriete van Achthoven sees in the reflection her past life's image of herself. If only her beloved could see she is the same person born with a different face.

The fog covered Naarden, the Netherlands, and our home which backs up to a lake. My forefathers had converted some parts of our land to accommodate a mystical lake with weeping willow trees covering it like an arbor.

The centuries-old oaks are meditation chambers as my mother believes people can attain self-realization by meditating under centuries-old trees. For the trees were there before us and so they will still remain at the same spot even after our time. This lake was created through years of hard work where my ancestors used a dam to divert some quantity of river water to our lake. Tulips, anemones, and calla lilies dance in the winds as the colorful roses remind all visitors this is Lake Vrederic, as named by my ancestors.

Memories of time traveling through the tunnel of light bother me. As a doctor, I do believe in dreams, yet my personal experience bothers me. I know somehow my family and I have changed history, so my family members don't cease to exist. Yet I wonder have we changed the future too by performing this act?

My heart had an empty space where I had placed my beloved Margriete within. All my love my dear beloved, I have given you. Eternally I shall keep this chest empty only for you. In seclusion, where no one can see me, I will shed my tears for you. Yet I will through my memories love you and hold on to you my evermore beloved. No one will ever be able to take your place, as I don't need anyone in this life reminding me of you or our eternal love story but your memories.

When a certain person called Margriete comes and enters our home referring to herself as my Margriete, it infuriates me beyond my character. The very arrogant and selfish Jacobus van Vrederic is now the loving son Jacobus Vrederic van Phillip. I will protect my family members from your evil hands gently in a gentlemanly way. I don't know what you want but you will never have me or win my heart, as my own Margriete has taken all the available space of a twin flame.

The morning fog covered my home and it actually allowed the fog within my chest to be lifted a little. I wondered why the skies were covered in fog. Was Mr. Sky missing his beloved, so he too had a heavy heart? My family members' dreams had bothered me for a while as they kept on repeating the same dream ever since our return from the tunnel of light. I had chased away the fake Margriete from our home very rudely. I did not even ask my parents if she was okay or if she did go home safely.

Voices came in from the carriage house that was converted to guest quarters. I wondered how we had guests in the house, yet I had no clue of who was inside and who went out. I knew Uncle Matthias had returned from India and had taken the room of his childhood in the main house. I never questioned anyone about all of these things as I usually left the home and am often traveling overseas for days on medical emergencies with Doctors Without Borders, or as a surgeon performing emergency surgeries for free.

Then I saw Mama come running toward me in a panic. She said, "I can't believe you have been so insolent. You don't even care about your own nephew, your brother. You know Andries is my life and whatever this world says I don't care. He is a part of my soul. He is not well and why is it you can't fix him? Go do something and make sure he is completely healed; you do call yourself a doctor, right? Jacobus say something, you were again passed out for days and on top of treating you, the poor girl has been treating Andries too."

I was in a state of shock. What was wrong with my nephew? He is a part of my soul too. Yet I wondered who was treating him? And where was I again? I can't believe myself, how was it that I have been passing out for days?

My father walked in and said, "Anadhi, leave my son alone. You had a fever Jacobus, and you were in and out for days. The doctor had said your fever has passed and you are doing well. It's your first time walking through the tunnel of light, and we were told by the doctor since you had found your twin flame and again had witnessed her death, it's normal to be in shock. Yet she did say not to keep your feelings to yourself but rather talk about it and release the pressure."

I watched both my parents and told them, "I am just tired from traveling and something called jet lag. I was working with the police to solve the murder mystery of my brother which is still an open case as some things did not add up. I will be fine Mama and Papa. Who is treating me and for what? Also, what's wrong with my nephew and why was I not told?"

That's when I watched Antonius come in and said, "Big Bro, come quick. It's Andries, he is shaking, and we don't know what is wrong with him. He is a healthy boy, yet something is not right."

I ran to my nephew's room, where I saw the windows were open and the room smelled like fresh bread and had the fragrance of a woman's perfume in it. I was familiar with my mother's perfumes as she always uses her Vincent Camuto

27

ones. Nothing else would please her other than any Vincent Camuto perfumes. Katelijne also picked up the same ones as my mother takes it upon herself to gift everyone the perfumes she loves smelling.

The bundle of joy was on his mother's lap which was strange as he always stays with Mama but only goes to his mother if he is not feeling good. He calls his own mother "Woman" and Mama "Big Mama." The little joy of our home jumped up as he saw me walk through the room.

He said with a sudden pouring of tears, "Big Bro, fix me! I am scared. Why were you not here to fix me? I can't believe it! I am not well and where were you?"

I recalled my memories and knew my brother Andries was in there as with all his problems or not, he would walk into my office and say, "Fix me Big Bro." Yet when he did need me, I was not there. I felt like there was more to it than anyone else could see. I then saw a different flowery perfume that smelled like jasmine flowers was on a doctor who was sitting next to my little brother, now nephew.

She jumped up at my sight and said, "I never left this home as you had asked me to the other night, because Andries is my patient. I am his doctor. Yes Jacobus, as you know, I too am a cardiologist; however, I am also a pediatric cardiovascular surgeon."

Margriete watched over me as if she was trying to get her thoughts together or maybe she wanted to calm herself down and not throw her anger back at me.

She said, "I own a clinic in Amsterdam where we treat everyone. No one is turned away for financial difficulties. I started to work at the Vrederic Children's Hospital as my aunt who owns an orphanage takes all her orphans there. I wanted to be there for the children. Jacobus, you are the only doctor I know who has multiple specialties. How you did it is a miracle and as a doctor myself, I look up to you for it. Yet I wanted to work with children and that's why I chose my field."

Mama watched us and said, "I begged her to stay as it was late and my son Andries and you Jacobus fell ill after the dream tunnel journey. I did not want others to think my family members are crazy as they get physically ill after a dream. Yet Margriete knows as she too was a witness in waking you up. She also has been treating my baby Andries ever since we came back. She has been residing in the guest house. She has no family members she needs to go and attend to, so she volunteered as she usually stays in the hospital staff quarters as an emergency physician. Yes

Jacobus, our family hospital's emergency on-call physician."

I watched her and saw she is a petite woman with olive-colored skin and long black hair. Her eyes are beautiful and big like she could see the inside of my soul. I watched her and knew she is the most beautiful woman my eyes had fell upon in this life. Yet I never noticed her in the hospital which I had made in my family's name.

I don't like to be formally called by my last name. So, all the doctors working at Vrederic Hospital and Clinic are called by their patients and one another by their first name. I asked referring to her by her first name, "Dr. Margriete, what is wrong with my nephew? I know he has no physical illness that we know of and has no allergies. He is not on any medication."

She watched me and said, "Physically, he is growing at a faster rate than normal humans grow. So, he is two years old, yet he is like a five-year-old boy physically. He speaks normally like a seven-year-old boy. His organs too are functioning like those of an older boy. It is like he is aging faster than normal. I believe medically it's not normal but could be because he was exposed to some kind of radiation or growth hormones but it's going to be headline news if anyone goes public with it. I believe you all had some kind of radiation while you all had traveled."

Margriete walked by the window and was watching the lake and the trees. She said, "Everything changes with time. The trees you had planted centuries ago have all grown up and are still there witnessing you again in this life. It seems like they too knew you would return and just waited for you. I feel like Big Mama's prayers were answered and Andries has returned and is taking on his age faster than normal. It's a miracle and as with miracles, there usually is no medical evidence we could provide. Miracles are just that miracles, not believed by a lot of medical doctors yet are believed by all humans, doctors, and all others alike."

She then stared at me directly and said, "Andries will need help with his unusual growth and the physical impacts of it need to be monitored closely. Yet as of today, he has no physical problems, just the emotional toll of becoming a boy and maybe a teenager sooner than anyone had expected. He also is being impacted with his last life's memories. In reincarnation theories, it is believed children remember more in their childhood about their past-life experiences, then tend to forget as they age. However, some people remember everything and don't share, and some remember slowly."

31

I watched her as she just stood there watching me. I told everyone, "I will examine him myself and attend to him. I believe this is a family matter and we will survive and take care of it ourselves. I appreciate Dr. Margriete van Achthoven's help and won't need it as we will keep everything in the family."

Antonius watched us and said nothing as he sat next to his son and held on to his hands. Papa did, however, say more than something.

Papa said, "Jacobus, I have personally asked Margriete to help with my child as I believe I need her help at this moment. If you would recall, it was Margriete who had helped with Katelijne's pregnancy and Andries's birth as we needed a doctor who could help and keep things private. She was there when Andries too had passed away and when Andries's reincarnated form had been born. She was the doctor who had spoken with all the reporters while Antonius, Andries, and Katelijne had gone through the police reports and news media. I want her to continue without anyone's given or not given permissions. Any personal feelings must be kept aside while all of my children's lives are at risk, including your life my son. This life I will not walk away from any troubles, but I will walk into all the obstacles and remove them any way I can."

I watched my family members as I saw Uncle Matthias walk in and hug Margriete. He then gave her a cup of coffee. He whispered something in her ears and was upset at her answer. My mother, however, did not let the matter go. She walked over closer toward them and gave both of them a stare. I thought at that moment even Uncle Matthias looked scared.

She asked, "What is going on? I am assuming Margriete did not have any breakfast or dinner from last night. Is that true Matthias?"

Uncle Matthias watched Papa for some kind of help, yet he got none. My uncle attired like an Indian yogi, with his dhoti, a batik tunic, and open sandals. He stood up and walked toward my mother. I saw the height difference, my uncle is a very tall man like Papa around six feet, four inches tall, while my mother is a five-foot-four-inch woman. I wondered how my mother made people feel at home or like a stranger in a minute.

Uncle Matthias hugged Mama and said, "How do you just know everything. Is it because you are a dream psychic or because your heart is so amazingly beautiful? I always wondered what would have happened if I had found someone like you, I would have never let her go. Yet I am happy I found Margriete and feel like maybe I have some hope left. Yet she calls me Uncle Matthias and I feel like I am her father whom she so misses, and wishes was still alive."

He went and sat near Andries as he said, "Why don't you all go and have some breakfast and I will stay with my favorite boy Andries. I have so much catching up to do. Also, Margriete is diabetic and must eat on time. It's our responsibility to make sure our invited guests or doctors are not kept in the household without proper food or drinks, even though famous doctors like my nephew Jacobus might want to interrogate our guests."

I watched my very openly spoken uncle and just smiled and told him, "I will sit by my little Andries as then everyone else can go and take a break. I also need to examine him."

I watched Margriete run in front of me as she said, "If you examine my patient, I must be there, so then I would be able to answer all of your questions. Also, I always carry my diabetic energy boosting bars for emergencies. I am fine, but we must make sure Andries is doing better as I don't want him to have a panic attack. He wakes up at night screaming and calling the same name as he keeps on saying a woman called Aideen Bakker is at risk as everyone has it wrong. Everyone will get it wrong and they will trust the

34

wrong people. Aideen is crazy and mental as she was in a mental hospital all of her life. Yet everyone will let go of the real goons. Who is this Aideen and why is Andries involved with her? Is she the same woman from before, who had harmed Katelijne and Andries?"

I heard what Margriete said yet I was so worried for Katelijne and Mama. I watched both of them as did Antonius and Papa. Somehow, we all went near Mama and knew we should take her out of the room. Margriete watched us and knew she had said something that had all of us go into panic mode. She watched me and then the doctor in her took over.

She said, "There is nothing to panic about as with children and reincarnation, they often remember things from their past life but at times could be missing a big part. At no time should any one of you go and start investigating or worry about anything before we are able to figure out the truth. I have worked with a lot of children who have had a hard time through reincarnation."

She went and held Mama's hands in her hands. Both were very petite and looked like sisters as Mama and Papa seemed like they were getting younger after we all returned from our dream traveling. Yet I watched two women talk with one another without saying anything. Katelijne was hugging Andries in her chest, like a mother who wanted to protect her son from all the troubles of this world. I watched Antonius say something to Katelijne as she brought Andries to Mama.

Mama then placed him in her chest and said, "Big Mama's heart beats Andries. I will never let you go my baby boy, for my love and prayers brought you back to me somehow, someway. Never shall we be apart ever again."

I remember as does Antonius how Mama had stayed night after night at the gravesite of Andries, crying when thunder or lightning would come down. A mother would cry for her son. I promised myself I would never let any harm come to my family or the members of Kasteel Vrederic, be it today, yesterday, or tomorrow.

Papa came and took Andries on his lap as did Uncle Matthias. It was then Papa said, "Margriete, please help him and tell us how we could help him and not let the past harm my child in this life."

Margriete came and held Papa's hands as she said, "The past is always there as a lesson. The present is there for us to deal with it today, so in the future we don't live with regret. What happened in the past will be dealt with as you all are ahead of the game. For now, your enemies have the victim standing in front of them, returned in flesh and blood with all of his memories. The predators don't know of this nor are they expecting anything like this to come and haunt them from the grave."

Margriete watched me and said, "It is hard as there are people who remember everything but are at times accused of lying and making up stories. Yet if you only believe, it is then you can move on forward without wasting any more time. The days are lonely, and the nights are frightfully lonelier. Yet it's then you move on with your own memories. They are your gifts, and no one can take them away from you."

I knew she was talking to me as did everyone in the room. I only told her in my mind, then live with your memories Margriete for I shall bury myself with the memories of my own Margriete. I said nothing as I know my family loves this woman for she has selflessly given so much of her life to my family for years. Yet somehow, I never got to see her, even though she was standing in front of me.

I let my feelings die inside of my ruthless heart as I knew right now, I need to find out how Andries was killed and who actually did this. By God, what if we had everything wrong and the real killer or killers were all roaming around free?

Antonius stood by my side and said, "Big Bro, the wagon of karma waits for no one. This family must repay for our committed mistakes. This family had once wronged a child and let her go and be called the illegitimate, the forbidden daughter of this home. We shall all be punished as we have wronged Griet and now the spirits of Kasteel Vrederic are missing. They even guided us through Andries and Katelijne's murder mystery. I know my ancestors had said the child can't enter this house alive and so she entered in a coffin. Today as we try to move on, I promise to all of you, I shall bring her back somehow, someway. For I know it's only then the ordeals and the sufferings of this home shall be over."

I watched my family members as I told them, "I still suffer for my one mistake, yet it's something I will keep on suffering for. I only wish Margriete was here to share the burdens and all the pain that come afterward with me. For I know I must find her and Griet and Rietje to end my sufferings and ask for forgiveness. Yet now I must protect Andries and find out who did this to our family."

Antonius watched me and said, "Big Bro, I am here with you, and I shall share the pain of the past and the present and the blessings of the future with you as we are brothers throughout time. Never shall I let you or Andries or Big Papa or Big Mama suffer by yourselves. For it feels so much better knowing we are all in the tunnel together, and like I told you,

I will carry you back through the tunnel if I have to, to keep my family together. We will find Margriete and solve who had done this to Andries together. You must believe in this and not have any doubts for only then shall we be able to move on."

Papa came and held both of us and said, "Mistakes are made by humans and they are forgiven by God as that's why we have this life to rectify what we have wronged and those we are still doing unjust to."

I watched Katelijne touch her womb and say nothing. I thought I heard a child cry and say, "Please let the world know I am not the forbidden daughter of Kasteel Vrederic but the beloved daughter."

Everyone looked up and saw there was a big torch, a light shining even in the morning hours as the fog never lifted throughout the day. We walked outside and there seemed to be a small child sitting in a cradle in the lighthouse. We watched like a movie and knew she was our forbidden daughter.

I watched Margriete faint at the sight as she uttered, "My child, won't I be able to raise you even in this life?"

I could not even move and hold on to the small petite woman in fear of falling in love with the wrong Margriete.

Yet I watched Papa hold her in his arms and take her into the house.

Antonius had tears in his eyes as he said, "My child, you will be back in this home and I shall raise you as my beloved daughter. Your Papa shall raise you as his godchild, I promise. Your Papa and your Opa had cursed you but your Uncle Antonius never did. As I promised you in the tunnel of light, I shall bring you back as I too am a son of Kasteel Vrederic, and Big Mama is my mother who taught me to believe in reincarnation."

I went inside and knew I must not fall for the woman who somehow reminds me of Margriete as how I could forget my Margriete? I screamed and let my frustration out as I was in my room. Mama, Papa, and Antonius were watching me as they said they found a note in Margriete's hands when she had fainted, tucked away safely within her chest. It fell out as Papa was carrying her and Antonius had found it. They left it in my room. The note was a poem written by Margriete to an unknown person, yet it said, "To my Jacobus, the eternally beloved and evermore beloved of my life."

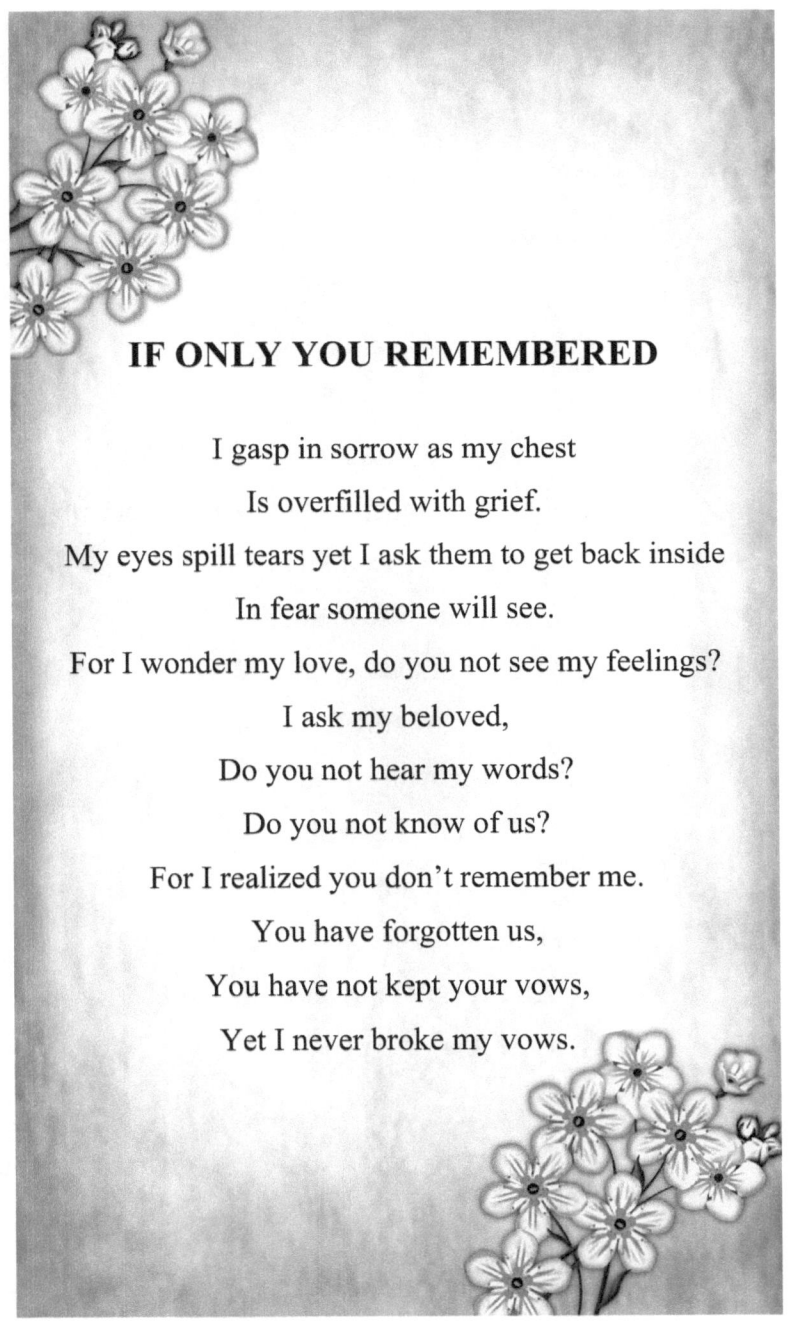

IF ONLY YOU REMEMBERED

I gasp in sorrow as my chest

Is overfilled with grief.

My eyes spill tears yet I ask them to get back inside

In fear someone will see.

For I wonder my love, do you not see my feelings?

I ask my beloved,

Do you not hear my words?

Do you not know of us?

For I realized you don't remember me.

You have forgotten us,

You have not kept your vows,

Yet I never broke my vows.

I kept them,

As you and I took them in my dreams,

Our promised vows.

My love, it hurts so much as I remember you,

Yet even in front of you,

I can't utter my memories.

In front of the only person

Who knows my feelings,

I remain silent.

For I do remember,

Yet I only wish,

If I could hold you once and share with you

All my untold memories,

All my hidden love stories,

All my unsung songs,

Yet it only could be,

IF ONLY YOU REMEMBERED.

-Margriete van Achthoven

I watched Antonius was still standing at my door. He came in and sat next to me on the sofa in my bedroom. He read my diary without asking and watched me for a long time.

Antonius my brave, loving, and honorable brother had said, "Jacobus it's good to conceal some feelings yet remember in this family we share all the secrets of one another. No secrets or hidden feelings. I know it hurts more than words could describe. Yet sometimes we just have to close the pain through sharing the wound. You my dear brother had told this brother of yours when I was still blind, it mattered not if I could not see because I could see through your eyes. Now Big Bro, even though I can see today, I can still feel through my sixth sense. Big Mama and Big Papa taught us to be completely honest with one another even when we don't agree. I would like to ask you to share your feelings. Please don't have the concealed heart."

I saw everyone had left me to be alone. My breakfast was sent into my room as everyone knew I needed time and so did Dr. Margriete. She must heal herself for the world needs devoted people like her. She needs to find her Jacobus wherever he might be while I need to find my Margriete wherever she may be. So today during a very foggy day, I too wrote a poem for my own Margriete to read when I do find her. For I know and believe I shall find her. I know if I was reborn again, then my Margriete, my twin flame who laid on top of me in the same burial ground, too must have been reborn again only for me. So, for you my beloved I write my hidden poems.

EVEN YOU

My heart throbs only for you.

Sleepless nights go by

As I stay awake wondering about you.

I ask the skies if you are cold and scared

As you sleep within the grounds.

Why have I awakened when,

You have not?

We went to sleep together,

Yet today I am alone.

My home is gifted with

Family members

Whom I love,

Yet why do I still feel so lonely?

I feel lost.

My heart hurts while I am awake,

It hurts even while I am asleep,

For my soul keeps on

Asking me a question.

What if I am wrong?

Are you there silently standing,

In front of me?

Why then am I refusing to see you?

I love you my beloved.

I live for my love.

I refuse to see maybe even you,

For would you not

Be angry if I, your beloved,

Watched and flirted

With another woman,

Making an excuse

As I thought her to be only you?

For you my love, I refuse to recognize

EVEN YOU!

CHAPTER TWO:

Effects Of Time Traveling

"Time travelers gain knowledge, yet they must come to a compromise and know through this journey, they have also lost so much. The compromise is knowing the stability between the loss and the gain."

Dr. Margriete van Achthoven asks the lightning bolt to take her life instead of her beloved's for it matters not he does not remember or love her, as she remembers and loves him.

FORBIDDEN DAUGHTER OF KASTEEL VREDERIC: VOWS FROM THE BEYOND

Today is another day, a new start, and a new beginning. The morning fog is nowhere in sight. It was a sunny and bright morning when I woke up today. I will close the doors to my own personal feelings. I will open the doors to my inner soul for my family members. My hands treat all who need my help, yet today I must close the door to Margriete and open another door where I am needed.

The Kasteel Vrederic library, where my family found the tunnel of light, was my sacred hideaway. The bookshelves, the study table, the sofa sets were all very warm and comfortable. The family portraits hanging on the six-hundred-plus-year-old castle remind me we actually did do the right thing. At any cost, our family tree must continue. So, I am extremely happy my younger brother is married and has a son. However, the feeling of something being wrong with Andries freezes my inner soul.

A sudden surprise actually stopped my feet on their track. A certain stranger bundled up in a hand-woven blanket was sleeping on the library sofa. I knew Mama always has guests and everyone is allowed to come into the library, which was my father's first, yet now I use it as he loves to work in his private studio next to their bedroom wing. The reason is my mother would wake up scared if she found out

Papa was missing. Anything about my mother brightens my inner soul and my day. My walking made creaking sounds on the old wooden floors. At the sounds, the stranger suddenly jerked up and we both screamed as I saw she was sleeping with a big stick in her hands.

Dr. Margriete, the stranger, kept on screaming. Then she said, "How dare you, a giant, enter my bedroom! Who do you think you are? Remember I am only here for a few days and as soon as I am not needed anymore or when or if my family members need me, I will be out. You are scaring me standing there so tall and looking at me like that. I sleep with a stick so I can tell the ghosts or thieves or crooks to not bother me while I am sleeping."

The sun was shining on her face as she somehow opened the thick drapes and let the morning sun come shining in. I watched the five-foot-maybe-four-inch-tall woman, who looked like a mix of Indian and Dutch heritage watch me with her green eyes or were they brown like Mama's eyes? She reminded me of my mother in some ways. My mother is a mix of Indian and Dutch-American heritage.

I asked her, "Are your eyes green or brown or black even though I know the color of eyes can't be black as they are actually dark brown? They are so mesmerizing."

She watched me and said, "They are brown, but my father's eyes were green so mine are just a mix. I told you my mother was of Indian heritage and my father was Dutch. Yet I was raised by my paternal grandmother in my parents' home in Scheveningen, The Hague. My parents went missing in a plane crash and never were found. I come from a rich family. Born into a well-off family, I had everything, yet I felt lonely. As an orphan, I knew I wanted to give company to other orphans, so they never feel the loneliness that had gripped me. I have an orphanage near Amsterdam where all children are welcomed and wait to be adopted. If they aren't adopted, then I take care of them. Also, Dr. Jacobus I am not mesmerizing for if I were, then I would have had my beloved with me somehow, someway."

She stopped and walked over to the windows as she watched the lake from the window and somehow went into silence.

She then said, "I hate dark rooms. They depress me, as do dark days. I wish I could just take this room and open up all the windows and place white curtains on them. The drapes would fly with the wind and the breeze would do wonders for one's health. Also, there could be a hammock on that big oak tree."

Margriete walked to another window and said, "That's Rietje's favorite tree. She had planted this tree centuries ago. She was a wild girl and loved to plant trees. It was a special time when actually Jacobus was away on missionary work. We did it to surprise him."

Then she stopped in mid-thought as she watched me and started to cry and just ran out of the library. She never let me say anything. I couldn't even argue with her and ask her how she knew the story of the oak tree when it's not even written anywhere nor spoken about. Actually, it even slipped my memories. I do remember little Rietje being so happy about the tree and how she wanted to surprise me. No one knew when or how it was planted as it was after Papa died in his last life as Johannes van Vrederic and before we all were born in this lifetime. Yet how she would know bothered me and I just wanted to justify it saying it's just a coincidence.

Antonius and Katelijne were waiting for me as I jolted out of my trance after being dumped in my own library by a stranger who thinks she knows the history of my forefathers. Antonius had a fresh cup of coffee in his hands which he was sipping from. I wondered why Mama never came with her morning coffee for me. It's a routine, either Mama brings me coffee, or I take it for her.

FORBIDDEN DAUGHTER OF KASTEEL VREDERIC: VOWS FROM THE BEYOND

I was eyeing my brother's coffee as he gave me his cup and said, "Here, have it. I had half. We can have fifty-fifty. Also, Big Mama and Big Papa had Andries in their bed last night. So, they are all sleeping in late. I saw Andries was much more relaxed with Big Mama than with any one of us. Margriete slept in the library to be close to Andries. I don't think the girl got any sleep at all. I really hope it did not bother you that she slept here."

I enjoyed my half of the coffee and watched my brother and his wife sit on the sofa Margriete was sleeping on just a while ago. I sat next to my brother and I knew I had to be strong for these two. Yet I also knew there was more they were not sharing with me. No one wanted to talk about the child's voice we all heard yesterday morning, as everyone was busy with Margriete and why she had fainted.

I told them, "No, it does not bother me who sleeps here as I actually like the woman's company. I don't know why though. Do either of you know why Dr. Margriete had fainted yesterday? Also, where did the child's voice come from? I know we live in a home which actually does talk or shows us things when we need them. Even though the Kasteel Vrederic spirits are missing, there now is a light glowing within the lighthouse lantern. How is it a child appears in it?"

ANN MARIE RUBY

Antonius got up and started to laugh as he said, "Big Bro, you know nothing is strange in this mystical home. People say all the mysteries in this world could have been solved if only walls could talk. In this house, walls can talk and do so much more. We all know if and where there is a problem, the lighthouse shines with or without the spirits. We asked her why she fainted, and she said it's because the lighthouse reminded her of her past life, her daughter, and her granddaughter. Big Mama told her it's because her twin flame was ignoring her in front of the lighthouse. She watched Big Mama and told her she is a medical doctor and could take care of herself."

I don't know why Antonius's words made me laugh out loud and I told them, "Antonius, I am a medical doctor too and I know at times we all need help. I know the truth of this home yet as a scientist as a medical doctor, I can't explain the scientifical aspects of it. None of this makes any sense."

Margriete came back in the room, freshened up, and had no traces of a long sleepless night on her. I knew in front of my eyes was standing one of this world's greatest doctors who placed everyone else before her own self. I had to keep on reminding myself not to be drawn toward her by her magical pull. I know I proved my Margriete was no witch last life during the witch hunts, yet I wondered if this one was a witch. Or else how did she pull me toward her like a charm? I was daydreaming about her while she stood in front of me. I wondered why and how I was being controlled by this charming witch.

She said, "I must talk about Andries as when no medical or scientific reasonings could be given, it's then we must look at the evidence in our hands. We have to work with treating the symptoms right now, while we try to figure out all the answers behind it. I want to monitor his heart rate as you will see it's fluctuating."

I told her, "I will personally work with you closely to figure out what's going on. Also, from where, when, and how did he get this? My conclusion is the tunnel of light somehow did something and I know it's not a scientifically backed solution nor any scientific reasonings could be given yet I know it's the truth."

Margriete watched me and said, "I agree Dr. Jacobus, I know it to be true as I am a witness. I walked into the room while you were all sleeping. There was a tunnel of light circling the room. I didn't know what to do but I somehow was burned by the light. I then saw you were having a hard time waking up and knew you needed medical help. Now I do understand I can't tell the world about what I saw or if I too will be affected by the light somehow. But all I know is you all needed my help and I will be there for you."

I worried if she too was affected by the light. It reminded me of the strange dreams my family members had about Margriete, how she was aging faster as Andries was aging faster too. Yet how come the dream had the rest of the family members not aging?

Margriete said, "Please come with me and examine him. His heart rate is not normal like what a toddler should have. Usually, toddlers have higher heart rates as they have small hearts, yet his heart rate is like that of a twelve-year-old child. Again, it is changing on a day-to-day basis. His oxygen level is normal, but he is having nightmares and I am worried his situation might get worse if we can't figure out what's wrong with him. He is stressing himself out through nightmares."

I got up and told her to follow me as I walked to my nephew's room. His parents, Mama, and Papa also came inside. I had asked everyone to step outside as I would examine Andries with Margriete. When we finished the examination, we decided he was completely healthy but had just aged overnight. I was so worried. I needed to convert my home into a lab and get all the supplies, I needed to do this.

I had to make some calls and get it done right away as things were getting out of our hands.

I was buried deep in my thoughts when Margriete said, "Jacobus, we need to check all of your family members. I am worried if there was some kind of radiation or something you all were involved with. If one member is having this kind of effects, then just maybe all of you will have some kind of effects. A child's body would react much faster than any adults and that's normal."

That's when we saw the lighthouse lantern above our home was blinking like crazy. The day was so sunny and bright, yet it was suddenly pouring rain and lightning was hitting our home. My mother and father were standing outside with me in the courtyard of Kasteel Vrederic. Antonius and Katelijne came outside as did my nephew Andries who looked more like five or six years old rather than two years old. It was then I saw my mother's two grandmothers who were both over one hundred years old and lived with us rather than an old people's home, came outside like they were in their seventies.

I wondered if the same radiation had affected them too as they were in and out of the room while we were time traveling. I noted in my head to get them checked up too. They saw the thunderstorm and one started to talk in Hindi and the other one in American English as they both said, "It's karma."

Uncle Matthias joined the group and said, "Looks like some kind of weird stuff is going on over here. What's new? It's Kasteel Vrederic and seems like even the castle is upset with us today. So dear home, please let us know how have we wronged you today?"

I watched my family and told all of them, "It's a thunderstorm and it shall pass, nothing magical or spooky. Everyone, please just calm down and don't panic."

My two great-grandmothers were walking in and out of the home like they could care less about what was going on around them. Somehow, they were busy in their own world.

Antonius screamed and said, "Big Bro, it's too late! We are already panicked overboard. Panicking has passed by us, now we are freaked out what's going on. If it is just a storm, then why is it only in our home and not anywhere else in the neighborhood? Someone will notice. That's it. We are going to be gone case, if even one outsider sees this. Okay they will say we escaped the witch trials but must be some sort of magicians or something."

Mama screamed and said, "Erasmus, fix it now! Fix my family members and all of you and your son's bad or good karma. Tell karma you are sorry for your doings of past lives. Apologize Erasmus now. Oh no! Watch the lighthouse and tell me what's going on in there."

A thundering lightning bolt shot out of the lighthouse and came near me. As I tried to balance myself, I saw Margriete with her small petite body stand in front of me.

She watched the lighthouse and said, "You can't take your anger-filled curses out at this man because all of this is my fault. Why don't you throw your curses and anger toward me? It was I who had gone mad and crazy as I lost you and your father. It's all my fault I sent you to your father and he had no clue I was even pregnant. Please send the curses toward me and let this man go. My curses were I could not even raise you with my own hands, I could not even touch you as I fell asleep, even though life never left my body."

I moved her away and told her, "Stop it! I don't know what you will get out of this, but you can't be my Margriete as I would know if you were. Also, I can take on my own curses and karma. Why do you want to kill yourself for a stranger like me?"

She watched me and I knew there was a storm inside of her as there was a storm brewing outside our home too yet nowhere else. I wondered what was going on as again I watched Margriete plead with the Lover's Lighthouse.

She repeated, "I call upon my own daughter to help me through this. For I know maybe even in this life I won't have my twin flame or you. So, I ask you, how could karma harm me, or harm the person who sent you away, or the grandfather who had not accepted you as he himself was not well? It's all the mistakes of life written only within the pages of my memories. I ask you to stop this boomerang and let me suffer even in this life but let this family be."

Mama got up and started to scream at Margriete as she said, "Dear child, it's not your fault that some arrogant men had their ways to kick out a woman when they so wanted or bring her in when they wanted to. It's all their committed mistakes and they have paid and lived a life or more for it. I don't believe karma is unjust and will haunt us in this life for mistakes we had no hand in."

Mama watched me and gave me the look and I knew I was in trouble. Antonius knew as he too looked away in fear of Mama's words now. Even little Andries laughed and knew I was getting it.

Mama continued to give us her famous stare and said, "I don't believe this is my granddaughter Griet. For she and her husband had vowed to be the protectors of this home, not the hunters. Also remember we did not have the children by ourselves, neither did Margriete as my son had slept with his married wife and had the child. So, mistakes had broken their home and separated their paths, they did not. I believe they paid for their mistakes already."

Mama watched the lighthouse and its fury and said, "I really don't believe our lighthouse is trying to harm us. Maybe it is trying to teach you a lesson Jacobus because time is running out and we need to bring back Griet somehow, someway. I only wonder, what if the lighthouse is trying to warn us that Griet would be lost in the tunnel of light, if we don't rush? That's how she is becoming the girl with the lantern. It's like you must love your daughter more than life Jacobus to let her go. Allow her to come back as she is permitted to come through the door of karma. Jacobus, set her free for only then will she come back to this house as a beloved daughter, not the forbidden daughter."

Antonius came near me and he held my hands as he said, "Please let me have her and let her go. Let me have Griet as I promised her in the tunnel, I will bring her back as the beloved daughter of Kasteel Vrederic not the forbidden daughter. Also, she told me she had no grudge but worried as she was not permitted to come and enter this home while she was still alive. So then how would she come through the door of reincarnation to the house she was forbidden to enter? I told her and I promise you, I will travel through

Heaven and Earth as I shall bring her back because I never had forbidden her to enter this home. I was not a part of this family then but through my birthright, I am now. So, I invite her back to this home through her birthright. Now while I do this, why don't you try to figure out who Margriete is or where she is? It seems like you are stuck in this wagon of karma because you don't express your feelings. Just do it Big Bro. See Margriete through your heart, not your eyes. Let me hold Griet within my chest with all my love."

That's when Katelijne cried in pain as we all saw a light appeared from within her womb and there in the light, we saw a child was standing. She looked so much like Antonius, yet she somehow also looked like Katelijne. I knew her so well as if she should have been mine, but the promise was, "If only you were mine."

The child stood there and said, "I am Griet, the forbidden daughter of this home. I was forbidden by the past inhabitants of this home, however, I never told my family members they were cursed for their actions. Forbidden I was by the family, yet I did not forbid or let go of any one of my family members. I had told my Papa, now Big Papa, 'I shall never let you go, if only you were mine.' Forever I shall protect my family lineage and the evil force that looms over the home is not I, but a woman named Aideen who had never left the tunnel of light and has been haunting my home to take her revenge. I shall protect you from my mother's womb. Karma strikes you through the lighthouse, not I, and a woman is looming around in physical form to destroy my family members for her own selfish reasons."

Griet watched Antonius, Papa, and me as she continued, "Papa Antonius, I, Griet, am back. Also, Big Papa Jacobus, I am on my way. Opa Erasmus, I will soon be home. Please find Theunis and Alexander as they are in harm's way and need your help. I pray in this life, I am not known as the forbidden daughter of Kasteel Vrederic as forever I shall protect this home even from my mother's womb."

We saw a light shine from the womb and burn down the lightning and the storms that were brewing around our home. We all watched Katelijne faint and knew she was pregnant again.

I saw Margriete fall to the ground and whisper, "What did I do wrong? I only hope I can sing to you once in this lifetime my child."

Then I saw Andries walk to his mother and say, "I will protect my sister from all scary storms. Come home to me and I, your brother, will never let you go. I pinky promise."

I walked over to Andries who was getting older, faster than normal. I knew he was somehow mature and very young at the same time. My nephew needed my help at this moment. The child Andries watched me and talked like my brother Andries who was murdered and whose reincarnated form this child was.

Andries said "Big Bro, I am back like I promised. I told Big Mama I would be back, and I don't ever want my Big Mama crying at gravesites anymore. I don't want Big Papa crying anymore, and I don't want you crying ever again. But Big Bro, aside from me, who else do you cry for? Who is Margriete?"

It was then we saw in front of us, Andries kissed his mother's tummy and said, "I will protect everyone somehow, someway."

He looked and acted like Andries, my little brother, and his father Antonius's twin, as they were mirror twins before and now, they are father and son. Life is a miracle, and I knew everything would be just all right. The Vrederic family members including my great-grandmothers never said anything nor did anyone question what just happened. They were busy cooking for the family. They came and watched us and thought to themselves, it was just another day at Kasteel Vrederic.

It was then we saw there was a crowd at the gate, and we worried who was shouting at the gate. The people had helped themselves in.

The crowd said in anger, "What was going on here? We all saw the lightning and thunderstorms and the weird lighthouse. All the magical powers of that lighthouse are nothing but voodoo. We wonder if your ancestor Margriete really was a witch. What's going on and why do you all have thunder and lightning bolts when it's a hot sunny day?"

I saw Margriete go and stand in front of me as did Mama. They spoke in Hindi and both knew Antonius and I both understand Hindi. Yet I said nothing while I watched the women handle this part of the problem.

They both said to the crowd, "We were having a movie shoot in the house. Everyone wants to make a movie using our home. They did a rehearsal, but we told them no, it's our home and we don't want any more disturbances. So, the camera crew, the producers, and the directors left. Please leave now and don't worry you probably will read it in the newspapers tomorrow. Film companies want to use Kasteel Vrederic as a movie set."

I watched the people take in the story and they actually were leaving.

Then one woman stopped and came back as she said, "I see you have a new member in the family, a young boy. I didn't know you all had a new family member here. Also, where is your baby son Antonius?"

Antonius said, "He is inside taking a nap. Also, I did not know it was a requirement we must announce who we have in our home as a guest, a visitor, or a family member. Our home is separated from all of you by acres of land. We never asked you how many family members you all have."

The woman said nothing and just watched my family like a nosy busybody. Antonius went to my petite mother and I really thought he was trying to hide behind her. Even though he was talking so bravely I knew it bothered him how these people were so nosy. I watched Katelijne watch her husband and was trying to say something with her eyes, yet Antonius was not good with body language as he until recently was a blind person and relied on sounds and feelings more than eye winking.

Margriete, Katelijne, and Big Mama were talking amongst themselves and Margriete said, "His name is also Andries, my cousin. We are traveling together and will be staying with the family."

Everyone left one by one as I wondered what just happened today. I watched Margriete give Katelijne a pregnancy test. Then she screamed and let the whole family know Katelijne was pregnant. The whole family rejoiced as we knew our beloved Griet was about to enter this home. I saw Margriete watch me and I could see her sad eyes search for patience to take the hurt of losing her child again, yet I could not give her my support as I did not know if she was real or had just read our family history and thought she is Margriete. I did not think she was lying as I knew she was genuine.

After the home was left in silence, I did a lab test, and I did complete physical examinations on my whole family. The test showed my mother, father, Antonius, Katelijne, and I were frozen in time at the age of thirty. It seemed like Andries was skipping ahead and was showing he would stop aging at the age of thirty. The strangest thing was Uncle Matthias, Margriete, and my great-grandmothers were affected by something, but I could not tell how much of it they too received.

Margriete came in and said, "I believe your family members have somehow found the tunnel of youth and have stopped or will come and stop aging at the age of thirty. That's why your parents look like your age. Also, that's why Andries too is catching up to the same year. I know we too have received some kind of radiation as we were touched by the light but not as much though."

Margriete walked back and forth as she placed her hair in a bun and watched Mama walk in and sit on the sofa next to her. I kept on watching her with some kind of pull in my soul.

Margriete then pulled me out of my thoughts as she said, "Maybe Big Mama can help us understand all of this. Please don't think of anything from this as Big Mama asked me to call her by this name. I am not trying to create a relationship with you through this. Also, it seems like you can't be my twin flame as you have stopped aging and I will age Jacobus. So, no illusions of you being mine or me of being yours, at least not in this lifetime."

Mama watched us as she walked over to me and placed her little feet on my lap. I knew it was a gesture for me to give her feet a massage. I automatically gave her feet a massage as I watched Antonius come in and give Mama's shoulders a massage. From the corner of my eyes, I did see Margriete wipe her tears, yet I remained silent.

All my family members walked in one by one as Mama said, "Seems like when we were all traveling through the tunnel of light, we somehow crossed between the different tunnels. We tried to get back into the dream tunnel yet somehow Jacobus fainted and wanted to go back to Margriete. I believe we must have then somehow walked into the tunnel of youth or had turned the age because we walked backward instead of walking forward. It is uncommon but happens with a lot of people who walk through the tunnel of light and come back from death or even through dreams. These people have found the youth tunnel. Some call this tunnel the immortality serum. It's like what people wish for, yet when you accidentally tumble upon it, you only want to move on with your life and not go backward. It's then people try to search for a reversal but can't find it."

Antonius was shaking his hands as he said, "But what about Griet? She walked backward to Rietje because before Griet could finish her journey, Rietje had walked into the tunnel of light. I watched a mother walk backward as she said she had never held her daughter alive, so she wanted to hold her. I pulled her back to me."

Papa was walking back and forth and shaking his head as Mama asked him, "Why are you doing that Erasmus? It's all your fault you know. Why did you go crazy for me and forget our son and his daughter?"

Papa watched Mama as he smiled and said, "I will do it again and again for you. It is my fault that I believe and know you are my other half. I don't want to breathe or live without you. If I must repeat and live without you, then I want to become mad and crazy and not remember you or our love story, ever again. Mad for you sweetheart, yet gone completely mad without you."

All the women in my household began making cute sounds for Mama and Papa. I knew the Kasteel Vrederic love stories had begun with Mama and Papa, but as I watched my whole family, I only prayed may it not end here and may it continue eternally.

A wild storm had started to brew in my home and all around the grounds. Loud crying voices were being heard all over the home and the grounds. Shrieking voices of women in pain could be heard from all the rooms. Lights flickered and supernatural figures were seen floating all around the house. It mattered not if it was daytime or nighttime, they were all getting stronger. I wondered what I should do to make our home free of all these supernatural beings. Who were they and what did they want from my family and me? I had worked with a lot of patients and thought if anyone had passed away and had a grudge against me.

Mama stood up and said, "I will not be terrified of dead people or hauntings. I am not afraid of ghosts, so scream and do whatever, I don't care. Remember Katelijne, we were good ghosts and we did take on humans as ghosts, so we can take on ghosts as humans."

Katelijne said in a very brave voice, "Yes Big Mama, we will fight once more for our home. We will get rid of all bad supernatural beings this time."

As she said the words, I watched a hand had appeared from nowhere and said, "Help me please. I need justice."

Both brave women, my mother and sister-in-law, jumped on top of their husbands and Mama shouted, "Erasmus, hide me!"

Katelijne screamed and said, "Antonius! Hide us! Andries and me now!"

Margriete broke out in laughter as she said, "Wow, I thought I missed all my favorite TV shows as a single woman has the TV and her favorite takeout for company. Yet you all actually really have a movie going on here. I can't believe you all are afraid of ghosts. I'm not afraid of anything except death, not my own death for then my journey would just end, but of those I love for I can't stand being alone. It's my only fear. I keep on seeing a man standing in front of me and he was shot by an army of some kind. I cried and tried to hide him within my body, yet he was so cold and did not wake up. I just don't want to fall for anyone or have any kind of love inside of my heart as it hurts too much to love and not be loved back or lose the love of your life."

I told her, "But I thought you were scared of the rain, thunder, and lightning. You hated it and always wanted it to go away."

Margriete watched me and said, "No Jacobus, I left my fears back in my past life as I know in this life, I must walk on my own and learn to live without my heartbeats. For how could my heart even beat if my twin flame's heart does not beat for me? I only have my memories and I shall live for my memories of him. My dear Dr. Jacobus Vrederic van Phillip, please know this. You can't take away my memories of my beloved even if you try. For always I shall tell him like a whisper, 'If only you were mine.'"

Margriete walked back in the pouring rain to the guest quarters. I watched her bravely walk and then she folded her hands in a tight way as she tried to open the doors of her temporary home, the carriage house where I had made love to my Margriete on our wedding night, for the first time in my other lifetime. I did not want to think of her or link her to my Margriete as I know if she was mine, I would have known.

Papa came and stood behind me as he said, "We must again solve a murder mystery to get to the end of these supernatural happenings. Also, we must find out a way to either get aging to stop, or stop Margriete from aging, as when you do remember her, it just might be too late. You don't want age to be an obstacle for you two in this life."

I watched Antonius walk with his son as he knew the child was growing older by the minute. He wanted to stop the time and enjoy his son.

He came near me and said, "Big Bro, I just wanted to say something in front of everyone but Margriete. As a child who was born blind and had to learn to see from within my soul, I know Dr. Margriete is our Margriete. Yet you won't see it as you try to see through your outer eyes, not inner eyes. I don't want you to see through my eyes but your own. I just hope it's not too late when you do finally open your inner eyes."

He walked away but then came back and said, "Margriete was writing this when we were all trying to cope with the unnatural storm. I pleaded to her if I could keep it. She told me yes, I could but not to give it to you. She did say if I could somehow through the library send it back to her Jacobus in the past. She said she heard and was here and saw how we had sent diaries back and forth before. So, if somehow, we could mail one letter for her to her Jacobus, not you. Here, take it and maybe you can leave it in your new diary and maybe it will travel time and land upon the person she cries and lives for."

I read the poem that spoke from the inner soul of a very frightened young woman. I was the most arrogant person who just allowed her to walk out alone in the pouring rain. I wondered if she was hiding her tears in the rainwater. Her poem I have included in this diary as the gut-wrenching poem hurt me more than I can express with words.

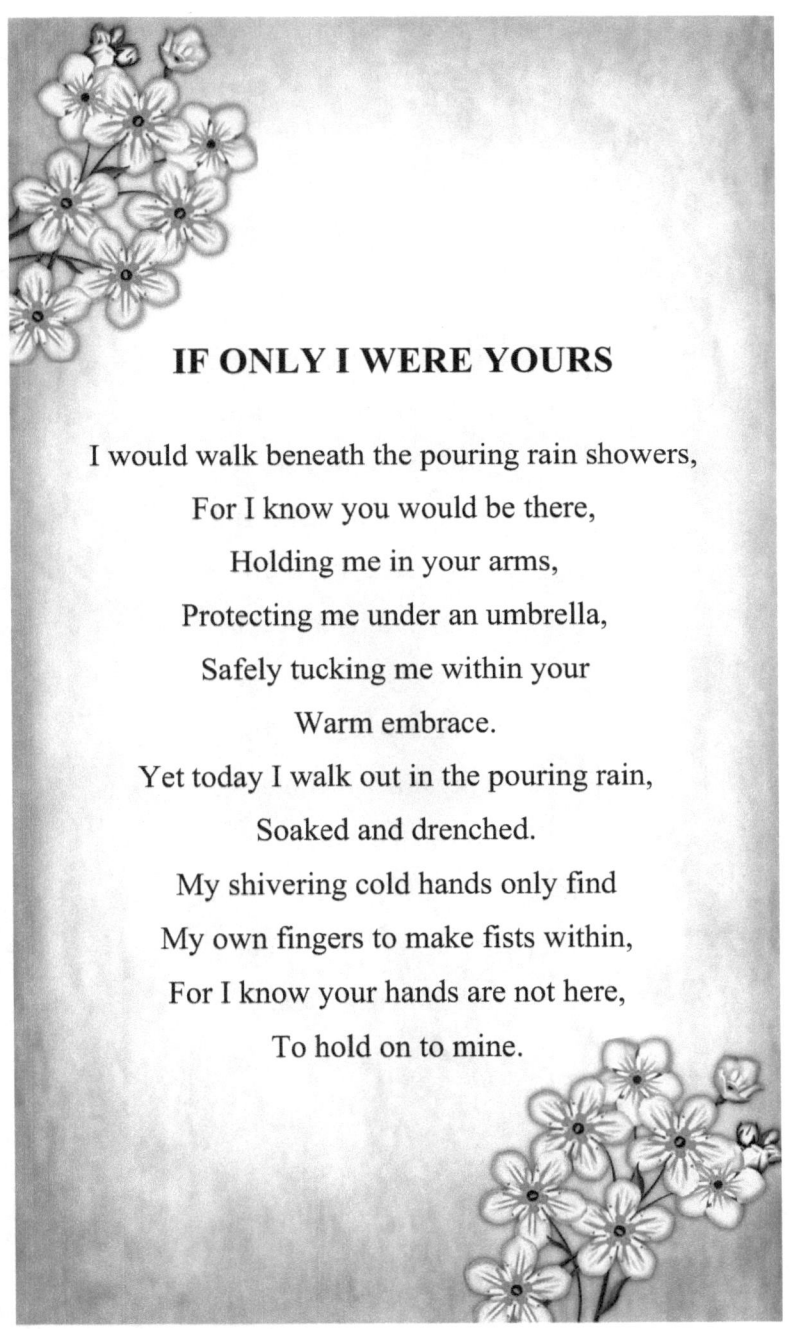

IF ONLY I WERE YOURS

I would walk beneath the pouring rain showers,

For I know you would be there,

Holding me in your arms,

Protecting me under an umbrella,

Safely tucking me within your

Warm embrace.

Yet today I walk out in the pouring rain,

Soaked and drenched.

My shivering cold hands only find

My own fingers to make fists within,

For I know your hands are not here,

To hold on to mine.

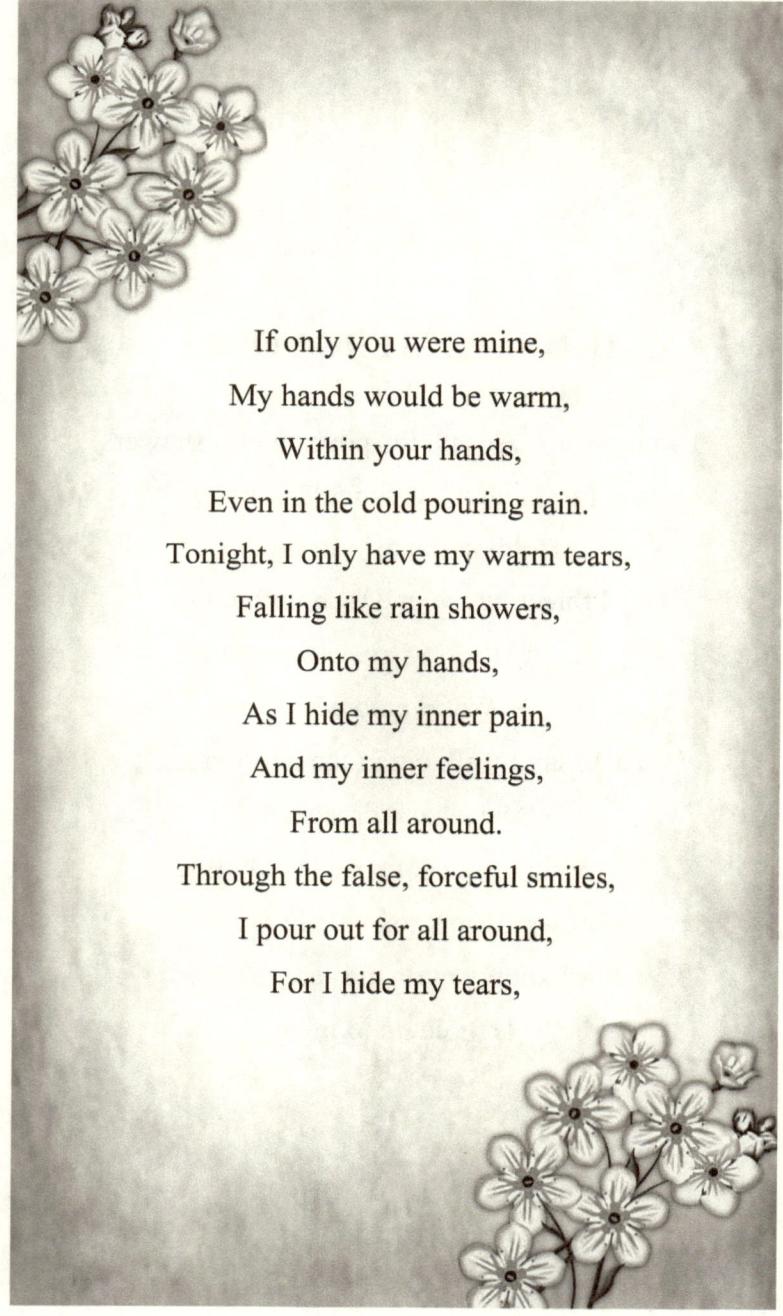

If only you were mine,

My hands would be warm,

Within your hands,

Even in the cold pouring rain.

Tonight, I only have my warm tears,

Falling like rain showers,

Onto my hands,

As I hide my inner pain,

And my inner feelings,

From all around.

Through the false, forceful smiles,

I pour out for all around,

For I hide my tears,

Within my eyes as I know

Without you, these tears

Too get lost within the agonies

Of the dark nights,

Where no one can see them,

Nor feel them,

For they only see the smiling face,

Of a stranger who walks alone,

Under the pouring rain showers,

Hiding the hot tears.

For I know these tears are lost,

And unknown to all as you,

My beloved, too ignore them,

So does this world.

For I am left alone,

Wishing under the starless nights,

Cold pouring rain showers,

Wishing and hoping,

IF ONLY I WERE YOURS.

-Margriete van Achthoven

I wanted to rip apart my soul and tell him to remove all the feelings of a human. For if you are my beloved Margriete, then I will never forgive myself. Yet if you are not, then I will never forgive myself for falling for you or feeling for you. Yet I only ask you why it is my soul calls out for you? I felt like holding on to you within my embrace and never letting you go. Yet I said nothing for I only love you my Margriete and never shall I betray you even for you. Maybe I am losing my mind for you, because of you.

Mama was now pacing fast in our room as she read the poem over my head. She slapped my head and said, "Jacobus, really? How could you be so mean? Does your heart not even beat for her and does it not tell you the truth? We must do something to stop the effects of time traveling."

After Mama left, I poured my pain through words on paper. So, here is another poem for you my beloved Margriete.

ONLY FOR YOU, I AM

You are my passion.

For you, I am the passionate

As you are my life.

For you, my heart still beats.

While your eyes fill up

With tears,

Mine dry up to allow yours to spill.

For when you seek my love,

And passion,

I have to say

I left all my love,

And all my passion

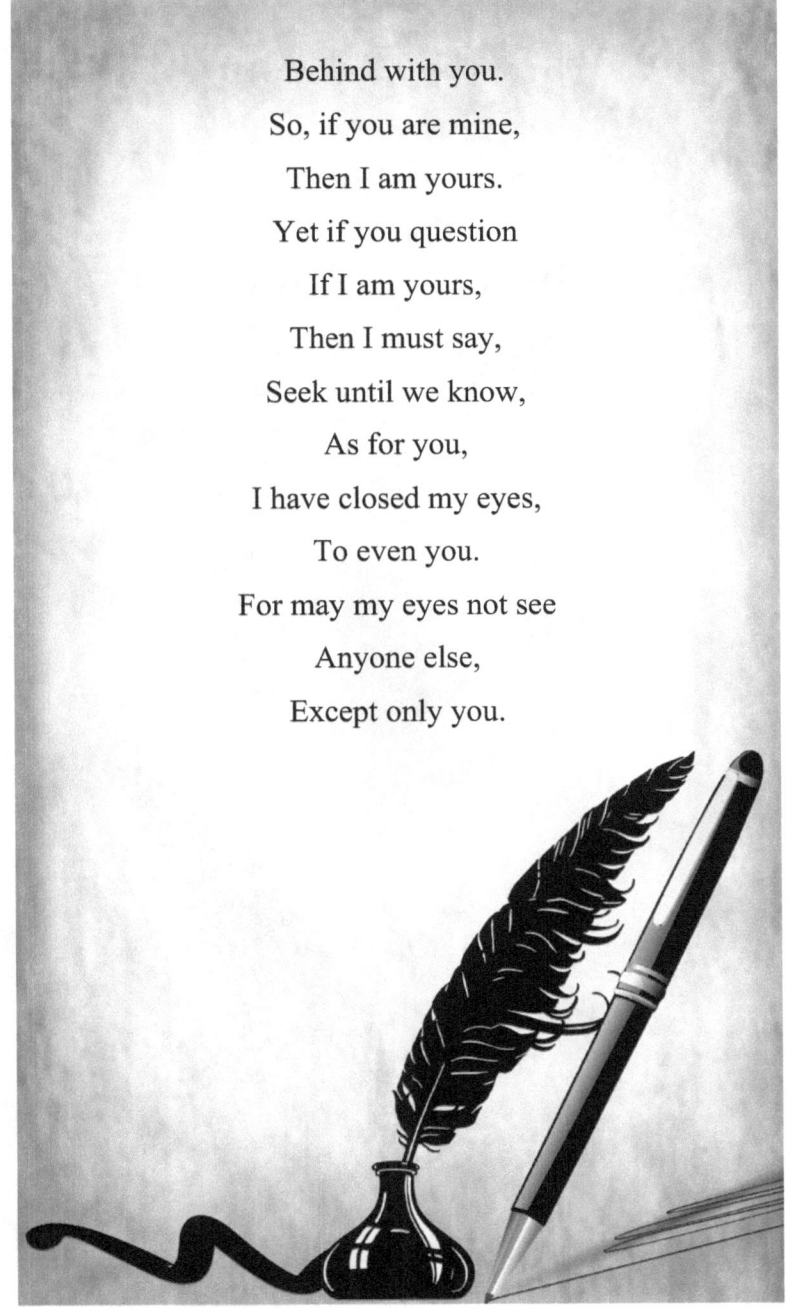

Behind with you.

So, if you are mine,

Then I am yours.

Yet if you question

If I am yours,

Then I must say,

Seek until we know,

As for you,

I have closed my eyes,

To even you.

For may my eyes not see

Anyone else,

Except only you.

Dear passion,

Dear beloved,

Know this today and

Forever,

ONLY FOR YOU, I AM.

CHAPTER THREE:

Confined Predators

"Predators can hide throughout time, yet when the truth serum comes and hunts them down, it is then the predators become the prisoners."

The reincarnated forms of the honorable soldier Theunis Peters and the brave knight Sir Alexander van der Bijl try to find bread, butter, and milk from the hidden cupboard.

Life in Kasteel Vrederic is never gloomy, even though the weather outside was very gloomy. Chilling rain kept on pouring all night. I wish it had poured louder. I love watching the storms outside as it gives my soul so much peace.

I felt like I was not the only one who had a storm brewing inside but now Mother Earth too had one brewing outside. Yet I am glad it did not pour or bring along with her lightning and thunder for a certain brave woman who slept all alone in my family's guest house would have been frightened and terrified. Why my heart sought this woman's comfort or safety was beyond my understanding.

I heard Mama's footsteps coming toward my bedroom. I counted the seconds as any minute the door would open with a bang. The door opened very slowly as I could smell my mother and her smell was familiar. I actually could smell all the breakfast items and my morning coffee.

All my life I waited for Mama to come and wake me up in the morning. She also woke up my brothers, one by one. Antonius and Andries too waited for her morning calls. Even after Andries was murdered, Mama always went and opened his room and would say until he is back. Now our little Andries is back and stays in his own room. My mother says it's a mother's love and belief.

She walked in and said, "Get up Jacobus and come with me to your brother's room."

I was actually dressed up as today was my day to visit our hospital. I love visiting my patients and know that's the other passion I have that I will never let go, trying to heal people or at least make it possible for them to be as comfortable as I can. I walked with Mama and saw she was knocking on Antonius's door as then she walked in.

She said, "Katelijne, Antonius, are you two up? If not, then get up and come downstairs. We have guests waiting for us downstairs."

I watched my brother Antonius was still in his pajamas sleeping and Katelijne was missing. I knew she was with her son Andries as even Mama stayed with Andries all night. Both women slept there until very early in the morning when both women went back to their rooms.

I asked Mama, "Who stayed with Andries this morning? Why didn't you call me? I could have stayed with him."

My mother slapped my head again. When she told me to bend, I knew it was coming. I wondered what I had said wrong and realized as soon as I saw Margriete walk out of Andries's room with a ten-year-old boy.

Andries said, "Big Bro, what are you up to this morning, and why are you bothering my Big Mama? Big Mama, Andries's heart beats Big Mama."

I watched a very tired Margriete and asked her quietly, "What's going on? How did this happen and why was I not called?"

She watched me and said, "Ask your parents why they did not call you, for I am very busy trying to figure out this myself. Andries was older when I walked into his room. Katelijne was panicking for her son as was Big Mama. I asked them to call you, but they thought there was no need, as we just have to let time heal all of this on its own. My only worry is how do I explain to your neighbors that my cousin has aged or I have a different cousin over here now."

I watched her and thought who cares about the neighbors? But I only told her, "We should all have faith in miracles when the subject or things are out of medical or scientifical hands. I just hope somehow the spirits of Kasteel Vrederic can guide and help us now, as we need them now more than ever."

Margriete watched me and said, "They are traveling through the tunnel of birth, at least one of them is. I do hope at least the other one is already on Earth. May he be guided to you and your family as you need him and as we were told by an unborn child, he needs you too."

I watched her hair flying in the breeze. Her gentle and soft soul had always thought of the others and never once did she even talk about herself. I did wonder if she had anyone at home who waited for her.

I so wanted to ask if she had any love interest waiting for her at home. I found myself burning with rage and jealousy at the mere thought of it. Yet again, I said nothing. Little did I know we had more bad news waiting for us downstairs in the parlor.

Margriete asked me, "Jacobus, where is Big Mama?"

Antonius, Katelijne, and Andries were following us as everyone stopped abruptly when we saw Mama was not with us. I heard Papa's voice coming from downstairs and knew his voice did not sound very kind or happy at the sight of our guests, who were waiting for us in the parlor.

Katelijne went closer to Margriete as she said, "I have a cold feeling in my heart. I am scared and am feeling strange. Hold my hands Margriete, I don't know why I am feeling this way. I feel like the same Grim Reaper who had placed me in the boat is close by somewhere."

Margriete stopped in place and held on to the hands of Katelijne and said, "I don't know the full story behind everything that happened to you. All I know is I was there with Jacobus when you were being operated on in Tennessee as one of the attending physicians. I know you are completely healed even as of yesterday. I did a complete physical on you and you have no signs of a heart transplant surgery. It's like another miracle had happened and it is as if you never were operated upon. That's the physical part of it. The emotional aspects of it, why don't you give me all of your fears and worries and just be fearless and know you have a beloved husband, a beloved brother-in-law, and a beloved son? You also have Big Mama and Big Papa, the most loving parents on Earth. Please don't ever forget you also are pregnant with one of the blessed spirits of Kasteel Vrederic, the beloved daughter of this home. You be strong my dear friend."

Katelijne watched me for a while and said, "Jacobus is not my brother-in-law but my brother. You too are not just my friend but my sister. Don't ever forget that."

Margriete watched all of us and said, "I will never forget, that's a promise."

We all walked into a very well-decorated, modern-day parlor. The white curtains were flying in the breeze. Colorful tulips were placed on the tables around the room. Soft blue sofas decorated the room not speaking about the wealth of the house but rather the modesty of the home. My mother's touches had made a cold castle into a warm home, where love and blessings were displayed.

I watched Margriete as I know my Margriete had made a hidden cupboard in this room, the cupboard where fresh baked bread would appear from nowhere. The tables would have bread and butter. If the bread had run short, Margriete would ask Griet to send bread to this secret closet Margriete had made.

The only three women who knew about this were Margriete, Griet, and Rietje. Theunis had discovered it as he had helped himself to the secret breads so many times. I always wondered how my two favorite spirits had always joined us at the dinner table like normal humans.

Tears fail me and that's why I don't ever show my feelings in public. Yet all the memories of Margriete only gift me with hidden tears that I only show my pillows and my shower stall. Margriete watched me and looked in the direction of the hidden cupboard.

There in front of the hidden cupboard hung a painting made by Papa and Antonius jointly. It was the first joint project that showed our home through the eyes of a blind painter. My brother had done this under Papa's guidance when he was completely blind. The painting of Kasteel Vrederic hung there as our family's pride.

Mama was very upset. As I saw her and her fearful looks, I forgot all my thoughts of Margriete and everyone else on this Earth. I wanted to run to her as I saw Antonius too started to walk toward her. Yet Mama said with her hands, no.

Papa said, "Jacobus, Antonius, we have Livina Bakker-Beenhouwer and Luyt Bakker, the owners of the famous Mirrorless Hotel here for a visit. They said they have very good news for us. They have brought another person whom they just met to our home. It seems Mrs. Bakker is a huge fan of Jacobus, the doctor who had saved her husband. Also, she recently read our family books and thinks they have a great surprise for us."

I watched the couple and tried to keep an eye on Katelijne, yet she was standing away from me near Margriete. Antonius, however, was standing next to me and he looked furious and upset just at the company. I knew their daughter was a murderer, yet I did not know why my family was furious at these people. I did not say anything as even my sixth sense told me, something was wrong.

Mrs. Bakker broke the silence and said, "Dr. Jacobus, I am so grateful for everything you had done for us and wanted to let you know what had happened to Aideen was all for the best. She was a horrible person and justice was done. Yet I have a gift for you as I think you actually will want to get acquainted with this person."

Then she asked someone to come into the room. She was talking with someone and actually the hidden person was not in my vision. Yet I knew my family members saw the person. Then like a strange lightning bolt in front of me, in my own home, was standing Margriete from the sixteenth century. The same brown eyes, brown hair, and pale white skin. The woman from the portrait on the walls of Kasteel Vrederic was actually standing in front of my eyes.

I wanted to jump toward her and just hold on to her. All my love that I had buried within my inner soul actually became even more cold. I wanted to hold her, yet I felt like something inside of my soul kept on saying, "Don't look with your eyes. If you are my twin flame, then find me through your heartbeats, through your inner soul, not your eyes."

Then the new woman said, "Jacobus, it's me. I am Margriete, your Margriete, and I was reborn only for you. I have been looking for you for so long that I almost gave up. Recently I was at the Mirrorless Hotel where I saw your pictures and knew it was you, my Jacobus. I told the owners my story and they told me about your books. After reading your books, I knew God created me for you."

Mama stood in between the woman and me as the woman started to walk toward me. I saw Antonius had his hands in fists. Katelijne was pale white like she just saw a ghost. She was speechless as everyone else was.

Then I watched the lights in our home started to flicker and angry sounds were being heard by everyone. The guests were given refreshments by my mother. I did not join them for breakfast, neither did Antonius nor did our Margriete or Katelijne. Mama and Papa, however, talked with them and I knew my mother was up to something.

I watched Katelijne's womb was glowing as was the lighthouse above our home. The open doors and windows only showed how the lighthouse lantern was moving in a circle. I only thought what I should do. There in front of my eyes was standing my Margriete from the sixteenth century. At least she looked like her. Yet there in the courtyard was another Margriete who looked so different from my sixteenth-century Margriete.

Then in front of Antonius and me, Katelijne's womb spoke and said, "Papa Jacobus, look from your inner eyes, not your earthly ones. Remember your promise as you had said you would recognize your twin flame anywhere, anytime. What if through the door of reincarnation, she has changed her eyes and her color and her looks? Would you not recognize her? Look at Mama Margriete, the mother who could not even touch me, nor could she be my mother in this life as you and Opa had cursed, not to bring the basket with whatever was in it to the house ever again. Remember, she promised to be with you and even gave up me for you. I speak from the womb of my newly found Mama for my Mama Margriete. Watch the lighthouse for it shall guide you always."

It was then I saw our Margriete was leaving the home. I ran toward her and told her, "Why are you leaving Margriete? Don't you want to see through the whole story? I would think you would want to stay until the end and see how everything ends."

I saw her hidden tears were stored to the brim, yet the brave woman only said, "Jacobus I have an emergency in my orphanage. There are two very sick toddlers. I don't know where they came from, as I don't question my aunt who brought them in as they needed a place to stay. The boys were only a few months old and no one has adopted them as both children have heart murmurs. They get ill very quickly, and I have to go and attend to them. I asked my clinic aides to bring them here with Big Papa's permission."

96

She ran toward the main gate as I watched two babies who walked on their own were brought to our home. One had blond bushy hair and blue eyes. The other one had dark black hair and green eyes. They ran with their little feet toward Margriete and hugged her.

One of the two boys said, "Where have you gone? I miss you. I was scared you too will let go of us. No one wants us. I am hungry and I feel tired. I want to sleep now, but before that I want bread please."

I watched them both and the doctor inside of me just woke up and I asked them, "Where does it hurt? I can fix you up as I can do magic. First let's have some bread and maybe some milk too, then we can kiss all the pain away. Give me your hands little one."

The older looking one said, "I am not a baby. I am three and my friend is almost three. It's his birthday tomorrow, so Margriete must be with us to cut the cake. It's our birthdays. Mine was yesterday and Margriete missed it."

I watched Margriete and saw she was crying as she held both boys to her heart. I watched the lighthouse was now dancing and there in the lighthouse was a baby girl and a toddler boy. I wondered who these two boys were as we took them inside to Big Mama. The two boys were looking at the house as if they were not guests but knew the house.

They went straight to the parlor and were looking at the painting hanging on the wall in front of the secret cupboard.

The two babies asked Margriete for fresh bread. One boy said, "Don't worry Alex, Griet is almost here. She will send the freshly baked breads over. Maybe we will also get butter and milk tonight as we are home."

Antonius just sat down holding on to his wife. It seemed like on top of being scared, they were both numb at what was going on in our home. I only wondered I might faint if one of them called himself Theunis.

Just then the boy named Alex said, "Theunis, where is the bread? I am hungry."

Mama said, "We did not have any bread today as I made Indian dishes, not bread and butter, but aloo naan and palak paneer. However, I will get them for you in a few minutes if you only wait a little."

Andries jumped up and said, "Yes Big Mama! Palak paneer is my favorite!"

Antonius joined him and said, "Big Mama, I love palak paneer. I was raised on it. It's my favorite first Andries!"

I watched them and knew when it came to any Indian food, my two brothers would jump for it as would I since we were all were raised with it. I wondered, however, if the two babies even knew what palak paneer is.

I told Mama, "They are babies Mama, and they are hungry. We can get them something for now and maybe later they can have other foods. They should have a lot of fluids as they both have a fever."

I watched Margriete walk toward the painting on the wall and take the painting off the wall. She then opened the old cupboard and in front of all of us, there appeared fresh baked breads. There were butter and milk too which appeared in front of our eyes.

Mr. Bakker stood up and said, "What is going on? How did the breads appear from nowhere? Also don't you think you should actually give some attention to this Margriete as she came all the way for you? We have come just for you, and actually even though the police have proven our daughter to be a criminal and we are happy she got caught, we never blamed any one of you for all of this as maybe we could have solved this differently. So, we are just saying if we could all move on with a new relationship and forget the past. This day could be a day to forgive and forget."

Big Mama came and said, "No, I shall never forgive your daughter for the murder of my son. You all can forgive your daughter, but we will never forgive or forget. I too agree my son could have been here if only you two had seen your daughter for who she was. A lot of lives were lost because of your daughter and it's really hard for us to move on beyond that but we are trying to be cordial with you as much as possible. Also, who is this junky you have brought? Why do you think my son is even looking for a look-alike and not for his twin flame? Don't say anything about her being his twin flame as you know our lighthouse is magical and shall speak when it is true or false."

That's when I saw the new Margriete was shaking in fear as if she was scared and really did not want to be here. She was looking at someone and just stood there like she was frozen. I followed her gaze and saw Andries was just watching the guests as he came slowly down the stairs. There in front of us stood a twenty-year-old Andries.

Andries kissed Mama and said, "Big Mama, why are they here? They are the murderers of your Andries and all the girls. They also kept Aideen as a prisoner in their home. Big Bro, everyone had it wrong as it was these people who did everything. Also, that woman is called 'Ella The Prostitute.' She tried to actually rape Andries as he passed away. Antonius had fought in his sleep and the spirits had arrived to save the day but Andries still had to go on a trip for a while, but I hear he is back."

The newly arrived guests stood up in a fury and started to leave as they said, "None of this is true and we will sue you for defamation. We will hunt down your family home until we wipe you all out. How dare you make up stories! Who are you anyway?"

Margriete came in front of him and said, "He is my cousin, and he is not well so he is saying things he actually does not know. It's just that all of this has actually placed a lot of stress on this family. Please let's call it a day. Why don't you all go home? And we will have this settled in a calm manner."

The Bakkers said, "You will regret this day. We only came to unite you with your twin flame as you have written about her. You have insulted us, and we will take revenge. We promise this home will be hunted down till it's ashes."

That's when I saw a little toddler stand up on top of the table and say, "I, Theunis, an honorable soldier, shall protect this home eternally."

Suddenly, I saw lightning appeared from the womb of Katelijne as she was shaking in fear and said, "I know you all had me raped and gouged. I forgot everything as I was dead and brought back to life, but I will not fear you all and shall testify against you. My loss of memories was only temporary, and I know I will remember everything. You all have been coming over to see my family not to be friends but to make sure I don't remember anything."

The guests left in a rush as I knew my family had placed all of our lives at risk. The Bakkers were filthy rich and would take revenge. I believed even people in the police force were in the game as this was an international crime that was being investigated.

For today though, I only hoped my family would stop talking and not tell them everything. My mother came over and again stood in front of me as she gave me her stare again.

She told Antonius, Andries, and me as we all stood next to one another, "How dare you three do this to me all over again! Won't you three ever learn? Now our whole family is at risk. How do we deal with this? We can't even talk with the police as then we will all be held in prison for having no proof."

Andries watched Margriete and asked, "Margriete, I am physically all right, or am I still in danger?"

Margriete said, "You are more than all right. You have just become an adult and so for that I am no longer your pediatrician, but I will still be your family doctor. Now your brother, the famous doctor, can take care of you."

Andries watched me as I watched over him and I asked him, "How does this relationship feel like Andries? It's not regular for people to wake up with all the memories and grow up overnight."

Andries laughed like his own self and said, "I am blessed to have this family and I made a promise to my Big Mama. In all my rebirths, I want to be only hers."

Papa came and said, "There was a fire in the courthouse and a letter was left behind. It read if we have spirits to help us, they will have evil spirits to help them. The Mirrorless Hotel will become our worst nightmare. They said the war has begun as they will hunt us down in our own home."

I told everyone, "I think it's time we all plan our next move as we have an honorable soldier and an honorable knight in the house. So, I know Griet and Rietje too will soon be here."

As everyone stood around the parlor worrying about our next move or what we should do, I told Margriete, "I still don't believe you or anyone to be my Margriete. I respect you and believe you have convinced yourself to think you are Margriete. Yet I will not believe you until my heart too knows of the truth."

ANN MARIE RUBY

Margriete told me loudly in front of all, "Jacobus, I really don't care what your cold heart believes or does not. For how would you even know who I am as you don't even have a heart. It takes a heart to feel a heart. You don't have any."

Antonius laughed so loudly everyone thought he was going berserk. He said, "Hey it was funny! I love the tension and the fight between them. I can't wait to see what happens there, between these two."

Andries was deep in his thoughts as he said, "I will catch them for my murder. I have them confined in a web. They don't know who I am and will never know. Yet I know who they are and how they work. I will catch them in their own game. Can you all believe a murder victim returns to catch his predators? I will punish them within their own games. They are thinking of spooking us out of our home. I wonder if they are thinking they can take over our home by frightening us with false booby traps and fake ghosts and goblins. Wait till they see we have real ones. We have real ghosts, spirits, and seekers. I saw Aunt Marinda on my return journey. I also met up with Aideen on my return trip. She is really bad, a pure rotten apple, yet she is mad as hell at them as they only used her. Okay family, remember we know our predators as they are now the confined predators."

That night, I wrote a poem for my Margriete as I did not get any from Margriete.

ONLY FOR ME

Come and look into my eyes.

See the tears that never fall.

The words that I promised,

Will not be uttered to

Any other woman.

The words I will never allow

My ears to hear,

Said by any other woman.

For you, I have taken my eternal vows.

Only with you I shall again

Take my vows.

Now my beloved please come

And help me.

Say the words a man

Repeats to his beloved wife,

The words that tie

A man and a woman

Immortally,

The sweet tears

That fall with only sweet kisses,

The unspoken words,

That become blissful songs,

When a man

And a woman

Unite infinitely,

When two minds, bodies, and souls

Become one,

And promise to

Never let one

Another go

But be one another's

Throughout time.

How my beloved shall I break

My oath that ties me

Eternally

To you?

For you, I had taken these vows,

So only for you,

I shall again take my vows.

So tonight, my beloved promise

From your mind, body, and soul,

You too shall take these vows,

And you shall keep

Your vows,

ONLY FOR ME.

CHAPTER FOUR:

Heartbeats Of The Blessed Daughter

"Heartbeats can be heard by the beloveds. A mother, a father, a brother, a sister, or eternal twin flames can call on one another through the magical sound of heartbeats."

Dr. Jacobus Vrederic van Phillip and Dr. Margriete van Achthoven are being guided by their previous life's daughter Griet, the forbidden daughter of Kasteel Vrederic.

The hospital wings were filled with so many patients. I walked around doing my rounds all day. The gloomy weather outside brought a cold, spine-shivering feeling that was making my inner soul itch. Thunder roared outside as the lightning poured inside letting all know how furious Mother Nature could be. However, I knew if we only waited out the storm, we would see the loving side of Mother Nature.

Just being with my patients and making sure they get the best treatment medically possible or keeping them as comfortable as possible, make my days. I walked into the Vrederic Hospital and Clinic which now also includes the Vrederic Children's Hospital. My life's ambition was to have a hospital where we don't charge the poor and needy. I am blessed as my family members had all pitched in to convert this dream into a reality. Now each and every day, my family members get to see the miracles of medical science helping people from around the globe.

The children's hospital has paintings, hand drawn and created by Papa and Antonius, framing the corridors and all the rooms. Storybooks written for children were donated by authors worldwide. Each night, one of my family members tours this hospital and reads a short story to the young children. After we lost Andries, this hospital was my mother's thirst as she found Andries in all of the children, and she gave them all of her love.

Busy within my own thoughts, I ended up in a lounge and waiting room for toddlers and young children. I saw there in front of me was Margriete, walking with her files, busy reading over some reports. I watched a devoted doctor in Margriete, whom my this hospital was proud to have. I could just stand and watch her for hours. I don't know why I felt this pull toward her. In my heart, I knew there was more to our relationship than just a man and woman or just friends. I felt like I had waited for her for hundreds of years.

I knew she left with the two boys right after the Bakkers had left. She told Mama she had to take them back somewhere. They were too young to get involved in all the spiritual activities of Kasteel Vrederic. No one could explain the certain knowledge the children did have, or the ways they had behaved. How they called themselves by those names, I did not ask Margriete either. I knew in Kasteel Vrederic, miracles do happen, and no one talks about them but just allows time to divulge with the answers.

Margriete suddenly looked up and moved her silky black hair that got out of her hair bun from her eyes. She had her glasses on and her white doctor's lab coat on. I wanted to just talk with her. I wanted to listen to her voice. Yet I knew if I started talking, I would pour all my unjust angers toward her. I wish I could be like Papa or Antonius and talk poetically or musically. Words come out of Antonius like musical notes. From my mouth they pour out as dry and irritating scratches. Yet I wondered if only I too could talk to you dear Margriete, ever so tenderly.

Out of the blue, Margriete said, "Jacobus, is everything all right at home? Are Big Mama and Big Papa all right? Oh no, is it Andries? Or Katelijne? Are they in trouble? I am so sorry I had to come to work as there are so many cases I have to deal with. They all need my help and I told Big Mama I would be a call away if you all need me."

I watched her for a while and then told her, "Everyone and everything at home is okay, Margriete. I called the police and told them everything. They have sent security to the house and are trying to keep an eye on the Bakkers. They told me they will keep an eye out for any new developments. Papa and Antonius have gone to Amsterdam for their art show. It's a big day for both of them. Today I guess our grown-up Andries is keeping an eye out for his mother and his Big Mama. Uncle Matthias and my two golden great-grandmothers are all home. I know Andries is probably keeping an eye out for them too. He loves our great-grandmothers as they think and know he is their old Andries."

She watched me and said, "Walk with me. Why don't you come and observe my young patients? They are here getting physicals done and are frightened like children are. Yet they are so busy with the kids' storytelling group, they forget all about their pain and worries. I love what Big Mama and Katelijne have done here with the storytelling time. The kids love listening to the stories and being with one another even if it is just for a short while."

Then I saw Margriete was silent for a while when she had stopped in front of a room which she watched like a mother would. Yet she was so brave, she opened the door and just smiled as we saw the two boys who had paid our home a visit last night. She walked in and the boys jumped up and started to cry at the sight of Margriete. They held on to her with all of their little fingers.

The boy who had blond hair and blue eyes said, "Where did you go Margriete? We cried for you! How could you be so mean? We were crying Margriete. Did you not even miss us?"

The boy with black hair just cried as he kept his lollipop in his mouth. The two boys became louder with their sobs as both boys tried to get onto Margriete's lap.

They saw me and the one with blond hair stared at me and said, "Why are you here? Where is Griet? You're so cruel. I am telling you, just go home. She needs you now. Go home please."

I watched the two boys and told them, "I am here to make sure you two can come back to Kasteel Vrederic as we have so many toys there for you. However, before anything, I will make sure you are feeling better and can go home with Margriete."

I checked the boys as we both read their charts and went over all the reports. The strangest thing was none of the boys had any sign of any heart murmurs. They were completely healthy boys who were either misdiagnosed or maybe a miracle had happened, and they were completely healed.

I told Margriete, "I will have all of these reexamined and make sure everything looks good. There was some kind of misdiagnosis as sometimes kids are misdiagnosed and that's why we need to reevaluate these situations. Who brought them to you?"

Margriete said, "Aunt Marinda, my aunt. My father's distant relation. He always saw the sisters Agatha and Marinda as his own sisters. Aunt Marinda is a nurse who never married, and Aunt Agatha is a Catholic nun who had opened a very small orphanage for the kids. I have converted the small orphanage into a bigger one. It's named Agatha and Marinda's Children. I grew up there as my grandmother raised me over there when she too donated most of her money to the orphanage. My grandmother's house in Scheveningen is my main home."

I went silent at the names of the two sisters. I knew the names were linked to my family for centuries. The Vrederic family's Aunt Marinda, the psychic, had traveled time and tide for us as she had said, when and where we would need her, she would then arrive at our home with or without our knowledge.

Margriete then said, "My aunts brought the children to the orphanage as their parents or maybe an unwed mother had left them under her care. Like I told you, I never asked as with Aunt Marinda you only ask when you know she wants you to ask. She is a psychic who is very knowledgeable with things we the normal humans are not aware of. Yet I would argue with the theory as I believe your family might be one family who would know her and her ways."

I was too much in a shock to say anything as I went into my own thinking world. That's when I saw lightning bolts were coming toward the room we were in. Margriete closed the drapes and tucked both boys in.

She told the boys Aunt Marinda would come in a few minutes and take them home as we left them. The two boys were overjoyed at the name of Aunt Marinda. The young boy's words bothered me a lot as I tried to call Papa and Antonius on their cell phones. No one answered their phones. I saw Margriete was looking at her pager for a while.

She then looked at me and said, "I have a message from Andries's phone. It's strange as he had never pranked, nor had he ever played games with me ever since he had become a grown-up young man. He will write he is hungry or if I could get him his favorite burgers, pizzas, or junk food. Yet this message only has one word typed all in capital letters. It says, 'HELP.'"

I took her pager as she just gave it to me without even arguing with her or rethinking anything. I did not say anything but started to run like my life was at risk. Margriete ran with me since somehow it felt like we could read one another's mind.

As we were running to the car, I watched Margriete was wearing a fancy dress and she looked so delicate as she was running after me. For some strange reason, I did not compliment her on her looks. She looked like the embodiment of forget-me-nots. Instead, I told her, "What's wrong with you? Why all the makeup? And the fancy dress? You don't need any. Actually, you look beautiful without anything. Oh, I am sorry. I am assuming you have a hot date somewhere with someone."

Margriete watched me for a while. She looked hurt and said, "I was going to the fundraiser event for underprivileged kids. I donate a portion of my income to the kids and I can actually decide how the money gets to be used or for what."

I knew I was in the wrong yet somehow, I guess I was jealous she looked so beautiful. She wore a light blue dress and looked like a princess who should be held within the arms of her beloved like the magical forget-me-nots she wore in her hair.

I only told her, "Please excuse my words. I can't express my feelings into words and when I say them, I sound arrogant. I guess I can write them out easily, yet I can never say them out loud."

Margriete watched me for a while and said, "I know Jacobus. I feel like I know you better than you know yourself. Maybe someday you will know how well I do know you. Until then, please let's not say anything or else we may leave words out that we both shall regret."

We said nothing more on this topic and started to run toward the car. I gave Margriete privacy to change in the car. She changed into a simpler dress and put on her white lab coat over it. We both carried our stethoscopes and doctor's bags with us. Margriete put her blue dress in the car as a keepsake.

She said, "Jacobus, try calling Big Mama or Katelijne or Uncle Matthias or maybe your great-grandmothers, even though I know they don't hear anything. I am fluent in Hindi and I try screaming on the phone and your Indian great-grandmother, your Nani, keeps on saying, 'Don't prank.'"

I laughed out loud at her words and told her, "I know both great-grandmothers do that for attention, so you would go and visit them as you would then get worried. I called everyone but no one was answering. I am worried because one of the boys from your orphanage said Griet needs me. How does he know Griet and why did he say his name is Theunis?"

Margriete watched me and said, "That's what Aunt Marinda named him and christened him by. Maybe you could ask her. I don't and did not as I don't question Aunt Marinda."

I thought to myself I will ask her when we finally do meet. Then I saw Margriete was typing something on her pager back to Andries.

She wrote, "Andries, behind the bookshelves in the library there is a stone wall. Push the wall from the bottom. There is a small black pedal there, barely visible. Push inward then toward you with your feet. A secret door will open. Get inside with everyone and close the door. No one knows about it as I hid there with Jacobus once before. Please go in there. I hope it still exists. You will know as I wrote on the wall M and J as our initials for our future generations to find us if we had died in there."

I watched Margriete as I thought how she knew of the one secret only my family members knew, and never shared with anyone on this Earth. I knew the only person who knew how to open the door and close it was Margriete herself. For my old Margriete was the one who had that lock made. Rietje kept it ajar as she could not open it otherwise.

I watched the woman standing next to me who looked nothing like Margriete and knew this must be my Margriete. Reborn with a new face and new look. Is it to test me Margriete or punish me? Yet how do I know for sure? I knew it was not the time and place to ask or know.

FORBIDDEN DAUGHTER OF KASTEEL VREDERIC:
VOWS FROM THE BEYOND

We both decided to leave the car far away and walk from a distance. I got a message from Papa who wrote, "Almost home but something is wrong as Antonius and I tried to get in through the gates, but the electricity was cut, and the gates can't be opened. Our phones were cut by someone saying we ordered them to be disconnected immediately. I hope you get this message as I am typing from a stranger's phone to your hospital pager. Pray for your Mama and Katelijne. For unknown reasons I am frightened to death for them. Jacobus, call Theunis and ask for help. He never refuses your calls."

Luckily our hospital provided all doctors with pagers enabled for long messages. Margriete just took my pager and read the message and said, "Strange as my phone was off too. I got the message from Andries on my pager too Jacobus. I gave him the number for emergency needs, as he had to page me for health reasons. I am so worried Jacobus. How do we enter without anyone knowing we are over there? Call the police Jacobus. Call for help please, I am really worried. I don't know how your sixteenth-century Theunis would be able to help."

I worried how do we enter without anyone noticing we were in the house. I did not want Margriete to panic so I told her, "Maybe they are all having a party and somehow did not notice they blew a fuse or something."

My words gave Margriete no peace as she knew Mama would not even allow any celebrations in the house without Papa. I prayed to the spirits of Kasteel Vrederic for guidance and a way into the house. That's when I saw there was a lantern floating somewhere near the lake. It was dancing with the winds. I watched the glow and it seemed like the lantern was moving. There was a small girl with neatly brushed brown hair, about two years old running with the lantern.

Margriete saw the lantern and the baby girl. She smiled and said, "The lake house, Jacobus, don't you remember? Alexander had built the door and the underground tunnel to the library safe house just before the home was besieged by the Spaniards. You were arrogant and ignorant then and refused to hide in the safe house and were shot. I see you have not changed much even though you have traveled through the door of reincarnation. Very arrogant and selfish."

I thought yes, arrogant definitely, but my dear Margriete I have no selfish bone in my body. But I avoided saying anything. For some reason, I knew I should support her and be there for her.

She somehow started to run and said, "Jacobus, it's Griet. She is guiding us. Theunis must be here somewhere. I don't remember if Alexander and my little Rietje ever married but I am positive they did as you all have arrived through the same tree again. Come follow the lantern, it's guiding us into the house. I know it's the same spirit with the lantern as the spirit in the lighthouse."

I wondered why I did not remember Alexander making that tunnel or the entrance to the safe house through the lake house. That's when I saw Margriete observed me for a while, as if she remembered something.

She said, "I forgot you were wounded at that time. You went into deep sleep on and off. It was Alexander who with the help of our spirit twin flames, Theunis and Griet, had completed the project. I remember getting in there, yet I really don't remember getting out of there. I don't know why. Maybe we didn't make it out. I just hope my baby girl Rietje made it out."

I watched Margriete and knew what she was talking about, as the reincarnated twenty-first-century Jacobus had seen this part during our family's time traveling journey.

I only told her, "I am positive Rietje and Alexander had made it out as I was there present at their wedding, and that's how we, my family members and I, are stuck at age thirty."

She saw me and said, "Yes Jacobus, my last memories of you were at that safe house. Somehow, I thought you became young again. I worried why you looked so young, and why you were so distanced from me. Even though I never let you go, from breath to breath I only wanted to breathe for you and with you. That was my last memory."

I saw my inner feelings and my rock-solid arrogant temperament I had built around myself crumbled like a block of a sand fortress. I knew in front of me bravely walking was my twin flame Margriete. Yet how would I tell her I know who she is? How would she believe me that I say this from my inner soul, not from my appreciation for all that she is doing for my family?

So, I said nothing as I let silence chill and freeze all my feelings and the air around us. I permitted silence to remove all the unseen tears that I rolled back into my eyes. Yet I asked my heartbeats to at least feel and touch her heartbeats at least once in this lifetime. I had sprung on to her and did feel her soundlessly. When our bodies touched, I knew she was my twin flame or as some call it, mirror soul.

Just her simple touch awakened my inner soul. I guess it was like looking into the mirror and finding your twin flame.

She felt me and whispered, "Jacobus, quietly follow the lantern please. We must jump into the lake and find the underground tunnel and the door. I hope it is still there, as it will lead us into the lake house and there is another tunnel in the cellar of the lake house that goes into the library. It sounds hard but as the lake is small and the tunnels are really small, it's like a total of five minutes in swimming and walking time. We should be able to get in there quickly if we hurry now."

She said the words and jumped into the freezing cold water. I followed her in there. I saw she was a good swimmer and a fast thinker as she had her underwater cell phone lights on. I realized her phone worked underwater.

Margriete then followed the lantern and was at the underwater gates that looked like they were left open maybe by our ancestors. We jumped inside and saw the tunnel was dark but Margriete's phone light led us to the lake house very quickly. Then as we entered the cellar of the lake house, there was a door and at the door, we found Andries waiting for us.

We were both soaked in water, yet somehow the fresh air had dried our clothes faster than we thought it was possible. I actually thought we felt dry as the lake was magical. I told myself it could be my anxiety of being so close to Margriete and then not wanting to let her know my inner feelings. With all the actions taking place around us at the moment, we both ignored the details about our damp clothes.

Andries, a young man around twenty-seven years of age, was standing in front of us. I watched the brother I had lost only a few years ago standing in front of me. Even though he was Antonius's mirror twin, he looked completely different.

Yet somehow, I knew there in front of me was standing the famous pianist who had left this world and his family only too early. It hurt to know the same people who had killed him last life were again after him and my whole family. I took an oath, not in this life my little brother, you will not be going anywhere.

Andries watched me as I knew he could read my mind as he said, "Big Bro, don't worry about me. I am back. I had to come back as I promised my Big Mama, my mother bear, I will never let her go. I had to keep a son's promise. Now I have to save the other mother who gave birth to me in this life even by risking her own life. She is hurt. The goons were firing at the house and a bullet brushed either in or by her. Big Bro, they tried to hurt my woman, my mother. Some people dressed all in black entered the house somehow. The heavily armed guards were poisoned, and all have fallen asleep. I remembered what Margriete had told me about the hidden safe house if anything or anyone does happen to get in. So instead of fighting with them all alone after we got the one goon, I carried Mama with help from Big Mama and came into the safe house. The great-grandmothers are out touring Margriete's orphanage with Uncle Matthias and a certain nurse. She came and said today she would like everyone to just come with her and tour the orphanage."

He took a breath, and I knew he was shaken up beyond normal. What was normal for this young man now standing in front of me was again a question. He was dealing with all of the changes happening in his life like a true superhero. I knew it was Andries's character not to worry and live life like it's only a day.

He spoke again, "Somehow Mama fell ill and said she was having breathing problems like heart palpitations I am guessing from panic attacks. We all got scared and Big Mama worried she might get ill, so she stayed back at the house with her. I wanted to stay with her as I wanted to make sure the woman takes care of my heart that beats in her body.

It's true you know, my heart beats that woman's name literally."

Margriete asked Andries, "Did Aunt Marinda say anything? Did she give any instructions at all?"

Andries watched Margriete and said, "She told me to give some herbs to you when you come in here. She said you would know what to do. She also told me to SMS you if I find myself and my family members in trouble. Also, she had asked me to take a blanket, some dry food, and water with me if we happen to be stuck with a pregnant woman for more time than we should be. She also kissed Mama and Big Mama as Big Mama swore, she met another woman years ago with the same name and same face. Then, she said it can't be though. But your aunt said, oh yes it was her. She had visited Big Mama in Seattle."

I watched Margriete as I knew she knew what was happening and was worried why Aunt Marinda was here. I knew Aunt Marinda was a time traveler. But I wondered how the time traveler was related to Margriete. I knew this was not the time for my curiosity to take its course.

We rushed into the room Katelijne and Mama were sitting in. I saw Mama was giving Katelijne some kind of herbs that Aunt Marinda had left behind. I rushed in and began my job as a doctor to treat the woman I had brought back to life only a few years ago, with Andries's heart. Margriete sat by me on the cold floor of the safe house and I saw a doctor, Margriete, had begun her job too.

Mama said nothing as she cried and let her tears roll over. Katelijne said to Mama, "Big Mama, no tears. Only smiles and good vibes. My doctor brother is here. He brought in with him Dr. Margriete. I am in the best hands possible. I will survive and I shall give birth to this bundle of joy. Antonius already has the basket all the breads came to this house magically in. He got it ready for the provider of the breads. He painted with his own hands on the basket, 'The Beloved Daughter Of Kasteel Vrederic.'"

I froze from inside at the words and the memories of the same basket that was rejected by this home, the same daughter as we told her she was the forbidden daughter of Kasteel Vrederic. Margriete touched my hands for the first time. She placed her small soft hands in my hands and just watched me. I knew the other person who would know how I felt was Margriete. This child we did not get to hold or have as Papa and Mama when we were together, or when we were separated. I was too arrogant, and life was not fair to us either.

Margriete said, "May you always be healthy and may all the pain you bear for this child be mine and only mine dear Katelijne. May you only have good health, lots of love, and a loving husband. May you always have a loving family by you, during and after her birth. I also pray you be able to hold and bring her up with love and joy. Also, Katelijne, may I be able to hold her in my arms at least once as I will give her all my love and blessings in that one kiss from a mother who also gave birth to her yet never got to hold her. Now get well and never be hurt ever again, my dear sister."

I felt like waves of emotions burst inside of my inner gut. Yet I must really be strong, or I actually was thinking. I must be made out of rocks. For how I was able to just keep quiet all along I had no clue. I realized here Margriete who had once tried to hold her child in her arms now wished she could hold her child in her arms at least once.

My curse, my karma, came back and touched a mother who had no hand in this. Yet she, like a true mother, had given up her child. I prayed please karma, now release Margriete from all of your karmic actions and give all the punishments to me.

Mama was quiet and she for the first time said, "Margriete, I am here, and this child will be ours. She is the blessed daughter of this home. The lucky one, as they say in India, a girl is called Lakshmi. You and Jacobus can behave as you want to, but God has been kind and has given you both a second chance to raise this daughter in a joint family all over again. We here in this home don't have any strangers as all of the children in this house are mine and your Big Papa's. You too are mine as is Katelijne. Whatever happens between you and Jacobus does not matter as I have chosen you as my daughter like I had chosen Katelijne. So, this is one family where all the children are ours."

Katelijne said, "Okay you guys, Griet and Andries are both your children, like do you really think I can raise a young man and a newborn baby by myself?"

Andries laughed as he kissed his mother's head and said, "Woman, let's get you and everyone out of here first. Your bleeding has stopped, and you look better too. I hope Big Papa and Buddy are back."

I laughed as Andries to this day does not call his father Papa but only Buddy. At times he calls his mother Mama and at times only Woman. They both have accepted him just like himself.

I knew the electricity was back as the lights came back on, and I guessed the backup generator too was back on. All of my cell phones also started to come back on.

I got messages from Papa which read, "I hope you all are safe as Antonius and I will be coming into the safe house. I know where it is as we all ended up in there through our dream traveling. Don't come out until we enter and give you all the all-clear. The police are here sweeping around the home and the neighborhood, but we only have proof of people being here yet no one in sight. The goons left broken windows, doors, and bullet holes all over like they wanted to ambush all in the house. Will be there soon. Stay put everyone. I do hope Jacobus and Margriete were able to go there and have Katelijne healed. The cameras showed she was shot on her thigh by a person who had on a ski mask and was wearing all black. I saw my brave wife fight out the shooter with her screams as she shocked the intruder with her screams and Andries had jumped on him with our family sword. He is still nowhere to be found. Only his blood remains from the injuries."

I was furious with the women of my household and Andries, after reading the details on how they made it to the safe house.

Margriete beat me with her screams as she was reading over my head and said, "Andries, I told you to never risk anyone but to quickly hide. Big Mama, you could have been shot! How could you just get in there without protecting yourself?"

Then she saw Katelijne and said, "I left the pepper spray I made with my own hands near your bed to start spraying if you need to."

She then hugged Katelijne and said, "I will stay with you from now on until these goons are caught. I won't risk you or your baby for anything. I got a promise I could hold your baby and be involved in raising her. I will hold on to you and your child within my embrace eternally."

Katelijne then cried and said, "Margriete, it's illegal to have pepper spray in the Netherlands. Yet since it is just a homemade juice which I do keep on my bedside table, I did throw it on him. As he screamed in pain, I ran and Andries was able to take him out as did Big Mama."

I watched Margriete say, "It's juice prescribed to you by your physician for your good health."

Then we saw the doors of the safe house open in front of us. Andries was ready to attack as was I if there was anyone else. Yet Antonius and Papa were there with terrified looks on their faces. Antonius hugged his son first and then Mama and Katelijne. Papa went straight to Mama and both of them just hugged quietly. I actually never saw Mama that quiet in my life. Then I saw in the dark room, her tears were falling over the brink at the sight of Papa.

Mama hugged all of us in a group hug and said, "My four men, my three sons and my husband, are here with me on top of the two daughters whom I never knew I had but am blessed to have. I am not worried anymore as I know there is nothing our family can't do or achieve if only we want or try. I just want to make sure I can hear the heartbeats of our beloved child, the beloved daughter of Kasteel Vrederic, and know that she is just fine."

That's when I told them, "She is fine as I checked her heartbeats first. Also, the beholder of the lantern who brought us here is the spirit of the lighthouse. Remember in the lighthouse, there is a lantern that my beloved daughter had carried all throughout her afterlife. Today, she guided all to safety through the lantern. Now she has guided us to her mother and the blessed womb that carries a blessed child. She will be fine. I know I heard the heartbeats and followed Margriete as she followed the lantern into this safe house. Yet I must say I had no idea about this tunnel as it was completed when I was shot and wounded and had passed away in my last life. Yet Margriete remembered as she saw Alexander complete the job in her last life. I believe she is the only adult reborn on Earth who knows about this tunnel. It was never mentioned in any one of the diaries as the one who knew too had passed away before she could write about it. I know Rietje and Alexander never wrote about it as it probably slipped their minds too."

Margriete watched me and said, "The heartbeats are so strong, they lead all of us to safety. Yes, I followed the lantern of the young girl who was holding it. I watched a child run holding the lantern as we entered the safe house following the lantern. I too heard the heartbeats of the lantern's beholder. The light just went into the womb of Katelijne, who has a pure and blessed soul. In her blessed womb I heard the heartbeats of the blessed daughter."

That night, we all stayed close to one another as I stayed close to my family members.

I asked Margriete, "Do you need to go home? If so, please let me know and I will drop you off myself. I don't want you going on the bus or taking a cab by yourself. Please Margriete don't go, if you don't have to."

Margriete watched me and said, "I called Aunt Marinda and she told me she has the boys back at her home, in the orphanage. She also advised me to keep an eye out for the child Katelijne is carrying. She told me to give you a message and tell you, she will come over and meet with the whole family as you all know her from before. Yet she told me the life of the blessed daughter is at risk. We all must keep an eye out for her at all times and make sure we protect her like she has been protecting this home for centuries. I talked with Antonius and will sleep in Andries's nursery as he has now gone back to his old bedroom."

She then watched me for a long time and said, "Good night, Jacobus. I hope you understand, and I really don't want to talk about anything right now. I am not looking for any understanding, any sympathy, or any love from anyone. I am tired of trying to prove my past that exists in my heart yet it's not there. I cannot see him or touch him or even look at any of the portraits as everything that was, still exists in this house. It's just that I don't. With a new face, I have been reborn Jacobus and I will never again try to prove anything. For me, it's a lot to handle as I feel like I just lost my husband all over again. Just today, again I walked out of the room I had lost him in. Right now, I need time and space to mourn him on my own. For I know you too would have known how it feels if only you had remembered."

She went upstairs, closed the doors, and turned the lights off. I knew my Margriete would cry out all of her tears in the dark. I told her mind-to-mind I don't need the dark to spill my tears dear beloved, as this world had turned me into a rock. That's why it mattered not how much I hurt; the tears don't find a way out of my eyes. I felt like they poured out for you in the safe house or during the short journey to the safe house. Yet I found my tears left my eyes dry. I only knew my heartbeats too heard the heartbeats of a certain woman my heart had beaten centuries for.

Today, however, you were so close to me for as you touched my hand by mistake or maybe in fear you gripped on to my hand, I knew the touch and didn't need my eyes to know or feel you. For I knew it's my eternally, evermore beloved, twin flame who walked with a different face to only tease me. Yet I the cold-hearted soul had again sent her far away through my ignorance and arrogance.

This cold-hearted Papa of Griet who never got to hold her once in my arms while she breathed on Earth, today after centuries I have heard her heartbeats, the heartbeats of the blessed daughter.

A poem for you my beloved twin flame as today again your simple touch had magically melted my cold soul.

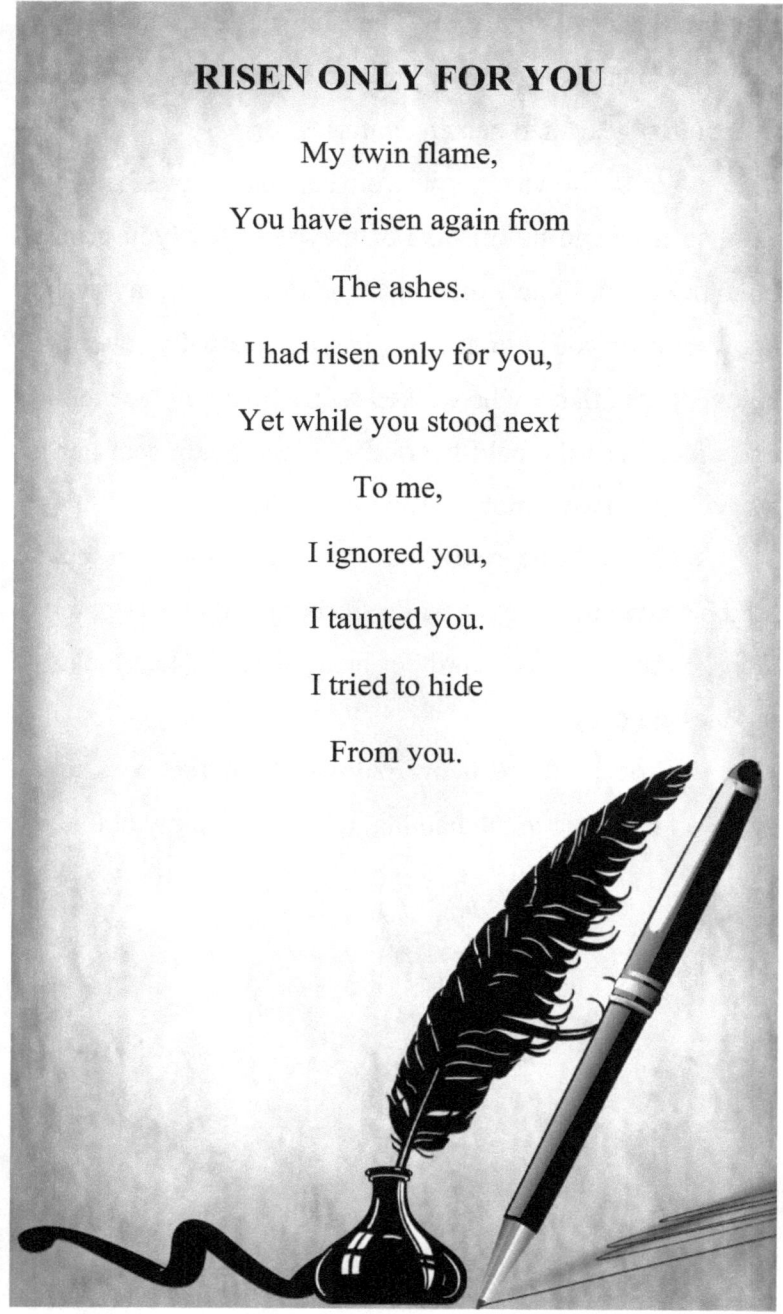

RISEN ONLY FOR YOU

My twin flame,

You have risen again from

The ashes.

I had risen only for you,

Yet while you stood next

To me,

I ignored you,

I taunted you.

I tried to hide

From you.

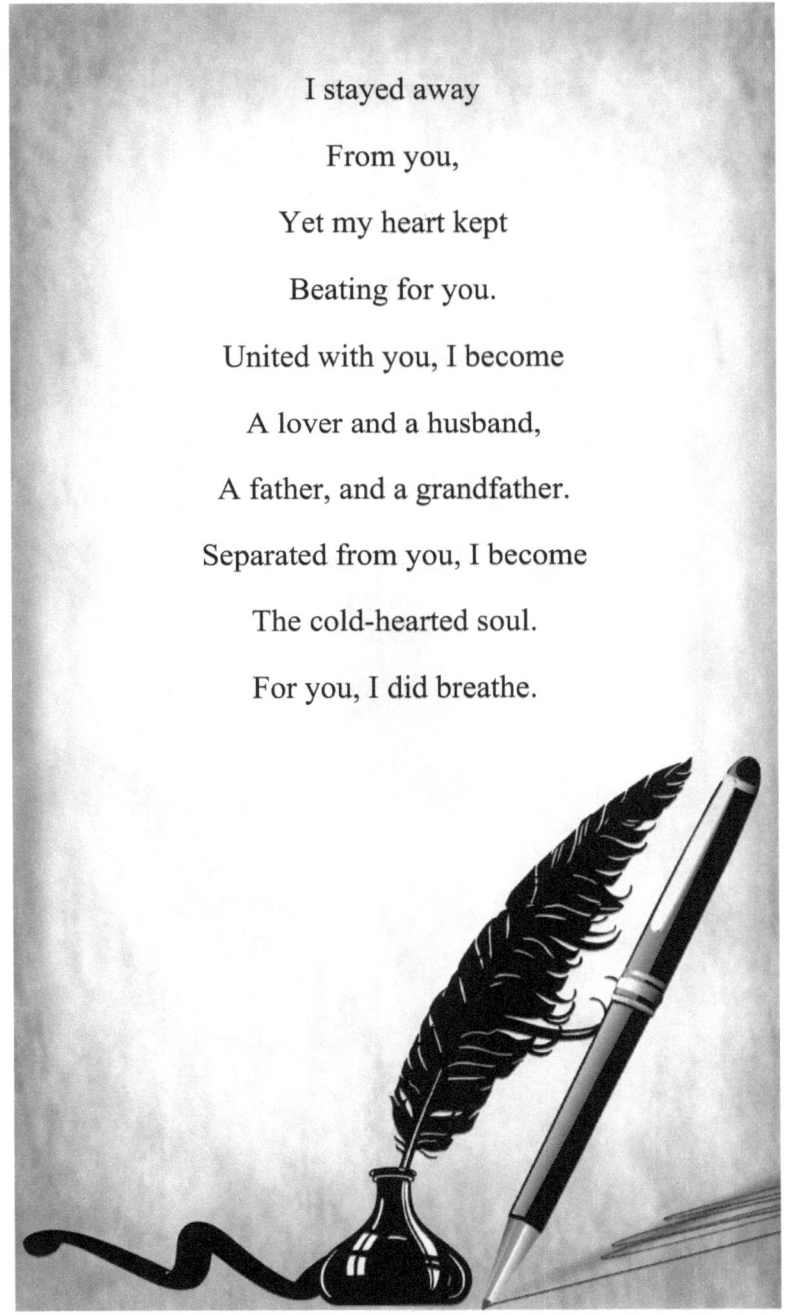

I stayed away

From you,

Yet my heart kept

Beating for you.

United with you, I become

A lover and a husband,

A father, and a grandfather.

Separated from you, I become

The cold-hearted soul.

For you, I did breathe.

Without you, I still do breathe.

Yet I felt lost and breathless.

My dear beloved,

Hold my hands once again,

And be my last hope.

As with your hands

In my hands,

I am once again

Able to love,

And be loved

By only you.

As my

Twin flame,

Please know,

Like the rising phoenix,

I have once again

RISEN ONLY FOR YOU.

CHAPTER FIVE:

Kasteel Vrederic Gets Protection From The Womb

"A mother protects her unborn child within her womb. Yet an unborn child too protects her mother from beyond the womb, and the mother who gave up her child, only to save the child, are both protected through eternal love and tears."

The forbidden daughter becomes the beloved daughter of another son of Kasteel Vrederic and is giving protection to her home from the womb.

Mist formed from Lake Vrederic and created a ghostly atmosphere around our sacred home. Evaporating fog that was over our lake made it look like steam was rising out of the lake and I knew it was only fog, yet I felt like there was more to it.

Mama taught me at a very young age if I could see further away, then it's mist not fog. When there is fog, it's harder to see anything. Yet I only wondered why mist was there rising from the lake. I wondered if someone was angry or was trying to say something or maybe send a message.

My thoughts drifted off to Margriete and what she was doing at this moment. I knew she was in a room across from my own room. I got to see the lake and Margriete actually had a view of the mystical lighthouse as our inner courtyard was also in her vision.

The amazing fountain that dates back about five hundred years still stands tall in the courtyard of our home under the mystical lighthouse lantern. I had stood in front of the fountain in my previous life and wished to find my twin flame who would stand by me eternally. She did stand by me until my last breath as she too came along with me and did not want to be left alone all by herself.

146

FORBIDDEN DAUGHTER OF KASTEEL VREDERIC:
VOWS FROM THE BEYOND

I had prayed in front of the fountain in the courtyard under the lighthouse lantern this life again for my twin flame to arrive somehow, someway. I also prayed may I hold onto her till my last breath for I don't want to live even a day without her. For you my dear beloved, I shall breathe, yet without you, I don't want to take even one single breath.

My phone was buzzing, and I really did not want to pick it up, but I did. There was a strange voice on the other side who said, "Jacobus, is that Dr. Jacobus? This is Theunis. I am three years and one day old. I really need to talk with my doctor girlfriend. I am scared Griet is in trouble. She said she is worried about her Mama. Her Mama might be dying as the bad people are hiding in your home."

I heard on the other side, a very young boy around the same age ask Theunis, "Did you tell the angry man Rietje is also in danger? She needs to find the way home, or she will get lost."

Then the boys were crying as I heard a woman enter and ask the boys what happened and why were they crying. I could not hear, but I heard soft singing in the background and knew a woman was trying to get the boys to calm down. I walked outside and headed straight to Margriete's room. Yet I did not knock on her door. Rather I went to Antonius's room and knocked on his door.

Antonius was so worried, he jumped out of bed and opened the door as he asked, "Big Bro, what's the matter? Are you all right? Is Margriete all right? Okay are Big Mama and Big Papa all right?"

Then he started to run toward Andries's room and without knocking or warning, he walked in screaming Andries's name. I ran after him trying to stop him and to make him listen to me first but being two years younger, he ran faster than I did. I just watched him and waited for him to come back to me. His loud voice, however, woke up the household members as I believe everyone was on the edge anyway keeping an ear out for one another.

Margriete came out in her white batik print nightgown. She had her hair out loose and sandals on her feet. She looked like an Indian princess who just woke up from her sleep. Katelijne came out slowly as I watched Margriete give her a helping hand.

Katelijne screamed and said, "Someone tell me my son Andries is all right please."

I watched another mother run from her room screaming, "No one touches my Andries! I just got him back from the Grim Reaper and I don't want to go back to his gravesite and wish for a miracle to happen."

Papa walked calmly behind Mama and said, "Stay calm sweetheart, everything will be all right if only you are all right."

I had to stop this and shouted above my lungs and screamed, "Family members, just be quiet! I just wanted to talk with Antonius for a minute. He shouted and ran toward Andries's room, I don't know why."

Margriete came close to me and said, "It's the first night Andries is sleeping in his big man room as he is a big six-foot-two-inch man. Yet Antonius refuses to see that and treats him like a baby boy."

Mama said, "Erasmus, get your boys under control. Tell them all to come to the library and we will all have hot chocolate and cookies and fresh bread and then we can listen to Jacobus."

Our family members were all over the edge with their nerves and everyone woke up with fear. I didn't want my family members to live within fear as no one should live in their own home in fear. This is our sacred ground, and we were being hunted down in our own home by the goons because they did something wrong.

I watched my mother make hot chocolate and lemon ginger tea. She brought out fresh bread and butter that always arrived within our home when we asked for it. She also got cookies out for Andries and Antonius to dip in their hot chocolate. I watched Mama and watched her make coffee for Papa and me. Margriete was there helping Mama as Katelijne sat on the reclining sofa with her feet up.

I went to Katelijne and asked her, "How is your pain? Let me check on your thigh and see if it is healing. Are you in any kind of discomfort? I know Margriete has been checking on you herself."

Katelijne said, "I am fine. The herbal things Margriete's Aunt Marinda had sent actually healed my thigh and it's like there was no bullet scrape. No pain either. My nausea also stopped, and I feel better than before."

I kissed her head and told her, "This Big Bro will always be here for you eternally. You don't have to take the pain all by yourself."

Andries walked in with Antonius and both boys went straight to Mama as they asked, "Big Mama, are you all right? Did you have a nightmare?"

Then they saw the cookies and chocolate milk and said, "Oh snack time."

They both went and sat by Mama's feet and Mama automatically started to rub their temples like she always had. I watched Margriete serve everyone the hot and cold beverages. She then sat down with her hot lemon, ginger, and mint tea.

I watched her give Katelijne the same drink and ordered her to drink it like a good girl. Margriete the doctor was visible to everyone's eyes. Yet within my eyes, there were signs of tears and a sadness that she buried within under a doctor's cloak. I saw Papa watch me and so did Mama as they both saw what I saw yet permitted silence to hide all the secrets of Margriete's inner soul.

That's when I saw Andries was watching me and said, "Big Bro, everyone is acting to be cool and sophisticated and patient, but please let us know what happened. There is no way you would have Buddy wake up the whole house unless you wanted all of us to be in the same room together. Also, I know our great-grandmothers and Uncle Matthias are staying as guests at Margriete's orphanage so they could be kept away from Kasteel Vrederic. But my question is why?"

Then before I could answer, he said, "Oh yes Big Bro, before you ask me how I knew you woke up the whole house through Buddy, it's because we all know he will panic and go shouting and asking for each and all family members one at a time before he calms down and he too knows when you call him at night saying you need to talk, it's you who is setting the Buddy alarm. A painter who never panics until it's his family. Also, you never get this worried unless you know something we don't."

I told my family about the strange call I got from Theunis, the three-year-old baby boy. I told them "The strangest part is I don't know how he even got a phone and my number. He was crying and told me Griet's life is in danger. Strange thing is he also told me about Griet and Katelijne before when Margriete and I had rushed to the lake house. Yet tonight I heard Alexander talk from behind and say Rietje's life is in danger as she is waiting in the tunnel and will be lost unless we can get her soon."

Margriete came near me and for the first time since I knew her, she said in a loud voice, "You took away Griet from me, I said nothing. You will not take Rietje away from me Jacobus. For it was and always is Rietje for whom I lived on and my heart still beats. If anything happens to my Rietje then all the mothers on this Earth would be put to shame, as a mother's love saves a child. My love brought my daughter back in the same household as my sister's daughter. Don't you take away the heartbeats from my inner soul Jacobus. I will never forgive you. Don't remember me, but how could you take away my Rietje because you don't remember me? I will protect her with my dead body like before."

Mama stood up and went in front of Margriete and said, "If you were still a three-year-old girl, I would have slapped you, but we promised never to hit our children no matter how mad we get. Take back the words you just recited in anger. Karma is always watching over us and you don't want words to become a circle. If you die, how will my Jacobus live on? I can't lose another child because you have lost it. Fight for what is yours and don't give up because life is hard. Rietje will come only if you too live for her to come to you."

I watched Mama and then saw Margriete get in Mama's arms as she broke down within her embrace.

Then Margriete said, "I take back my words and may no harm come from my words upon my children, my Griet and Rietje. May my love protect them eternally."

Papa came and said, "Anadhi and Margriete, it's my karma and my past life's curses we are all living within. Yet I will fight with my boys this life to make sure our home finds peace. Also, Jacobus please tell us what else can we do? Or what else is going on? Can anyone else help? I feel like we need to get those two boys in our home, not for our protection but to protect them from all the unknown enemies. What if their lives are at risk? I won't be able to forgive myself."

I watched Antonius and Andries finish their chocolate milk like it was the only thing they could concentrate on. Yet I knew my brothers and knew when they get worried, both of them eat. Everyone in the room was watching Antonius and Andries.

As Mama slapped their heads with her soft hands, she asked, "You two, are you two even here? Are you listening?"

Andries said, "Big Mama, we were trying to not waste the milk. You made it with your blessed hands."

I watched Mama now kissing their heads. Yet I saw Katelijne was somehow very uncomfortable. She said, "Big Bro, I don't feel good, as if the baby is talking from within my womb. It's strange but I can hear words. And it's getting louder."

That's when we saw there in the room, a light had appeared from Katelijne's womb and in front of us was standing a small child with a lantern in her hand. She was crying and walked over to Margriete. She watched Margriete and just stood in front of her for a while.

She then said, "Mama, please don't cry for I love you more than being born. Please with love and blessings give me your permission to be born from your sister Katelijne's womb. For Uncle Antonius had brought me back to this home with love and blessings and because of his innocent calls, I am home again."

Griet then came over to me and said, "Papa I have forgiven you last life, for how could I not forgive someone I loved with all my heartbeats? Like I had said, I shall never let you go, if only you were mine. Yet now through Uncle Antonius, I will be your niece and then I shall never let you go."

She then walked over to Papa and said, "Opa, I know how hard you tried to save me last life, even with your memories gone you fought. I had entered after death to this home only because I forgave my family members. I love you all and know last life my heartbeats had stopped only wishing to be with all of you. This time, I shall be with you all as the blessed child of Kasteel Vrederic and may this world remove the curse and erase my name from the forbidden daughter of Kasteel Vrederic."

Griet then walked over to Andries and said, "Brother Bear, I need your help as some bad people are hiding in our home. They have entered the castle and still hide in here. They will try to attack from within the home. They were not found as they live inside within the hidden walls of this home. They are dangerous as they hear everything and can see everything. Please get Theunis and Alexander back inside the home. As you should know, Theunis is the main protector of this home. It was Theunis who brought me back to this house and it's within his hands the protection of this home lies. For when he is here, it is then I too shall protect my home from even within my mother's womb. Brother Bear, remember it is Mama Katelijne they all want to murder as they don't want her or you to testify in front of the world against them."

The light evaporated and we were left in a room where everyone within the room was filled with tears. If only tears could create a river, then we have flooded our library. I stood up with dried eyes and knew if I control myself too long, I will have a broken heart that will never mend.

Margriete got up first as did Katelijne and both hugged one another. Margriete said, "We will fight with everything that we have. I will ask Aunt Marinda to bring the boys back home to where they belong. I will not allow anyone to even come near Katelijne with my life. Jacobus, help me please. Our children are at risk. Big Mama, do something. Big Papa, please. Antonius, Andries, get up and let's get ready to fight once more. This time we fight with the hidden invaders of our home."

Antonius got up and saw there was a sword left from Theunis that was used to get rid of the goons of this home over and over again. I knew that sword belonged to Theunis and then his daughter Rietje, who was trained to be one of the best swordswomen during that time period. We shall again protect our home with the same sword.

I told everyone, "We already have the sword of Theunis as he had gifted this to his only child Rietje. With this sword we shall begin to get our home free from the twenty-first-century invaders."

I then told Margriete in front of all, "I must go and get my pickup truck from the road. I had parked it far away, so we don't give out our arrival to the invaders. Also Margriete, where is your car? You came here in mine."

Margriete watched me strangely and said, "I don't own a car Jacobus. I ride my bike. Why would I waste money on gas and bus if I could save some and give it to my children in the orphanage?"

I only saw her and worried where did I go wrong as I couldn't live without my car and pick-up trucks. I watched Papa as he too avoided my eye contact. No one said anything for a while.

Then Andries said, "So Big Bro, your truck is home. Buddy and Big Papa brought it home, as they have the duplicate key. We should worry about calling the cops and somehow, we must come up with a story as to how we know the invaders are hiding in our home. Also do you guys think we are safe in this room? Is that why Griet brought us to this room?"

I watched Andries and told him, "I had installed a special detector in this room which not only detects any cameras but also turns off all cameras and sound systems trying to look at or hear anything in this room."

Mama then watched all of us and said, "My babies, then I take the loveseat and let Katelijne and Margriete take the reclining sofa. You all just take any other seat or the carpets and let's get some sleep as dawn will break soon. Jacobus, call your inspector friend and tell him everything. Let's be ready as they are all ready. Also remember in this room, we have the escape route and the secret room we can all hide within if needed."

I watched my mother who was wearing her simple white pajama dress and had her long black hair in a bun. She looked no more than thirty years old. Papa, the tallest in the Vrederic family with his brown hair and his light French beard also looked like he was in his thirties.

Now the whole family looked like we were all in our thirties, excluding Margriete. She was younger, and I believe she was still twenty-seven years old. I knew we would have to deal with all of our age progression or regression issues next. Tonight, I just wanted to hold on to what I had and not fail any one of my family members.

Antonius came closer to me and whispered, "Do we all need to sleep here? Is that really needed? Because we don't want anyone to know we are all weak and frail and scared. Also, I believe this way we will all scare ourselves even more. Let's tell Big Mama we should not frighten away from danger but face it if it comes in front of us. I am scared to sleep in the library Jacobus."

I watched my brother and wondered why he was so uncomfortable to sleep in here. I tried to read his blank face as he was looking at Mama and did not know what to say. I wondered if I should just ask him for the answer.

So, with a lot of hesitation, I asked him, "Antonius, the truth please. Why are you scared of sleeping in the library?"

He watched me and said, "Because last time we did, I almost lost you. I will not have it anymore. I could take a lot of loss but losing you or Andries or anyone else in this household, I don't think I can handle the pain of it. Big Bro, you almost quit on us in this room, remember?"

I touched his back and told him, "I am not going anywhere. Also, to answer your question, no I don't remember. I only went to sleep and as I woke up, you all, including Margriete, were hovering over me."

Andries was standing next to us and started to laugh as he said, "Big Bro, at least you had familiar faces hovering over you. I went to sleep, and I woke up after a nightmare of traveling through tunnels to people going 'goo goo ga ga' over me. I wondered why I could not get my words out or tell you all it's me Andries. Then I had to learn to walk and talk all over again. It's hard as time was passing by, I was forgetting my memories. I only survived knowing now Big Mama can sleep in her own bed. Jacobus, I watched Big Mama cry over my grave, over and over again. I felt her pain and her inner soul was ripped out of her. It was really painful to see her in that stage. Worse was knowing I caused pain to my mother, and I could not do anything to erase that pain. I prayed to be with her once more so I could tell her my heartbeats belonged to her and when they stopped, they still called her name. I just wanted to be back with her."

Antonius and I just watched our brother recall what he felt and saw from beyond the grave. I wanted to ask so much more but I knew it was not the time. I saw Mama watch me and I knew she was worried for all of us. I will never let my mother go through this pain ever again.

FORBIDDEN DAUGHTER OF KASTEEL VREDERIC:
VOWS FROM THE BEYOND

I saw Katelijne and Margriete were watching us as they were sitting on the reclining sofa under a soft blanket cuddled together. Mama and Papa were on the loveseat cuddled up next to each other. Mama fits on Papa's lap so easily as she was so small and petite.

This time I said quietly but loud enough for my brothers to hear, "Must protect Mama at any cost."

Mama asked us, "My boys, what is it? Why are you three whispering? I don't like whispers; it makes me think something is wrong with my ears."

Margriete watched her and laughed out loud as she said, "Big Mama, you have two doctors in the house. Your son is one of the world's most famous doctors. I am positive you are always in good hands. I think it's his fault. A doctor's voice is always like a whisper. It always irritated me, so I make sure I don't whisper with my patients as they are children, and they don't hesitate to tell me the truth."

Mama watched us and we knew we better tell her something otherwise she would get worried. I watched my brothers and knew Andries would do it, and he did just that.

He said, "Big Mama, Antonius farted. He has been farting, so he does not want to sleep in the library, and everyone is annoyed with his farting noises and not to mention the smell."

Antonius watched everyone with a blank face, and he gave Andries a look like you will pay for that look but did not say anything. None of us said anything as we swore anything for the woman whom we all call Mama.

I watched the two women cuddled on the sofa say nothing but place the blanket over their faces.

Mama watched them and said, "Girls don't cover your faces. I like to know my children are breathing. Keep your faces uncovered."

The two women who walked into this house as strangers knew they too were my mother's children. No one said anything and the whole room went into pin-drop silence. That's when a sound from the house broke everyone's sleep.

I told Margriete, "Take Mama and Katelijne and go hide in the safe house now."

Papa came near us and asked me, "Did you call the police? Were they told about how we suspect there is someone hiding in the house?"

I told them, "Yes I did, and they said they had sent extra police to do rounds and keep an eye. They also said on top of sex traffickers, now we are dealing with drug dealers as the Bakkers were found to be tied with both crimes. They have a big case reopened and placed it against them. Somehow our family had to get involved in it. They believe as Andries was trying to save Katelijne, he somehow saw the drug dealers and the sex traffickers. It is possible he or Antonius did not even realize but somehow, they thought Andries saw everything. So, they used Aideen to kill Andries with injected drugs. Aideen, however, might have thought she was giving him diabetic injections as she was found screaming and saying, 'The guy is diabetic, and I was told to give him insulin.'"

The sounds disappeared as I continued, "All of this was disclosed to me a few hours ago as one of the sex traffickers has volunteered to help in return for lesser punishment. So now they are saying Aideen was helpless as she was mentally disturbed. She was on heavy drugs and was kept on various medications and could not even remember what she did and did not do. She was evil, however, and had committed a lot of sex crimes but did not want to harm anyone with death."

That's when we heard gunfire and what sounded like alarms and fighting going on outside. We also heard sirens warning us the police too were here. That's when I saw again a lantern appeared and there in front of us was a young girl who was shining and glowing like a lantern.

She said, "Get into the safe house everyone as the police too have gone bad. A lot of them are involved with the drug dealers and will betray you, as their names would otherwise be disclosed as corruption beyond normal. Please, time is being wasted. Go and hide. Do remember not to tell anyone about this hiding place. Otherwise remember Big Papa, Papa, Opa, and Brother Bear, a life could be lost too early and too soon in this house, then Rietje would be at risk. Please keep everyone safe by staying together, not separated."

Griet was in the form of a young girl, the girl with a lantern was real. It's my baby girl Griet. She then watched all of us and said, "Please remember as you all had left me back in the tunnel of light to enter the reincarnation zone, I had seen a very old Rietje enter the tunnel. I saw my own child for the first time and knew I had to hold her at least once. I ran backward as did Theunis. Yet he stopped running first, then I was stopped by my father Antonius as he held on to me and I cried as I saw Rietje was walking alone. That's when I saw Papa Jacobus had gone backward even though he was on my father Antonius's shoulder being carried. Yet Rietje was then picked up by Papa Jacobus not far behind me. I watched Alexander had walked into the tunnel earlier as did Theunis. They both went ahead. So, remember my warnings. It's Rietje now whom you must protect."

Griet was becoming nothingness as the light was fading. She said still trying to rush her words, "If I am forbidden, then all my lineage is forbidden, and so are all of you. From me, all of you had come all over again. From Theunis, you all had come all over again. So, find him and bring him and Alexander back home. The protection lies in the hands of the ancestors of this home. Theunis is the only one who can help you all. Alexander too could give some protection."

I got up first as did Andries, and we moved everyone into the safe house, one by one. Antonius, Andries, Papa, and I went last. The lightless room was shining as again there was a lantern shining in the safe house miraculously. I only wondered how will my little Rietje will come now. I wondered what was going on and how will everything be solved?

Mama told us, "Reincarnation is strange. At times, children, grandchildren, nephews, or nieces can be born from one another. I believe Rietje too will be born near to Griet as Griet walked back in time. She had waited for her daughter and now they will be born as either sisters, cousins, or just friends. I am not sure or even though I did see this part years ago in my dreams, I won't share until it's the proper time. Let's try to survive this trauma first."

That's when our lantern had gotten brighter and glowed with its beholder. We saw there in front of us was a basket of freshly baked breads, butter, and warm milk. I knew it was almost dawn as breakfast just arrived. I only hoped with the first sight of dawn, we would find ourselves safe within our own home. We just needed to settle down until dawn appeared within our lives. We all could not see dawn or the morning skies, as this room was blistering cold and dark even in daylight hours.

No light streamed into the safe house even through the newly installed window through which people inside could see the outside world. Yet from the outside, the window looked like a part of the cold stone walls. This was completed for situations like this. I knew even if no earthly humans could see the cold walls, one person I knew who had traveled time and tide to help us would know and see. This one person could see through any barrier, be it a wall or be it even time.

I then saw Margriete sitting on the cold floor at the corner of the safe house. She had bad memories of this room that had covered her soul. I only wished I could erase those memories and give her better ones to forget them by. I thought she was a mind reader for what she said next shocked me. I thought did I say that aloud?

FORBIDDEN DAUGHTER OF KASTEEL VREDERIC: VOWS FROM THE BEYOND

She watched me and said, "Jacobus, please don't worry about me or my memories. I know you want to erase them as it hurts to see me this way. Yet dear Jacobus, I don't ever want to erase the memories of my beloved, whether they are bad ones or good ones. For me, life is nothing but a love story which began in the sixteenth century and still continues in the twenty-first century. My daughter did not live long, yet she lived enough time to carry on the Vrederic family lineage. I am blessed I have always had her by my side as a spirit. A mother protects her children Jacobus, but my child has protected her family members and me from the beyond. Now she is protecting all from her new mother's womb, which I her mother still am blessed to be a part of. I won't change anything Jacobus as I lived for my beloved and had died on his chest and that was my love story I would treasure eternally."

I stood up and told her in front of all, "For you Margriete, I forgot to love. I buried myself in your memories. In front of my eyes, you stood with a different face and different looks, yet you were still yourself. I realized it when a look-alike of your past life's face came and declared herself as you. I knew then it mattered not what you look like, but I could see you through my inner eyes. My beautiful Indian princess or Dutch princess, it matters not as

I only wish and pray may you never let me go, as I promise in front of my family members, you have me or not, I shall never let you go. Now I also keep as my witness my daughter who has returned once again as our beloved daughter."

Papa spoke after a long time as he said, "We shall survive another war, the emotional and physical war we are about to face as now through our beloved daughter, our home Kasteel Vrederic gets protection from the womb."

In the dark room as we waited for dawn, I wrote a love letter to my beloved through a poem.

ALL MY LOVE

Sacredly kept my

Mind, body, and soul

Hidden in a box

Called arrogance.

Some call it ignorance.

Some call the box,

A cold

Freezer box.

Yes, my beloved,

They also call it ruthless,

The one who is

Heartless.

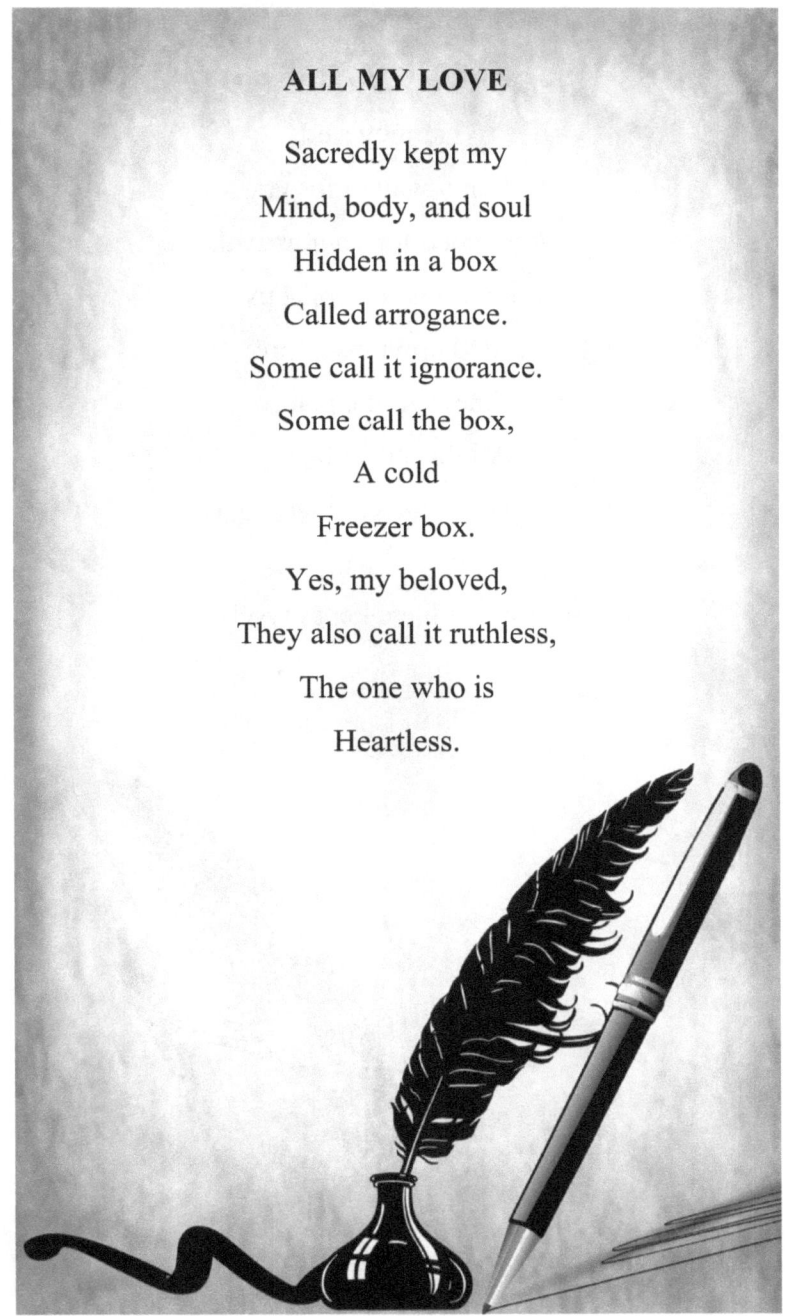

It mattered not
What they said
As I only waited for you.
I only hoped for your arrival,
For with your footsteps
Printed upon my shore,
I knew all the pain,
All the sufferings,
The name callings,
Would end.
For you, I have kept myself
In a box,
Hidden from all

The hurtful,

And unjust words

Of this society.

For I know

Your words,

Your loving gazes,

Your understanding

Of all my pain,

Would only

Make all my

Dreams to become true.

So, my beloved,

I only ask you,

Even though everyone

Misunderstands me,

Don't you ever

Misunderstand me,

For I became like this

To keep myself

Hidden in the box,

Only for you.

So, when you do finally

Open the box,

You will see,

In this box,

Which is my inner chest,

I have hidden,

For only you,

ALL MY LOVE.

CHAPTER SIX:

A Righteous Soldier And An Honorable Knight Return

"Reincarnation is a blessing if only you remember, yet reincarnation is welcomed in my home even if you don't remember. For through this door, I get you and will have you from far away even if you don't remember."

Dr. Jacobus Vrederic van Phillip stands in front of the secret window and finds a canoe appeared in the lake.

The morning mist had a visitor today, as there in the sky was a sunbow. A sunbow is an arc that appears to look like a rainbow. Yet it actually is formed by the sun shining through the mist. I wondered if Mother Nature was giving me a sign that even through the dimness, we will have some kind of light that shall guide us out of this darkness.

Margriete was up and checking on Katelijne. I checked on Andries and knew he had stopped aging and was around the same age he had passed away in his last life. Mama came and stood in front of me. I knew it meant she wanted her shoulders massaged. I kissed my mother on her head and automatically massaged her shoulders. They were so stiff I worried she was worrying more than she showed any one of us.

Papa was talking with Katelijne as he asked, "Are you comfortable, in this cold place? Do you need anything? I am worried in your condition you should have good nutrition, get some light walking done, and get a lot of rest. At least that's what we did when your Big Mama was pregnant with Jacobus."

I knew he was right, and we should get her out of here but how? I tried to make eye contact with the other doctor in the room. Yet I saw her wondering in her own world. Somewhere in her world, I did hope she found some place for me too. Yet I wouldn't ask as she still believed I was just accepting her as a gesture of goodwill. How would I tell her I had blocked off all of my feelings because of her? I was determined to win her over with all my love. I would not pressure her nor would I make any move on her as I would make sure she too loved me back. Now I was jealous of my own self of the sixteenth century. Yet I told Margriete in my mind, I love you too much to let you go or pull you in.

Andries screamed, "The phone is buzzing! It's someone's cell phone. Whose phone is buzzing? Guys, check your phones."

Papa screamed back, "It's my phone! The police commissioner has called back. He has become a friend and tried to help and has been in communication ever since Andries was murdered."

Mama got up and sat next to him. She tried to read Papa's mind as he was only saying, "hmm" and "yes" and nodded his head.

Then Mama said, "Erasmus, speakerphone please. We will stay quiet, but I can't take the anxiety much longer."

I saw Papa turn the speakerphone on. The conversation was one-sided as the police commissioner said, "It's a very risky and critical situation as they have moved into your home. We too tried getting in but could not find anyone as of yet. They can't hide in the forest as we have surveillance there. Somehow, we believe they have taken homes around your home. We are trying to check on all the tenants and people who have bought properties in the last few years around your home. The drug dealers are trying to go under. The Bakkers have not been caught as we think they could be anywhere in Europe. All of their hotel chains have been frozen including all their assets and bank accounts. I know we will get them. It's a matter of time."

Papa said, "So if you don't know where they are, why have you asked my family to stay put in one room and not go anywhere?"

The police commissioner took a break and then said, "We have picked up some dead bodies from your neighborhood. We believe they are young women who were raped and left for the wild animals. We also found some more bodies of very young boys. I believe there were drug dealers trying to get these boys to sell drugs for them. We believe these are just simple threats. And we did get a letter asking us if you would leave your home and give it to them, then they would leave you and your family alone forever. They told us then they would also take their business to another place."

FORBIDDEN DAUGHTER OF KASTEEL VREDERIC: VOWS FROM THE BEYOND

Papa said in a very cold tone, "We the members of Kasteel Vrederic know how to fight our own battles. With or without your help, we will fight and not be intimidated. This property belonged to my ancestors who were all noblemen and noblewomen. It will always remain in the family, which is still known as a principled family. Never shall this home fall in the hands of the dishonest, duplicitous, or fraudulent people. I thank you for all that you are doing and hope as it's your duty to get the criminals, you do get them. If you don't or for any other reasons refuse to catch them, then my friend you too shall become an enemy of the inhabitants of Kasteel Vrederic eternally."

I heard on the other side the voice was shaking in fear as I knew no one wanted to be an enemy of the famous spirits of Kasteel Vrederic. Yet the police commissioner only said, "Erasmus, we will not give up and shall continue to search all around the country and beyond, until we catch them. The property should be safe as we have very high security involved, yet there are still murders and rapes going on somehow. We only ask you to be careful for a few more days as we try to resolve the situation."

The phone was disconnected by my father who never gets angry or shows a temper. I heard him breathe hard through his nose.

Antonius said, "Big Papa, you are breathing through your nose, that means it's now all right to panic."

Andries looked at Antonius and said, "It means now Big Papa is upset and we should all run away and maybe go to one of our vacation places for a while. Big Mama, you still own your homes in Seattle and India, we can go there."

Margriete said, "I have a home in Scheveningen and in San Francisco. I also have one in Los Angeles. No one would even think of going to my homes as they were my grandmother's. After her death, I now own all of them. My distant aunts whom I never knew existed had invited me to live with them in the orphanage which I now co-own. So, all of the houses are open for all of you to just go and be in for as long as you need them."

I watched Margriete and told her, "Maybe we shall take you on your offer and go on a vacation after this ordeal is over. Yet now I will stay here and protect my ancestral property. For I know help will arrive soon as the sunbow that appeared this morning over the lake in the skies is my evidence, someone is trying to perform yet another miracle."

Andries said, "I have returned from beyond death not to give away our home. I have come back to be with my family. I shall also take revenge on my death, and for making my mother, my Big Mama cry for all those nights. So, I call upon the one and only ancestor who had protected this home eternally from beyond, also for whom and through whose bloodline we have all returned."

It was then through the miraculous sunbow that had created an arc, a bridge over Lake Vrederic, we all saw a canoe was approaching our home. We could not see if there were people in the canoe as it was covered like a fishing canoe, providing shelter for rain. Yet it just came closer and closer toward the lake house. We all hoped if there were goons in the canoe, it would just pass by as it is impossible to find the hidden tunnel through the lake into the lake house, then through the underground tunnel to our safe house.

Margriete came and stood by me, somehow touching me from behind. I knew it was her even though I did not see her. I could smell her, feel her, and knew she better move away if she did not want me to kiss her in front of everyone.

Oblivious to my feelings, she screamed, "Aunt Marinda is here! That's my aunt and her centuries-old canoe. That kind of canoe is not made or found anywhere else on Earth. They stopped making that for centuries. I would tell her she is a witch or maybe just a seeker or a time traveler who travels to places or people she loves. She says she will appear if and only when you need her."

I watched my family members come one by one and stand next to me. All of them were pushing me forward. They did not even leave a gap in between as all wanted to see what was going on.

I shouted and told them, "I will fall out through the window if you all don't move back."

Everyone moved backward and Mama said, "I want to see who is coming Jacobus. It's not fair you are watching but not telling us what you see. Someone should be on watch who would say or tell everyone what is happening."

Everyone at once said, "Antonius."

I knew everyone agreed Antonius would repeat everything to the bullet as he saw them. Yet how could I tell my family we don't want any sounds attracting anyone toward us through their retelling of the sight-seeing tales? I did not want any alarm bells going on but how would I say it or not say it? I saw Andries watching me.

He said, "I can hear them, the newcomers. They are talking to me mind-to-mind. Actually, they are talking with my sister in the womb. I guess I can hear all of them as I too shared the womb with my sister. She is calling them and asking for help. They are asking me to convey the messages to you all to not do anything until they arrive. Also, one of the boys asked if he could use the potty. The other one is

182

asking for his bread and butter. Big Bro, I think we are getting an army of toddlers as help."

Margriete jumped up and said, "My boys are here. My miracle babies are here. Theunis needs his bread and butter. Alexander needs to use the potty as I just potty trained him. I knew it, Aunt Marinda is here with the boys."

I had my arrogance or maybe the scientist in me think to myself, okay so we have two toddlers and a woman who is so old that she is thought to be maybe centuries old. I did not know if I should be happy or worried now that we were risking the lives of three more people. Yet how could I again say something and get everyone's hopes crushed? I only hoped my Theunis Peters from the sixteenth century could have arrived to be by my side. I miss you my buddy. Yet I kept quiet and hoped if we the inhabitants of Kasteel Vrederic couldn't do anything, then Kasteel Vrederic would be able to fend for herself.

As we all waited, it seemed like hours went past us, although we all knew it was only a few minutes. Margriete was so worried for the toddlers, she almost started to cry. I realized how hard it must be for all the orphanages to raise a child and then let the child go. On the other hand, I knew people like Margriete would just set them free to be adopted by a well-off family who would give them love. The children would give the parents a family. Yet I knew these two boys belonged in this house and should stay here as I knew I shall never let Margriete go, if only she were mine.

The doors to the safe house opened and there in front of us was standing Aunt Marinda from the sixteenth century. The same Marinda who had helped me save Margriete and set the witches free. The same Marinda who had traveled time and had helped Mama find Papa. She also helped Antonius and Katelijne find one another.

I wonder if she had personally brought Margriete into our home to once again help a cold-hearted man who needed to find his own heart and the beholder of it. Now again it was as if time had stood still for her as with the same appearance and looks in front of us was our favorite psychic who had for years predicted the unseen and unknown futures of the inhabitants of Kasteel Vrederic. The same psychic who had taken a vow to protect Kasteel Vrederic and her inhabitants throughout time.

She arrived with two little boys who were holding on to her hands like their lives depended on how strong they could hold on to her. They both saw Margriete and let go of Aunt Marinda and ran to her. They both jumped on her lap and kissed her both cheeks from two sides.

The blond-haired one, I assumed Theunis, said, "Don't ever let go of me ever again. I missed you so much woman."

Alexander who was one day younger said, "How could you be so mean woman? I cried for you and am scared now to let you go ever again."

Then Aunt Marinda said, "My dear niece, you do have a way of making elders even older by making them worry for you. Now go on, get everyone out of here and let's go to the parlor and have some food in our bellies first. No worries now. Just make sure you don't ever let these boys stay away from you even for a minute. It's to the very uttermost urgency that you pay heed to my words. If ever you need to be away from these boys, then you keep your mean old Jacobus near you. His cold heart will get warm from it and maybe he will remember you through his inner soul."

She then watched Papa and said, "Johannes, how are you? It seems you have found my Anadhi and are behaving in this life. I am glad I was able to help."

Then she saw Katelijne and said, "Dear child with the sweetest and most loving soul, I see you now bear within your womb another child of this home. This time you are giving back the home's soul through the blessed daughter of

Kasteel Vrederic. Yet do remember the original mother of this home too bears the soul of this home. She must never leave this home crying or hurt, for then everything in this home shall again go into the darkness that evolves around the home even now."

Aunt Marinda walked to Antonius and said, "Dear son with the blessed soul, I am happy now you have eyes to see with, yet even when you did not, it never stopped from seeing the truth. I bless you with happiness forever."

She walked and kissed Andries and said, "You are a true warrior and shall always be. The sacrifice you made for an unknown woman was not a simple sacrifice as this sacrifice gave both of you another chance at life. Karma had you enter her womb, which was your world before this world. It's true a mother's heart beats for her children, yet this mother can always say her son's heart beats within her."

Aunt Marinda went to Mama and Papa as she said, "The love story you had woven throughout centuries has come true through your belief in one another. Your vows from the beyond had made you one another's destiny. I am honored to have known you and your love story."

Then she came to me, "Dear Jacobus, we do have a wonderful history together. We rescued your beloved with the help of the honorable soldier Theunis and the honorable knight Sir Krijn. Today in front of you, you have Sir Krijn's nephew the honorable knight Sir Alexander and the honorable soldier Theunis standing in human form. Don't be fooled by their age, as they have an old soul which they have brought on with them in these newly found earthly bodies. Also, Jacobus, the wife you had sought and fought to rescue even in the sixteenth century is and was standing in front of you. I had found her and had sent her to your home. Yet I hear you could not recognize her because of her newly found earthly veil given to her by her Creator. Yet I wonder is she the one with the veil? Or is it you who has worn your veil?"

She said nothing more as we moved back to our home and were in the parlor like nothing had happened. There was food on the table and all the drapes were open. It was like we had been in the home all along. I wondered who had opened the drapes.

Aunt Marinda warned us as she said, "Don't eat the food. It was not made by me or anyone from the house, yet it was made by some of the corrupt police who had moved in thinking you all have left. They have opened the drapes to keep an eye over you all, not to protect but to make sure you don't return. Not all of the police are good, as some are corrupt and bad and have given a bad name to all the good police. I wonder do you really trust your friend, the police commissioner? How long have you known him? Why is he so involved in this case? Keep an eye on him. Also don't share all the details about our home with him."

Papa said, "I don't know but I thought I could trust him. Yet I do wonder then who can we trust these days?"

Aunt Marinda said, "Trust in yourself first, then the members of this house, your family members, the inhabitants of Kasteel Vrederic."

She then walked around the house and said, "Anadhi, I shall stay in the room with my Margriete so make sure we are both comfortable in there. The two young boys shall stay with Andries as he now knows he can mind talk with all of them. We shall win this war as long as we can keep Margriete alive till Rietje returns."

The nightfall came and we were all worried where we should all sleep and if we should be separated or hang around together. I had faith in Aunt Marinda and knew not to ask her any more questions other than what she had volunteered to answer. Yet I was bothered why she said Margriete is in danger. I would protect her with all of my being even if it meant I must stay awake all night to keep the Grim Reaper away. I must talk with her privately and ask her more questions as how was it she did not age at all from the sixteenth century? Was she reborn like all of us or how is it she appears where she is needed?

I watched the two little boys playing in the family room with Margriete, Andries, and Antonius. The room was converted into a playroom for young boys. Papa was busy getting toys and setting up the playroom as Mama was busy making snacks for the boys. I saw Katelijne napping on the sofa as was Aunt Marinda. I worried what to do as nightfall was approaching, and everyone was trying to act normal. Yet I knew it was all an act. My father never stayed away from his art studios and neither did Antonius. I had to do something. I had to talk with Aunt Marinda before nightfall.

That's when I saw from the corner of my eyes in the room was the honorable soldier, Theunis Peters, and the great knight, Alexander van der Bijl, standing and watching me. Everyone in the room was shocked to see them except Margriete who was now carrying both boys on her lap. They were fast asleep. They laid on her lap with their feet spread over Katelijne. Margriete was patting the children slowly to sleep.

Theunis watched me and said, "Buddy, can you really see me? I was trying so hard to get in touch with you and talk to you, but my three-year-old brain just wants to be busy with all the fancy toys. By God, I look so strange as a toddler. At least I am one day older than you Alexander, so I will turn into an adult one day earlier."

I watched the young man with dark hair and green eyes watch me as he said, "It's a pleasure to be back in your home again Jacobus. I know you must rush and get into the original knights' quarters in the cellar of the castle for it is where they hide."

The two men had everyone's attention as Theunis said, "Where is my sword? I left it with my daughter Rietje. She was one of the best swordswomen in this world. I hope you won't be foolish and risk her life too. Jacobus, please confess what is in your heart and move on, for if you keep on burying it within yourself, you will end up walking with a heavy brick on your chest. No doctor will be able to remove it then, not even a famous doctor like yourself. Share your stories, otherwise, all your untold and hidden stories will remain unknown. Burying your own secrets won't be buried from you as you know where they are buried."

He then watched Margriete and said, "You my dear mother-in-law are still so beautiful and graceful. Remember you had created the Lover's Lighthouse with your words and prayers for this home to be blessed eternally. So, within your hands are the keys to the eternal lighthouse. I know through your blessed hands, the blessed daughter who was called the forbidden daughter shall again enter this world. Yet please remember not to let go of my daughter who held on to your hands until your last breath. She is on her way to you, yet you must accept her and open the doors for her. If you ever leave this home in anger or hurt, then the lighthouse, Griet, Rietje, Alexander, and I too will be no more as we will be with you forever eternally yours my dear mother-in-law."

I stood up worried what all that meant. I didn't ever want Margriete to feel pressured to have to stay here if she did not want to for that will hurt even more than knowing she just did not want me anymore. Who would want a cold-hearted person like myself anyway? I had to get a hold of myself and find out more about the invaders.

Alexander read my mind and said, "Cut off the bridge to this home first. Then cut off the bridge to the lake house from the lake. Block the woods by placing a high-voltage electric fence so no one can enter through there either. Then the only place anyone could enter through will be air. Get police protection and share this plan with them. The invaders will be trapped in the house and you can have the upper hand as you know they are here, yet they won't know you know. Cut off all modern connection you all have electronically so they can't be in touch with the outer world.

The message is, don't become prisoners but make them your prisoners."

There was pin-drop silence in the room as everyone went into their own world of thoughts. Maybe everyone was worried how to get all of this into action as no one knew how to lead. I realized everyone thought the other person will lead and just did not want to be the first person to lead or fail. Again, I wished I had adult Theunis or Alexander here to lead. Yet I saw I had the sleepy baby boys resting on Margriete's lap so peacefully, I did not have the heart to say anything and wake them up. I only remembered how I had placed my granddaughter Rietje on my chest and let her sleep on my chest. I wish I could still hug her one more time.

Life is about moving on, yet how do I move on if my life is missing from me? I watched the beholder of my life watch me without a blink. I knew everyone was watching me and somehow, I needed to say something.

So, I said, "Opa's heart beats Rietje, the only sentence that gave a heart to the heartless man last life again needs my heart to beat. Yet the person my heart beats for does not even know my whole mind, body, and soul only belong to her. I started the journey from this home to find a small child I had lost. I ended up taking many more journeys through my different lives, to only seek and find people I love and had lost. Yet tonight I ask all of you, please find me as tonight I am lost, and I need you. Griet had said, if only I was hers, she would never let me go. I ask you dear child, how could I not be yours, as I only searched for you all of your living life? I had never let you go even after death. Margriete, you too blame me for not remembering you? Yet don't you ever see that I only loved you, so for you I kept all my love and chose to forget everything else?"

I saw Mama walk over as did Papa and told me, "Dear son, I fought to find you and brought you back from the grave as I stood there and told you, 'Mama's heart beats Jacobus.' My love brought to me my three boys. Your love will bring back your Margriete, Griet, and Rietje somehow, someway."

I watched Margriete walk toward me and she stood there in front of me with tears in her eyes and two little boys in her arms sleeping. She watched me with her tear-filled eyes and said nothing. As I stood there in front of her, I also said nothing. No words were exchanged. Nothing was given or taken yet it was as if everything was said and all the words that never came out of my lips but froze on the way, were said. I knew she understood me, even when no one else did.

Papa said, "You two go to the other room and talk it out. Get the words out once and for all, and don't make any more mistakes as we all have made mistakes and now have a second chance to rectify our wrongs and do the right thing."

Nothing was said by either one of us as we both had one thing in common, we let our silence talk. My brave and courageous twin flame then said, "Big Papa, all the never told words have been told. As I know even if the whole world does not understand, Jacobus does. He knows what I just said and told him through these tears. If my tears could talk then you too would have known. Yet even though my tears have no words, I know Jacobus reads them all very clearly."

I did and I hugged my beloved within my chest so hard, I just wanted to hold on to her, and never let her go.

I only told her in a whisper, "I shall never let you go."

The two sleeping boys then said, "Down please Margriete, for now I call upon my sword."

We both realized the sleeping boys were in the middle when I held on to Margriete. We both realized these two boys were a part of our two girls so actually it felt good. That's when we saw there was a shining light that had appeared in the room and we saw a sword was floating in the air. The sword flew into the hands of Theunis as it made itself into two swords and one flew into the hands of

Alexander. Then I saw two toddlers had two tiny swords in their hands.

That's when I saw there behind the toddlers were the adult forms of the two who said, "To protect and preserve the honor of this castle, this home, we have returned as I am known to this world as Theunis, the righteous soldier, and I am Alexander, the honorable knight. In a new body and in a new time zone, we stand yet our souls shall guide even our younger selves to protect this home from all harm's way. Until we are of age, our spirit form will always guide our child form."

I knew now in front of all of us stood the two toddlers and in spirit form, their previous life's adult form. Who says a house can't talk? From beneath the walls of Kasteel Vrederic, a righteous soldier and an honorable knight had returned. Then, in front of everyone's gazing eyes, I kissed my beloved Margriete. A passionate kiss from a beloved to a beloved.

A PASSIONATE KISS

My beloved arrived

Tonight,

Within a bewitching

Dark and stormy

Night.

For thousands of nights,

I sought

Only you.

Within the stormy oceans,

I floated alone seeking

Only you.

I listened to all

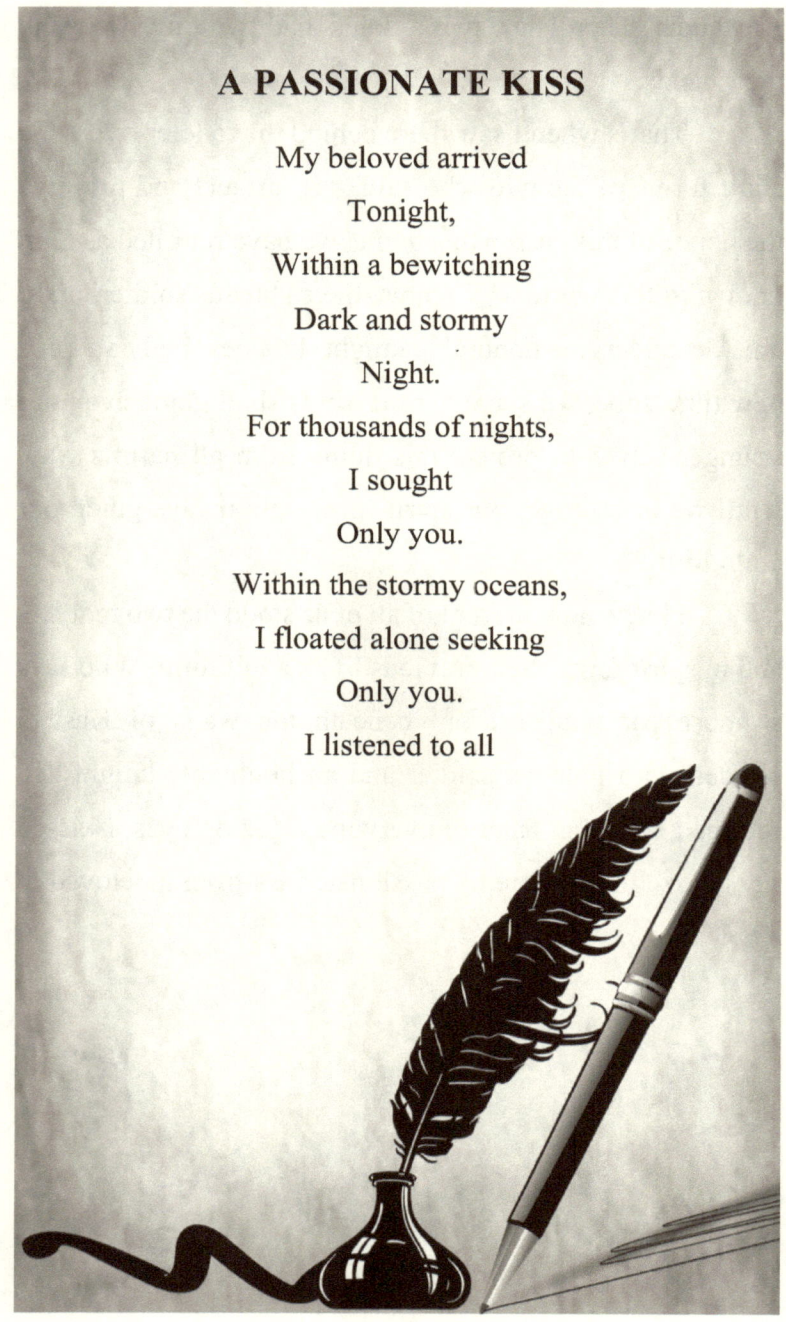

The lonely hearts,

Hoping I would

Amongst them,

Maybe find you.

I sat under the

Lonely skies,

Wishing upon

A star

For only you.

I asked the glowing moon

To seek you,

As I wondered

Were you too seeking

Only me?

Were you asking

The lonely skies about me?

I only hoped

One day,

Or maybe one night,

You will arrive

In my home,

As you my beloved

Have imprinted

My mind, body, and soul

Eternally.

So, as I sought, asked, and knocked

Life after life only

For you.

Tonight, within a stormy night,

In the midst of the ferocious

Thunder of my heart,

Lightning pouring out of

My inner soul,

And pouring tears,

Creating a heavy rainfall,

You have arrived.

You placed yourself,

Within my chest.

Eternally and evermore

Beloved of mine,

Has come back,

To be mine.

So tonight I

Too promise to be your

Eternally and evermore

Beloved.

I seal this vow

Of mine with

A PASSIONATE KISS.

CHAPTER SEVEN:

Never Let Me Go

"For you I am and for me you are.
Bonded together eternally
For one another.
Everything and everyone
Leaves me,
Yet my beloved promise
You shall never let me go."

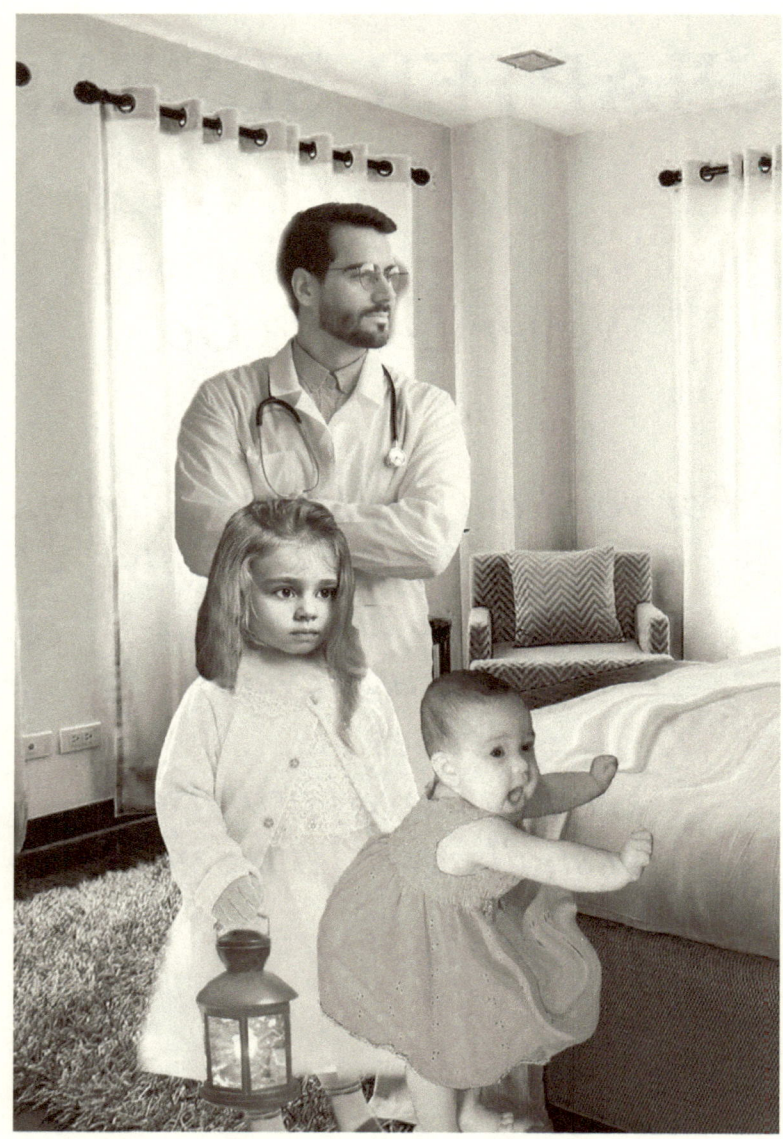

The forbidden daughter becomes the girl with the lantern and gifts her baby Rietje to Dr. Margriete van Achthoven as they both want to be born in this life as daughters of Kasteel Vrederic.

FORBIDDEN DAUGHTER OF KASTEEL VREDERIC: VOWS FROM THE BEYOND

A sixteenth-century heirloom sword had appeared from nowhere, then it multiplied itself into two swords. The historical sword that belonged to the Kasteel Vrederic ancestors followed the toddlers everywhere. The storm that had brewed outside brought in explosive lightning bolts and loud claps of thunder into the centuries-old building. Yet the dancing swords following the two boys around distracted everyone from the fearful storm brewing outside.

I knew I had to start getting the house ready like the two men I admired most in this world had asked me to do. Fear grips everyone and converts a person to become her prisoner. I told fear, she will never control me or get me as her prisoner for I would fight until my last breath for my family.

It seemed lately Mama never slept as she was cooking nonstop. I wanted to help her as I thought maybe she needed company. As soon as I went and tried to get close to her, I watched like a storm, Antonius and Andries were standing next to me, like they were somehow glued to me.

I asked them, "What is it boys?"

Antonius said, "You are going to see Big Mama. Why? What's wrong with her? Is she all right? I am freaking out Jacobus, is my mother okay?"

Andries then stood by and somehow I think damaged my eardrums as he yelled, "Big Mama, are you all right? They are not saying anything. Big Mama, they never tell me anything. It's not fair. If something is wrong with my mother, I have the right to know what's wrong with her."

I told him, "Andries, little brother, don't ever scream like that. I feel like you ruined my eardrums."

I watched Antonius rub his ears as he said, "I am worried if I can hear anything anymore. Big Bro, please check my eardrums. You are a doctor, right?"

That's when I saw like a storm appeared my running Papa, as he screamed even louder and said, "Jacobus, where is your mother? Is my wife all right? Move from here and let me into the kitchen!"

Andries stared to laugh proudly as he said, "Ha ha ha, I take after my father. See like father, like son. We both scream."

Amongst all this mess, I saw Mama watching us from behind and she said, "Why are you all screaming? I am fine. I was trying to analyze some of my dreams with Aunt Marinda. I sent Margriete to the kitchen. She is cooking for everyone. The noise and banging are coming from the kitchen, all thanks to my new daughter. I am, however, worried as Aunt Marinda said Margriete doesn't know how to cook anything. Forget Indian food or Italian cuisine, she can barely toast bread. My boys only eat Indian food. Yes, I know Margriete looks Indian as she is half-Indian; however, she was raised by her Dutch grandmother. Margriete actually can only reheat food, not really cook. I was raised by my Indian grandmother and so I was taught to cook Indian food. I did not have a choice. I will teach her just like I taught Katelijne."

Then I saw Mama was wondering in her mind and said, "Yet I seriously wonder if she can learn. She was staring at the food and asked how all of it comes together. Then she started to cry and said she had never once in her life turned on the stove. She said she missed Bertelmeeus, as he had done the cooking, then her grandmother, and now Aunt Marinda. I told her not to worry as Jacobus knows how to cook and can do it next. Yet she said she wants to try the way she always does when she wants fancy food."

I watched Andries go into a laughing fit as he was having so much fun. I still remember how Andries was treated like the youngest even though he was Antonius's mirror twin. Yet, Andries would have so much fun if ever Antonius or I got into trouble. For a minute it felt like my family was all back together. This mess felt really good and like a blessing.

Papa was worried as he said, "Maybe we should go in and help the poor child. She won't say anything and cry like she usually does. Maybe Jacobus could go and help, or maybe Anadhi and Katelijne can go and help her. We can all pretend we don't know anything."

Aunt Marinda came in and joined the conversation as she said, "I would not worry about her. She probably will do what she usually does when she needs to cook fancy food. I also believe her surprise is probably about to come in there for the first time. Margriete will get a good surprise herself, as she is trying to surprise all. Either way, I believe even if Margriete does not remember this new help who is about to arrive actually is someone Jacobus will remember."

She just went and sat down in the family room as she called the two toddlers to her. Then she was either telling them a story or having a grown-up conversation with little boys who surprisingly looked very interested. I wondered if nothing made any sense anymore or that's how it was in my home.

Papa looked very short-tempered and kept looking at his cell phone. He was expecting a call from the police commissioner for any updates. I only hoped nothing out of the normal would happen and we could just get out of this storm very soon.

Margriete came in very happy as she said, "The famous Chef Bert is here and has taken over the kitchen. He is one of the chefs who volunteers at our orphanage and at the hospital when we have fundraisers. I know I should not have called him, and the truth is I did not, he called me. He said Aunt Marinda called him to help us out for a few days as a friend. He is also an armed policeman who works as a special security for famous families. I never met him before, but he looked so familiar as if I had known him sometime somewhere. I only wish I could remember and not mistaken him for someone else, or someone else for him"

I had to take advantage of the situation and said, "Really Margriete, you too don't want to confuse one person for another? Oh, don't worry I won't hold a grudge as it does happen. Do you share your personal feelings, or just wait till the veil is unveiled?"

She watched me and said, "Jacobus, it's different. It's me and it's you, how could you not know? If only you had touched me, then you would have known."

I smiled and before she realized her mistake, I told her, "Ooh sweetheart in this house my mother taught us boys to be a gentleman. She would kick out any and all girls before we could even go near to touch or kiss a girl. I did not know you actually were hoping I touch you. For how can twin flames just stop at touching Margriete?"

I heard Andries say, "Ooh Antonius, Big Bro is in love and he wants to kiss Margriete."

I wanted to tell them it's true I do, for the first time in my life I actually knew I had found my twin flame, my other half, and I was not embarrassed to say it either. That's when I saw Papa was on the phone worried and had an expression like he just saw a ghost.

He said to the person on the phone, "I will share with the family that you have proof there are some goons hiding in our home in the cellar or somewhere in the castle. You have found a person beaten up who refused to harm us. So, he confessed. Yet I am worried why you have not shared all of these findings with us until now. I hope you don't mind me saying but my family members are now worried if they should even trust the police force."

Papa placed the phone on speaker as we all heard, "I know it's hard to trust the police force as a lot of things are happening at the same time. Yet I must warn you this family is really powerful and are way ahead of us since they have had a lot of time planning all of their actions out. A woman who claims to be Aideen has been found and she said she never wanted to do any of these things. Yet her biological mother was being held a prisoner and so she participated. We did find someone's body who the Bakkers had said was Aideen but checked out to be Aideen's twin sister, who was mental and held a prisoner for years. We have her in prison, and we have a few more of their goons in here. They were caught trying to run away from your home. They were all trying to scare you all out by pretending the castle was haunted. Yet they are saying the home is really haunted and they don't want any part in it. I will call you with details soon. So, it seems like there are more than two Aideens. Somehow the one Aideen is using look-alikes to do the dirty work for her. This way, she can be at multiple places at the same time. Also, she is trying to confuse everyone through her actions."

I watched my father and knew something was amiss as he should be happy our spirits were now active and were doing their best to scare off the uninvited assailants.

I told him, "Papa, sit down. What is it? It seems like you saw a ghost. You know it's not strange in our household. Finally, even the police know the truth now. They are working and so are our spirits. All we need to do is stay put until all of the goons are caught or sent away."

Papa said, "Bertelmeeus was in here as I was on the phone, yet he watched me and left. I wonder if he too is now a spirit in this house."

Anadhi and Margriete got up together as they both ran toward Papa and sat next to him trying to understand what he was saying.

Aunt Marinda was watching everything and said, "Ask your friend to come in here Margriete. Why don't you introduce him to the family, if you really do know him, or have recognized him?"

Margriete said, "He is the chef who has helped me over the years like I told you, in the hospital and the orphanage. He is not Bertelmeeus or I would have known. Yet to the best of my memories, I can't remember his face. Oh my God have I too not seen him if it is really him?"

That's when we all saw there in front of us was standing a very young Bertelmeeus. He looked like not a day older than thirty years old. He was tall, maybe seven feet and two inches in height. He had no hair, blue eyes, and fair-colored skin. Yet I had seen a very old Bertelmeeus before and I am guessing so did Margriete. Yet my father knew him from a very young age, so he thought he had seen a ghost.

I walked to him and said, "Welcome back Bertelmeeus. I hope you have not lost too many memories.

Also, how long did you know and how does it feel to see everyone all over again? I wondered where you were as everyone had returned except you."

Bertelmeeus hugged me and said, "I remembered just as I entered the kitchen. I never met Margriete before but today I saw the woman who has been helping me become a famous chef for the first time. I feel like I was in a tunnel and just got out and found my way back home."

Then he asked, "Where is my baby Rietje? Is she back? What about our daughter, my great-niece Griet? Is she back home yet?"

He watched Aunt Marinda and said, "I should have guessed, you are never involved unless there is a story to it that is close to your heart. Oh Marinda, why have you not told me about my family and that they are in trouble? Who is it that is after them? What did I overhear you, Johannes, talking about?"

Everyone in the room was quiet as the night had become even darker as if it was even possible to have such a dark night. The storm continued outside as the storm inside continued too.

Aunt Marinda said, "First, his name in this life is Erasmus van Phillip. The famous artist and the owner of Kasteel Vrederic. Also, I had known this for a while, yet it's like a sleepwalker should not be disturbed but just observed, unless his life is at risk. Today one of the members in this household will be at risk. That's why I need your help. I want you to be around Margriete at all times. Keep an eye on her as through her your Rietje will again be back home. Also, your great-niece Griet is on her way as she is in her mother's womb right there. I will get you caught up on all the details soon. Tonight though, I want you to not forget you are also a police officer and are armed to shoot if needed. Now let's have dinner everyone."

I watched Andries and Antonius stand up and go closer to Margriete. Then I saw Papa and Mama both came and got closer to her. Margriete actually said nothing and just remained quiet for some strange reason. I did not ask her and gave her privacy.

That's when I watched the two young boys come in. Theunis told Margriete, "We are hungry. Feed us now woman. Also, girlfriend, I am here. Don't be scared, all right? I shall protect you from front and behind."

Then Alexander told her, "I shall protect you from side to side, don't worry. I am your knight in shining armor."

At their word, I saw the grown-up spirit form of the two boys were standing there near her. I only hoped she had some space left in her heart for me too as I wouldn't leave her for the life of me.

I had received a few calls from the hospital and had to call on other doctors to cover my shifts. I watched Margriete do the same as she was trying to get other doctors to cover for her. I only hoped I didn't have an emergency case where I must be there.

Papa sat next to Margriete and told her, "I need to talk with you and Jacobus. Please correct me Margriete if I am wrong. The terrible night when I had walked out of Kasteel Vrederic to find Margriete, I knew I kept on forgetting everything and kept on reminding myself I must stay awake and do this. I wanted to find my daughter-in-law and the child. I entered the church you were at and we talked for a while. I told you to come back with me as I wanted you to get your beloved husband and I wanted my granddaughter to have her home. Yet you said you were under the impression Jacobus did not love you. He only married you for sex."

I watched Margriete had agreed to all of this as she said, "That's how I too remember, but then I don't remember anything else as I woke up years later when Jacobus took me home. Our daughter had been buried and I raised my granddaughter as my daughter. I thought or rather assumed you did not want me as your daughter-in-law. I thought you were upset as my daughter looked Indian and you did not accept her."

Papa watched her and said, "Dear one, my beloved wife whom I had lost was of Indian origin. I went berserk as I lost her. How could I not love my wife's last images? I remember as you refused to come home with me, the church had collapsed as it was taken over by the Spaniards. A fire was set to burn down the building. I remember somehow, I did deliver your child, my granddaughter. As I watched the face of my departed wife in my hands, I told her, 'I shall never let you go.' Yet that's when I also was hurt in the same fire where you were hurt. When I did come through, I told Jacobus not to allow any baskets in the house as I didn't need anyone saying anything about my family. Little did I know in the basket of breads, was my own granddaughter. I had people search for you and everyone said you believed Jacobus never loved you, so you left. He loved you so much, he become a rock and never spoke to me till my last breath. You see I lied to him and told him I told you not to come as I never wanted him to know you refused to come."

I saw for the first time, there were tears in my eyes, not for anyone but Papa. I knew the same father who loved me more than his life could not have been that different even if he was buried in sorrow.

Margriete said, "Those were all mistakes, as I too was arrogant and listened to all the people who had said the Vrederic family members only use women as their one-night stand. Yet as I found out I could not live without him even if he did want to live without me, I was blessed to have memory loss from the burning fire. When I did get my memories, I was in Jacobus's embrace because of Aunt Marinda. Yet I did remember some parts of our conversations and had told Jacobus to forgive you as you had tried to unite us. Yet it was our fate I did not get to see you again. Reincarnation is, however, a blessing as I have you now."

Then Margriete stood up and told Papa, "Big Papa, please don't let go of me ever again as I promise I too shall never let you go as you are mine."

I watched them and knew I was having a hard time handling all of these emotions and watched everyone in the room wipe their tears. Mama came and kissed Margriete on her head and she wiped away her tears and Papa's. Then I saw the two boys were acting strangely as they kept on repeating, "NO" at the top of their lungs.

I saw Theunis appear in his spirit form as did Alexander. They were both running toward the windows outside of our parlor door. There in front of the windows, I saw a man standing with a huge gun in his hands. My two brothers were frozen as they said, "Move! Duck everyone!"

A man was standing inside our home as the windows were somehow blasted opened silently. Without any sound, we had goons inside the house who were all armed. They were all speaking in a foreign language and I knew they were drug dealers whom we had cracked and so they had lost their business.

One man who looked like a body builder came in front of me and said, "So you are Dr. Jacobus Vrederic van Phillip. For you, we have lost so many girls last year. Now you have single-handedly crushed our drug business. Since you have taken down our hotel, you too shall now go down with it."

As he uttered the words, within seconds he fired his gun and I actually saw the bullets come near my heart, yet I did not feel anything. All I remember was someone had pushed me down to the floor and was lying on top of me.

That's when I saw blood all over my face and saw black hair had sprawled all over my face.

216

I heard a faint voice call out to me. She said, "My beloved, I guess this life too separates us by a breath. Jacobus, please hold me in your chest and once please say it, you remember me and know I was and am your Margriete. Once please tell me you love me for I am yours and was yours and if not in this life, I will try to come back and unite with you in another life."

All I could say was, "Margriete, don't leave me. Take me with you for my heart only beats for you. Without you, I don't want to breathe."

I watched faintly there was a giant who carried me and Margriete by himself and took us to my room.

Then I heard Theunis ask me if I could hear him. I told him, "I guess I can hear you so I must be in the land of the dead. It's all right if only Margriete is here."

Then I saw Mama who said, "Get up Jacobus now, and please save Margriete. You are the only doctor who can perform this surgery and save her life."

I got up on my feet and there on my bed was lying the only person I never wanted to perform any surgery on as how could I open up the woman I loved eternally? I knew her life depended on it. My family members were all there with all of my medical equipment and there on live TV was Margriete's and my colleague Dr. Ray Banerjee.

He said, "As the police have the whole neighborhood under surveillance, no one is allowed to enter or leave. Also, the roads have collapsed, and the road crew is fixing them. They have tried to send a medical helicopter, but the weather has delayed it. So, my friend you must do the surgery as Margriete is losing a lot of blood. Is there anyone who can help you with this surgery?"

Aunt Marinda came in the room and said, "I can help as I am an herbalist and Bertelmeeus also is a policeman who could help but is hurt himself."

That's when I saw the TV screen went dark. I watched the two young boys enter the room and say, "We shall help! We will heal her as we promised to help her."

I saw they brought their swords as the girl with the lantern appeared at their call. She walked and dropped her tears on top of Margriete and then appeared another child. A baby girl who was chubby and cute like I remembered her from the past.

I watched my little Rietje sit on top of Margriete. She said, "Oma, please don't leave me again as this time, you must promise to bring me onto this Earth as your daughter, not granddaughter."

I watched Margriete move as I told my family, "I need space. Also, Mama, if you and Aunt Marinda could help me then we can begin the surgery now without any delay. You made me a doctor Mama, and now won't you help me save your daughter-in-law?"

The night was very long as I finished the surgery and was able to take the bullet out without much bleeding. I knew Margriete would recover completely, yet I had to take into account any infection as I must take her to the hospital or convert our home into one. I did the latter, as with the help of all the spirits and my family members I had converted our family room into a hospital as we had not one but three patients.

Bertelmeeus and Aunt Marinda were both shot in their thighs. The bullets brushed off of them as Aunt Marinda never felt anything and was walking around like nothing ever happened to her. Bertelmeeus, however, was injured and needed a surgery. He stood in between Margriete and the bullets as he walked toward the bullets.

Everyone said it was a miracle as there somehow were two baby boys who were fighting with their swords. No one had stopped them as they were at times floating and even grown-up men. My brothers had all become barriers for Margriete and myself. My mother bear, however, got kitchen knives and started to throw them into the air as she and

Katelijne practiced throwing knives. My father laid on top of me protecting my body from all the bullets.

I had asked him how he was able to carry Margriete and me both at the same time. I thought it was Bertelmeeus who had carried us. Yet Bertelmeeus was busy fighting off the goons as Papa ran to the other room with both of us.

He said, "It's easy my child as I am the tree, and you all are my fruits. Did you ever hear of a tree that can't bear its fruits? It's a silly question, don't you think?"

I asked my parents, "How did Margriete get shot and why did I faint with her? I know they were aiming at me."

Mama answered as everyone else remained quiet. She said, "Margriete screamed and jumped in front of the bullets. So, she actually made the gunman get nervous and lose his aim. If he had aimed correctly, you would have been hurt seriously. Margriete actually hit you and told you to never ever die on her again. She said she had to see you die once and there is no man or woman who will be able to take you away from her before her. She said she will die first as she never wants to see you die again."

That's when everyone had left us alone in the huge family room on a makeshift bed for two. I saw my family members sleeping on couches all around us trying to pretend they were all asleep. I checked on Bertelmeeus and saw he was out with heavy medication I gave him so he could rest the pain out.

I sat next to Margriete and saw she opened her eyes and smiled at me and said, "I love you Jacobus. I need to say it because I did not want to die without saying the words."

I whispered in her ears, "Dear beloved, I love you more than life sweetheart. Life is only with you and for you. I kept my heart closed to all only for you. Please know it's only you I breathe for and want to breathe with. I am breathless only for you. If I have to stop breathing it will be because I would be busy kissing you, eternally."

That's when my beloved whispered in my ears, "Jacobus, hold me in your chest and never let me go."

Dear beloved twin flame, as I held on to you so you would never leave me alone again, I heard your loving words. I promise through my virtuous words, I shall never let you go as you are forever mine. So tonight, I wrote this poem and named it as you had asked me to never let you go.

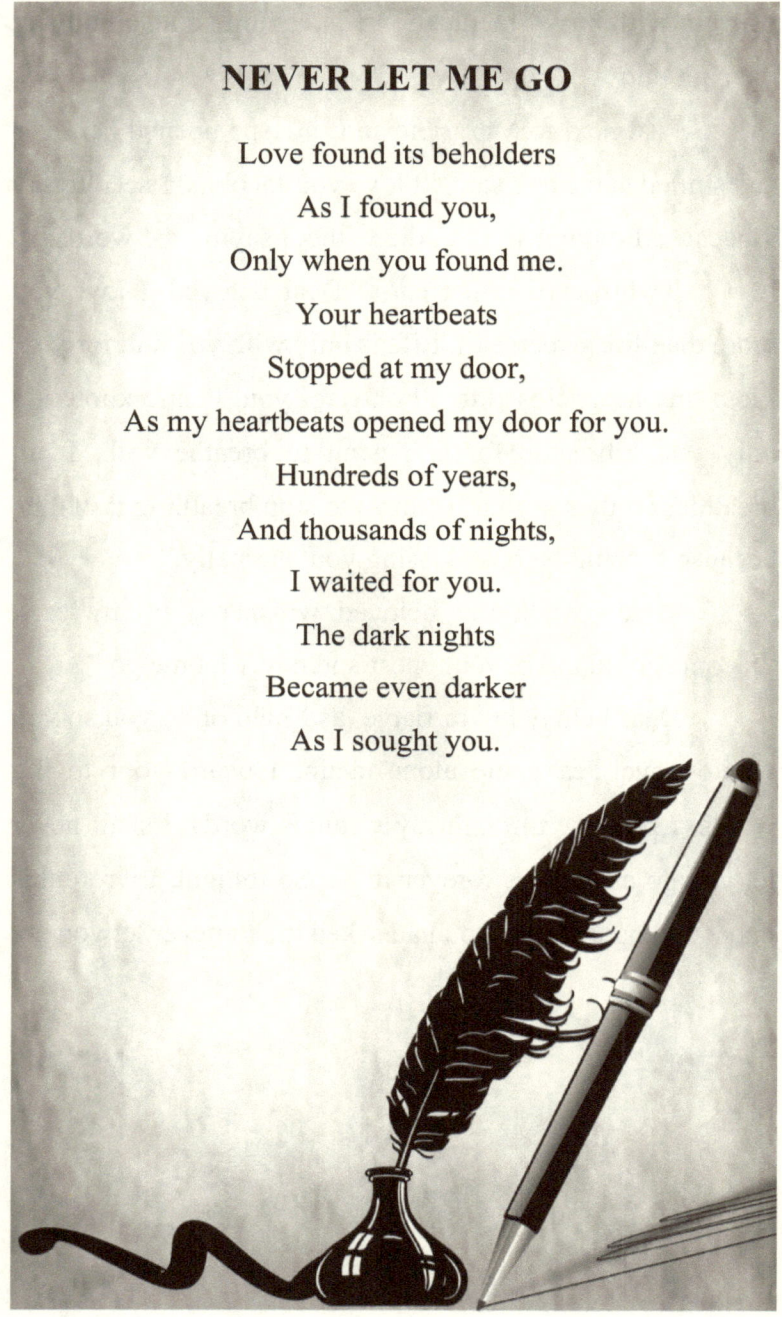

NEVER LET ME GO

Love found its beholders

As I found you,

Only when you found me.

Your heartbeats

Stopped at my door,

As my heartbeats opened my door for you.

Hundreds of years,

And thousands of nights,

I waited for you.

The dark nights

Became even darker

As I sought you.

FORBIDDEN DAUGHTER OF KASTEEL VREDERIC:
VOWS FROM THE BEYOND

The days were lonely

As they never found you.

Yet today as you have arrived

Through a stormy night,

The storm inside of my heart,

Was ever more powerful

As the need to hold on to you,

The want to just keep on

Watching you,

Became a struggle.

As I tried to ignore you,

For I know if I keep on

Watching you,

My beloved,

I could

Never let you go.

Yet tonight as we pass again

Another storm,

You whispered within my ears,

The only phrase my heart

So wanted to hear

For hundreds of years,

As you said,

NEVER LET ME GO.

CHAPTER EIGHT:

Father Of The Lighthouse Returns

"Vows are made immortally and kept even beyond death. For the vows given or taken create a magical path for the vow-givers to travel time and tide to keep their given vows."

Andries van Phillip monitors on a television screen the invaders of Kasteel Vrederic.

K asteel Vrederic looked and felt like a hospital wing. My family members, however, made it feel like a family reunion. Everyone stayed back in the family room. It was like no one wanted to leave the other person alone. The birds were singing somewhere in the forest nearby. I felt like maybe spring was arriving early. Or maybe finally in my life, spring had returned.

All throughout the night, I kept on checking on Margriete and Bertelmeeus to see if they were doing well or had any changes. I felt like my mother who still to this day enters our room and checks on all her three boys. She will touch our nose, then pinch us and ask if we were all breathing. She says it was something she did as we were all brought home from the hospital.

My two brothers were adopted by Mama and Papa after Uncle Petrus and his wife both had died leaving the twin boys to my parents. I never realized they were my cousins as they were just my younger brothers. Mama told them about their parents as she believed they should know their blessed parents. My mother, however, tells everyone she carried them far longer than a mother does so she is the mother who carried them too.

The love that had bonded this family was made in Heaven and has lived in this home throughout time. No one comes to our home and hunts us down as we shall take revenge. I saw Papa was up all night as his thinking face was so visible. I was actually worried for him.

I watched Uncle Matthias, my father's other cousin who decided to be a forever bachelor walking around the family room. I wondered when he came in and I thought he was with my two great-grandmothers.

Uncle Matthias said, "Erasmus, why did you not share all of this with me? I thought you knew your life, or my life only differs, by that I don't care about my life. Please remember if you are planning to join Petrus, you better let me know because I will forcefully bring you back."

He walked back and forth and watched how his loud voice woke up everyone. He did not mind though as he continued to pace.

Uncle Matthias said, "These three boys are also mine. I am their father as much as you are Erasmus. Jacobus, Andries, and Antonius are all mine too. We just got Andries back miraculously. Now what are you doing? How could you get this family involved with these types of goons? We are normal people. We don't get involved in shootings or drug dealings or any other crimes. We only get speeding tickets maybe if you have a car. I don't, so I don't even believe in that either."

He then saw Mama and said, "Anadhi, you are a dream psychic. You know these things beforehand, then why could you not prevent them from happening?"

I watched Aunt Marinda open the windows as she stood up and said, "Anadhi is a very strong dream psychic. That's why she tried to prevent Margriete from going anywhere. We also tried to keep the family together so if something does happen, then we would be able to help one another. It's like we take all the preventive measures yet still we can't at times avoid the situation. We just minimize our risks. Anadhi had spoken to me about her dreams as she is warned in her dreams. I, however, can just tell by observing a person and even then, I could not prevent the fall, but only reduce the risk."

I watched everyone and knew Papa was not paying any attention to anyone but was in his own world. I watched Antonius and realized he too was worried about Papa. That's when we all saw Andries walk in and stare at everyone. It seemed he was upset at something as he sat down without even saying anything.

Mama noticed immediately as did Katelijne. I saw both women run to him and saw Mama sitting next to him as did Katelijne. It was so strange to see how Katelijne was still attached to her birth son even though he had become an adult in two years.

Mama asked him as she rubbed his temple, "What is it my son? Don't ever be upset as this mother had begged Heaven and Earth to get you back to me. Always remember in this family we share everything with one another."

He watched everyone and said, "Well there are goons in the house attacking my family members. The woman who treated me like her own son was shot and is in pain. I somehow feel like it's all because of me. I must have seen something and was at the wrong place at the wrong time, so everything happened. Also, now who am I? Am I Andries who is twenty-eight years old or Andries who is a toddler?"

Papa spoke for the first time in a while as he burst out laughing. He went and sat next to Katelijne. He spoke very quietly like he was about to paint another masterpiece. He said, "Katelijne, scoot over and let Big Papa sit."

Then he touched Mama as she was on the other side of Katelijne. No one said anything as we all knew Papa takes his time to gather up his thoughts. He then continued and said, "Andries will be our original Andries. As I know Jacobus already has it arranged with the security. We had told everyone, that is Jacobus, Antonius, and I, that Andries

230

was hurt and kept away to recover. We kept him in hiding so he could gather his strength and his memories. It is essential for the police to keep him hiding as he is the only one who had seen all of the goons. We also told everyone Andries had gone through some reconstruction surgery, so he looks a little different, yet he still is the same person. That part was easy, as now you can just gather your old ID with a new picture and be yourself. The hard part is they have all asked where is the boy you all had said Katelijne had given birth to."

Andries stood up and said, "Cool! I am a superhero now. But what do we do about the baby me?"

Margriete woke up and was listening as she said, "It's easy! We can say it's Alexander as we will adopt him anyway, right Big Papa? We can say we adopted two boys and had both of them be Andries. It's because the family was adopting these boys anyway as Big Mama and Katelijne both love children and help children at the hospital and at home. Also, as you all realized these two boys were not being adopted because they were thought to have a heart problem, we all decided to show the society they are all normal children. It matters not if they are completely healthy or have some issues. We deal like a family."

Mama stood up and said, "There is no way I will let the father of the lighthouse leave this house. He is the original father of this house. Theunis is the one who created the lighthouse. It is his bloodline that continued to give Kasteel Vrederic her family lineage. If he had not married Griet and did not have their blessed daughter, none of us would be here."

She watched the two boys as she said, "Alexander, I know how you had single-handedly with the help of your spiritual father-in-law made this family tree. There is no way you can leave this house as this is your home and you two are back in your own home. I don't care who your biological parents are. I feel like somehow you have traveled from the past to the future and landed as babies in the twenty-first century."

Mama watched Aunt Marinda and said, "I had a dream a few nights ago where I saw Theunis and Alexander were both stuck in the tunnel of light. They were being told to go forward and not look back. They both stopped as they knew if they did go forward, the connection and bond they had with their twin flames would be cut off. Their twin flames were running toward one another. I watched Griet run to Rietje and try to be in the same tunnel. So, they will be born near one another, breaking the mother and daughter bond, and creating another one. Then I watched Theunis cry and ask God why he has to be separated from his twin flame now. That's when I saw Alexander walk in. He told Theunis he would help somehow, someway. Alexander saw me as he knew we were still in the tunnel returning home."

Mama got up and walked close to Aunt Marinda as she then said, "I called upon Aunt Marinda in the tunnel as I knew some people on this Earth are time travelers. I then realized our Aunt Marinda is one of them. I asked her to help unite Theunis and Alexander with their twin flames. I called Theunis the father of the lighthouse and Alexander the father who continued the lineage of Kasteel Vrederic. She then smiled and agreed to bring them back with her. She did, however, tell me they would not be born but would just arrive with her. This would be her gift to Griet and Rietje. However, the deal was the boys must come back home to Kasteel Vrederic."

Aunt Marinda watched our front garden courtyard as she was just standing there and watching the magical fountains. We all tried to see what she was watching and knew not to bother her as she was thinking and getting her thoughts together.

She then said, "It was all possible as Theunis had taken a vow with God to protect this home eternally along with his beloved twin flame. So, if one is born then the other one is allowed to come back home to the same place through the given vows. Alexander, however, had taken a vow to protect Kasteel Vrederic throughout time. He had said he would make sure the lineage continues through Rietje and him. So, he was guaranteed a return with Theunis through his given vows. By doing so, he has guaranteed a return ticket to his twin flame Rietje. Again, the deal was he must also be here at Kasteel Vrederic protecting the family and making sure Rietje too returns safely. So, it was Alexander and Theunis who found Margriete as when she walked into the orphanage, they were already in there."

I watched Margriete get up and say, "I was born with my memories of Jacobus. I used to cry for him even as a child. I learned to live with my memories and not share with anyone. Yet as I became the owner of the orphanage, I knew I would find him. I did not want any influences on my memories, so I never looked the family of Kasteel Vrederic up. Yet as I found Uncle Matthias and had walked with him into this room, all my memories flooded back to me like it was just yesterday. I knew it was fate which had brought all of this together. Now let's find a way out of this murder mystery together."

FORBIDDEN DAUGHTER OF KASTEEL VREDERIC:
VOWS FROM THE BEYOND

I watched Papa as he was smiling and said, "I have something to share too. With the help of Matthias, I searched all over the house for our old documents. Some documents actually my brother, Antonius and Andries's father, had stumbled upon when I had bought back my home from the bank. Years ago, due to my father's bad business dealings, our home had been foreclosed upon. The bank had foreclosed the home and to make matters worse, it was then my father had faced an early death along with his two brothers. After he passed away, my mother and her sisters who were married to the three brothers were asked to leave the house within thirty days. I had no clue about it, so when I did find out, I bought the house freehold within three days."

I watched Papa stop talking and go into a deep thought. I knew he was very emotional on this subject. It's very delicate as he had worked very hard to save our ancestral home on his own. I know at the time, he was the only breadwinner. Yet he made sure his extended family members never realized how hard he had worked to get back the house he himself had finished renovating in a previous lifetime.

Papa then watched me for a while as he knew I knew his emotions. He then said, "When I purchased the home again, we the three brothers decided to stay with our mothers, the triplet sisters, by taking turns. One of us would always stay here. That's when Petrus had found the original blueprint of the house. With the blueprint, we found all the renovations and reconstructions of the home that were done throughout the years. Petrus was a genius and loved working with electronics. He wanted to keep an eye on the three old women while he was away. So, with the help of some of his friends, he had single-handedly installed cameras everywhere in the house."

I could not take the excitement I saw that was going around us. I watched another electronic prodigy, Andries, who obviously got this talent from his father was jumping up and down.

He said, "Big Papa, please say Papa had wired the house with cameras that work even without lights. Did he wire the cellars and all the tunnels just like they would do in a spy thriller movie?"

Papa smiled and said, "Strange you even think like him. Yes, he did. He took the blueprint and went on a spy mission. He kept on saying, one day when he would be far away, these cameras would protect all of the children of this home. Remember Anadhi, you were pregnant with Jacobus when he would talk to the baby in your womb and say,

'Uncle Petrus will protect you eternally through these cameras.'"

I watched Mama cry and say, "It was so long ago, and life brought so much pain when we lost him and his beautiful wife. The rest of the stories just erased it from my mind Erasmus."

That's when we saw outside, there was a very heavy police presence. The police were touring the house and grounds as if they too had some news. We let them do their job as we planned to do our own job. We would not share this news with anyone other than our household members.

That's when I heard Bertelmeeus walk back into the room. He said, "I know I am a stranger, but I know I was a member of this family. I would like to help get rid of the goons."

I watched Bertelmeeus walk out and check on things as if he was not even injured. I saw the big guy and thought to myself where had he been all of these years?

I told him, "Bertelmeeus or Bert whatever your name is in this life, within my eyes and the eyes of the family members, you are always family. I hope you remember, we just saw you a few days ago walking Rietje down the aisle on her wedding day."

He saw me for a while and he said, "Jacobus, I do remember, and it still feels like yesterday. I actually thought something was wrong with my mind until Aunt Marinda showed up."

We all watched Aunt Marinda as she said, "They are moving in everyone. We must rush and find out where they are. My only advice is to work with the cameras you don't need to fix but can make do with because you don't want to go into their hiding areas alone. However, I won't guarantee others won't go in there. As we all know, the father of the lighthouse, the honorable soldier is back, and he will do as he pleases."

I walked into Mama and Papa's room with my brothers. I did, however, see there were two little pitter-patter sounds of two little boys following us. As we entered the room, we saw a door was left open in there. I assumed Papa had left it open and went to close the door as air was coming in through the door. I saw a little boy stand in front of me.

Theunis's young form said, "No, bad man in there waiting with gun. You stay here."

That's when we saw two men appear in the form of Theunis and Alexander in front of us who placed a finger in front of their lips and warned all of us to be quiet. I don't know what happened. As soon as they were gone, the younger boys returned in minutes.

I wondered what happened yet did not have the courage to ask such young children. Margriete, however, did and as she entered, she went to the boys and held them in her chest.

She then said, "Where did you two run off to? I was worried sick for you two. I am trying to take the pain of the bullet and you two are running off getting me even more nervous."

The boys then kissed her cheeks and said, "We are good boys. We scare them off."

They again walked out, and I saw in their place were Theunis and Alexander standing there with their swords. They were trying to see what Antonius was doing.

I followed their gaze and saw Antonius drawing over the blueprint over the missing lines or something. He was trying to touch the paper and do it with his eyes closed. I realized how Papa had taught him to paint as a blind painter. Antonius was actually helping him recreate the blueprint.

I watched Margriete and went closer to her and asked her, "Sweetheart, is it true you can't cook at all?"

She watched me and said, "Jacobus, Big Mama said you are a great cook. Also, Antonius and Andries are good cooks. Big Papa and we the girls can have our spouses cook for us."

For the first time, I held her by her hands and asked her, "Are you proposing my darling?"

Margriete watched me and said, "Really Jacobus, we have been married for hundreds of years, almost as long as this home has been standing. Why are you talking about proposals now? We already did all of that. Now let me see what's going on over there. Also, Jacobus, it's the man who proposes in this household as we are old-fashioned people here and I know Big Mama would have it no other way."

I saw my father and brothers were all watching us. Antonius said, "Jacobus, Bro, I want to listen to you two too, but I am trying to figure out the blueprint. Wait till I come, wait for us when you have some romantic lines to say to one another. It's not fair we missed most of it trying to fix the blueprint. We love that you two finally have figured out you belong to only one another. Also, Jacobus my dear Big Bro, it's the man who proposes in this home. I will be on team Margriete."

Papa was watching us and he said, "Boys, something is wrong. Why is Andries not coming out yet? He went to check something in the electrical panel box. Go and find your brother and then let's go and try to figure out the situation we have in our hands."

He then saw Andries come in singing to himself. Papa was very upset as I knew he knew something he was not sharing with us. Mama came in with a shocking face like she saw ghosts or something. I dropped everything and went closer to Mama and Katelijne.

Mama said directly to Papa, "Erasmus, when were you going to tell us the news? I thought in this house, we don't hide anything. I just saw the message on your phone. I was checking for any news when I saw your phone was left open in the family room for everyone to see."

Mama then went silent as she was now crying and then again asked, "Erasmus, why have you not told us?"

I panicked what was Papa hiding from us? He seemed really distracted all morning. I assumed it was because he wanted to find the blueprint of the house.

I asked Papa, "Please share anything that you have Papa. If it is not related then it's all right, but if it is related then please let us know."

He then said, "The goons attacked the orphanage and the hospital. I have my people over at the orphanage and have moved everyone from there including both grandmothers as they refused to leave the children. Matthias refused to go to a safe house provided by the police as he wanted to be here to help. The hospital is under heavy security and has been blocked off by the police and is safe. No one was able to get in through the security barricades. Also a few more people have been arrested in this gang and the police think the drug dealers have moved on. The gang leaders have been arrested and all the others don't want to be in a war with the whole country, so they have also left. We only have to find the Bakkers. The mother, the father, and Aideen are all missing. Remember they made the innocent sister fall prey to their scheme and had her murdered as a decoy."

He watched Mama and then said again, "I am sorry I did not share all of this as it was when Margriete too was fighting for her life. Matthias and I thought it would be better if we don't share as things were under control faster than we could have been there."

We watched Aunt Marinda walk in as she said, "I knew about everything Anadhi. I must say I requested Erasmus not to share it with you all as I needed Jacobus to concentrate only on Margriete and Bertelmeeus. The only things he could fix and control at the moment. Also, all my children at the orphanage are completely safe as I personally with the help of Erasmus had the orphanage under heavy protection."

Margriete stood up and said, "Big Papa, could we all go through the blueprint together? Then we could maybe figure out where the Bakker family is hiding if they have not left and gone yet. I really don't know why the cops can't just get in and get them."

Papa stood up and said, "Yes, we can go through it together now. Andries has a better idea as he has transferred it to the TV so we can all zoom in and see the blueprint. From Antonius's drawing, Andries has transformed it to 3D so we can actually see it on the television set."

Papa watched Andries as then Andries told us, "You see, Papa Petrus was ahead of his time. He had directly wired every single camera to the main electrical circuit breaker panel. When Big Papa had installed the new panel box, the original camera wirings too were redone with modern technology and were made up to code. All I had to do was figure out where all of it was, the subpanel box for the cameras. I knew I had something of Papa inside of me, and I thought where would he hide it? Then it was obvious, as I am positive all of my brothers and Big Papa would know the answer, right?"

We all said at once, "In Mama's closet."

Mama was watching everyone and said, "So everyone was watching me when I was changing?"

We all laughed as Andries went and kissed Mama and said, "No Big Mama. He hid it in a place where he knew it would be safe. Also, I know he did it because he trusted you the most. That's why he left both of us as your sons."

Mama watched all of us and said, "I carried you all for more than two years before I let you all walk on your own or be on your own. He left you all to me because you all are my babies, my sons."

Andries then told all of us to go with him to Mama and Papa's room. We followed him and even Bertelmeeus came inside as we closed the doors. The little boys were already in Mama's bed, sleeping on her pillows. Katelijne too went on the bed and got herself comfortable. I watched Margriete sit by Mama on a sofa as Papa sat by them too. The rest of us sat on bean bags on the floor.

Andries said, "Let's watch some movies everyone. Does anyone want some popcorn?"

The two bundles sleeping on the bed got up and said, "Me! I will have some."

I got the boys some popcorn as I knew Mama kept all kinds of snacks for Andries who was diabetic and still is. The seventy-five-inch TV turned on as then we saw so many screens appeared on the TV. It was as if we were watching a hi-tech security camera. There were pictures of the lake and the lake house. Then we saw the carriage house and I watched Margriete look away. We saw pictures change one after another.

Suddenly Antonius said, "Freeze it Andries! Look, where is this? How come I didn't know this room existed? Big Papa, what is this?"

Papa came forward and said, "To the best of my knowledge, I don't know where this place is. It's like a tunnel. It goes into another tunnel and there is a huge room."

Everyone watched the TV screen, and it was as if this room and the location were not known to anyone. It was as if our mind or memories had erased this from our brain. That's when I saw Bertelmeeus come and stand next to me.

He laughed and said, "Jacobus, the accused witches' room. We had brought them back from the gallows and the stakes, remember? We had kept them there until they had a safe place to go. You had through the years brought so many children, men, and women and kept them there and gave them food, drink, and sustenance until they were trained to work in the public and fend for themselves. Margriete, you do remember, right?"

It was then I laughed and told my buddy Bertelmeeus, "Yes, I do remember. How could I forget? Theunis himself, our spirit soldier, had helped make it as did Griet. She helped decorate it and you helped everyone to be safe in there until they were ready to reenter society."

That's when again as the toddlers were sleeping, I saw the two men standing next to us. One was attired like a seventeenth-century knight and the other one in a sixteenth-century soldier uniform. They were watching the TV screen and having the popcorn the children were eating.

I told them, "So now I know who is asking for the food when the boys are asking, Theunis and Alexander. It's nice to have you both back, at least until you two become toddlers again."

Theunis sat next to Margriete just like his toddler form does so many times and he kissed her head and said, "It's always good to be back and see my girl."

Margriete, Katelijne, and Mama were all sitting by them and were like mothering the two men. It was nice while it lasted until Bertelmeeus broke the silence.

He said, "Everyone, there is a pretty woman there. She is looking at herself and it actually looks like she is kissing the mirror. She is beautiful but I think crazy actually."

There in front of us on the TV screen, we saw Aideen in flesh. I wondered how they actually pulled everything off. That's when I realized she actually had the hidden dungeon decorated like a queen's palace. A nice sofa set, a bedroom set, and a TV. It's then I got worried.

I called Andries, "Andries check out her TV set. It's similar to your one. So, is it a TV or a security system she is monitoring us through?"

Andries told us, "It's a security system. That means she has been monitoring us for a long time. I can actually mirror her system without her knowledge, and we shall see what she can see."

It actually took my brother only a few minutes to do this. I thought to myself do give the chap some appreciation when our life is not in danger. He is a genius. I heard the popcorn eating sounds had stopped as both men went to Mama's refrigerator and helped themselves to Coca-Cola bottles. I was watching them as was everyone in the room.

Theunis said, "Come on Jacobus, these are amazing drinks. Did you try them? Also, this box keeps them cold."

I only nodded and went back to Andries as I watched Andries take a big move. He spoke to Aideen through her TV screen.

He said, "Hello little birdy, I hope you are not lonely for I can see you from beneath the Earth, where you had sent me. Remember I told you, I would come back to hunt you down. A promise is a promise little evil ugly one. Now I am back, and I will haunt you eternally. I will put you in a very safe place in my own house where you won't be able to breathe or see anything, but you will scream in pain. Little evil ugly one, remember that's when I will say these were my vows from the beyond. Oh, yes if you don't remember I am Andries van Phillip, and I am back from the grave to only take you into the grave."

Andries told Theunis, "Dear father of the lighthouse, would you not keep your oath and protect my family, your descendants? Within our bodies, runs your blood for we are of your bloodline and so you are the father of this magical castle, our home. Through you, our dynasty had continued."

That's when we saw on the TV screen, two armed warriors from the sixteenth and seventeenth centuries had appeared. They were standing in front of Aideen as they only watched her and let her see them.

She stood on her feet and said, "I don't believe in ghosts as I had set this TV to fool you all in the house. I pretended to be dead and a victim, so you all would get my parents and arrest them. I would then betray them and run away."

I watched our knight and soldier become big and place their swords on her chest. She screamed in fear as I watched the Bakkers appeared.

Mrs. Bakker said, "Aideen, you are trying to betray us because of a false ghost? You made the ghost yourself. We adopted you and your sister, gave you both a home. We had to dispose her to save you, and now you are saying you will set us up to be caught by the cops and just disappear? You plan to live in here eternally, do you?"

I heard Theunis say, "Shut your ugly mouth and remember no one hurts my dynasty for I am the father of the lighthouse and it is I who shall make sure you three never ever appear in my family home ever again."

There I saw appeared heavy lights as if a lady appeared and I saw Griet standing there and she said, "You touched my mother Margriete and have thus declared yourself as my enemy. I had taken a vow to protect my family home eternally. Now confess how you got in here."

I watched Griet was just standing there yet the three predators were having a hard time breathing. Then like a light flashing in from nowhere appeared a woman with a sword on a horse inside of the room that had no windows.

Rietje got down and said, "I am Rietje and this is my family home. You dare enter our sacred grounds. Did you not know this is my dynasty? These are my bloodline. I am known as the woman with the sword. I got rid of enemies from my Opa's house when I defeated the Spaniards. I banished all who touched or accused innocent people as witches or warlocks, and now you three are mere ants. So now you shall meet up with your Creator. But I shall wait a few more minutes as you must meet up with my family member whom you murdered so ruthlessly."

We had all made on our way to the hidden room that looked like a dungeon or a hideaway which our ancestors built to use as a safe hideaway for when we needed it.

Andries entered as did Antonius and the Bakkers were frozen in place to see the person they murdered was standing in front of them. Andries asked them, "Why did you murder me?"

Mr. Bakker then said, "It's because your piano student found out everything about us. She had sent you a letter before she was killed. We knew you did not receive the letter or the emails. So, we had to kill you and destroy your phone so no one could ever find out. She was a ten-year-old girl, a child who almost took our whole empire down. The drug lords, the sex traffickers, all of their names were on a small note. It's buried with her ashes. Just like you, we knew this home is haunted, so we are not afraid of you. Because you are dead, and we still are very much alive haunting your family members. We will leave the house as soon as we find your other phone, the one she sent the messages to. Also, all of the computers too need to be erased. We are almost there as your family members don't even know we are actually not going to hurt them, just scare them so we can erase all of the proof left by a silly ten-year-old girl."

He laughed out loud as did his wife and daughter as he then said, "You see I never actually wanted to harm you or your family, as your brother was my physician. It's that stupid girl you were teaching piano to for free at the church where Katelijne's father preached. So, I had to make sure Katelijne was hurt to the point she forgets everything. I tried to murder her too, then kill you, and your poor blind brother could not even see anything, so we left him alone."

Mr. Bakker then said, "That church and the pastor of the church were so annoying. We should have killed all of them. We left them as they were too stupid to even link the poor girl to us. Everyone thought the child just went missing and was never found. Now get lost and go haunt another house until we are gone, you stupid ghost. We will find the items we need, and we will leave in peace."

We had everything on tape as we watched the police force, rush in, and get the Bakkers. Everyone just watched Andries and knew what Papa had told them and said nothing. The whole thing ended very quickly. Then we saw there were only police officers who were asked to keep patrol of our home until the Bakkers were taken care of.

That night, I saw Mama, Katelijne, and Margriete put to bed two very tired toddlers in a room, the very same room I had Rietje in. I remembered all the nights I had stayed awake with her. I saw Bertelmeeus watch me from behind. There were, I saw, some escaped tears on his cheeks.

He saw me and said, "I wonder where my bundle of joy, my little Rietje is. I promised to never let her go, yet life let us be separated."

Bertelmeeus, Margriete, and I watched the toddlers sleep. Papa, Mama, Antonius, Katelijne, and Andries all were there just making sure the boys were still there. Aunt Marinda, however, was not anywhere we could see. No one said anything as we knew she is a time traveler who travels on her own time and to her chosen place. Yet she comes back as if she never even left.

I told everyone, "Look, he is back, our honorable soldier who has brought with him our brave knight. I feel blessed as tonight in Kasteel Vrederic is sleeping the father of the lighthouse."

As everyone went to their own rooms, I wrote to Margriete again, "Dear beloved, after tonight I knew our love and our union from last life was blessed as through the blessed union, we did have our daughter and her beloved husband, the father of the lighthouse. Here is a poem I wrote for you, celebrating love and all eternal lovers on his return."

THE FATHER OF THE LIGHTHOUSE

My beloved twin flame,

Ours is a love story,

That did not end in vain,

For it was written within

Two souls,

Two minds,

And

Two bodies.

Through love and promises,

The story was written.

Through tears and loss,

The story continued.

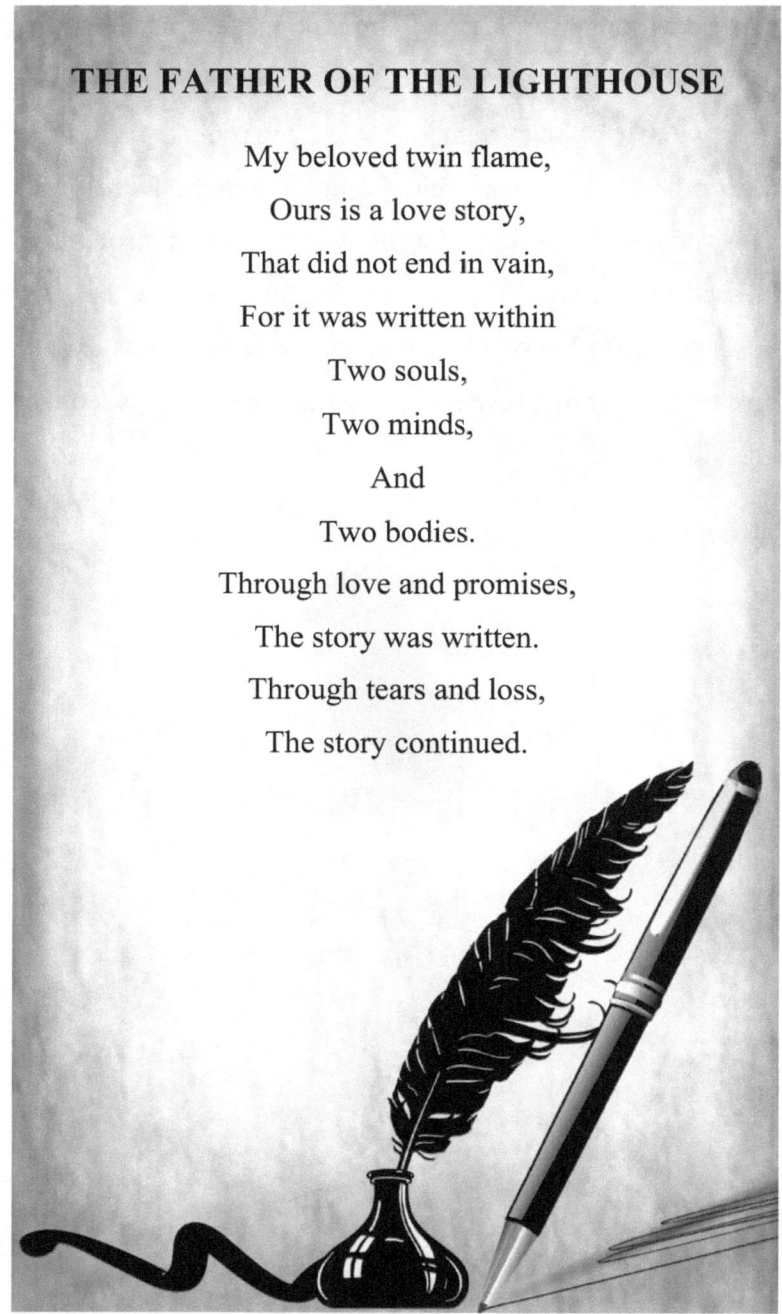

Mistakes rewrote

The love story.

Death had planted

Forget-me-nots,

Throughout time.

Yet throughout

All the storms,

All the obstacles,

The love story continued.

Even after death,

The love story begins again,

As now throughout the dark storms,

And better and worse days,

We made our love story

To begin again.

As we ended in a graveyard,

On top of one another,

We are then again

Given another chance

To rewrite our love story.

Just like a miracle

From beneath the Earth,

Comes to be within our love story,

He who stayed with

Our child,

The only symbol

Of our eternal

Love,

He who created

Another love story,

And continued our

Family dynasty,

THE FATHER OF THE LIGHTHOUSE.

CHAPTER NINE:

Twin Flames United

*"For one another, twin flames rise
like a burning phoenix from ashes,
yet if one half of the twin flames,
forgets and refuses to remember,
then the other half sings like a
nightingale and retells the love
story of twin flames."*

Dr. Jacobus Vrederic van Phillip proposes to his beloved twin flame after finally realizing how they both have risen like the magical phoenix for one another from ashes.

Life is made out of love, laughter, and tears. Life is complete only when there is someone to share life with. I watched the rainfall land on the ground and either make a puddle or just evaporate under the scorching sun. Yet when the raindrops land in the river, they eventually become a stream or a magical waterfall. They find peace as that's where they were meant to be.

What about twin flames and soulmates? What are they? Twin flames are one half of one another. When united, they are complete. Individually, they function yet in union they are whole.

Soulmates are complete individually yet are souls that belong together, like soul families. Margriete is my twin flame. When she will land upon my chest, I will be complete just like I know she too will be complete.

My family members are my soulmates as without them, I am not complete, and with all of them, I feel complete. Some members of the society who have come close to my family over and over again are also my soul family like Bertelmeeus and Aunt Marinda. Life after life, they are for this reason pulled to us as we are pulled to them.

This morning, I heard the birds singing as the wild deer were roaming around our forest. I wondered if life would be going back to normal for us. Yet what was normal I wondered.

The house was so quiet. I wondered why everything was so quiet in our home when suddenly my mind drifted off to the one person my heart freezes upon if anything is wrong or not. My mother, I have to check on her and see if she and Papa are all right.

Papa came running into my room. Mama and Papa never knock as it's not even in their mind that a parent has to knock to enter. Papa was looking strange as he walked into my room and first went to the windows near the front courtyard.

I keep the back windows facing the forest always open. Not the front ones. I am not fond of keeping an eye on who is coming and who is going.

Papa said, "Get up, stupid! Go and stop her from leaving! She is packed up and leaving. She is taking the boys with her and she said their job is complete here. Now life must go back to normal. She has to go back to the orphanage and the hospital. She likes to keep busy, so she does not have to be reminded about her loneliness. Jacobus, get up and stop her! I can't let her go. Not again."

I did not know what to say. I thought once Margriete had entered my house and my heart, she would never abandon me or my home. Yet I watched her in the courtyard trying to get her things in a taxi.

I ran downstairs unshaven and with my pajamas on. I watched the love of my life watch me and not say anything but just get her things in the car. The two boys were crying, and they saw me and ran toward me.

Theunis said, "Why do we have to go? You have a big house. How come we can't stay here? I like this home, as if it's my home. Also, Griet is coming here soon. I really wanted to make sure she is safe and not in any trouble when she finally does come. Also, Jacobus remember if and when we do leave, the lighthouse will be shut down. Margriete is placing everyone at risk by doing this."

Margriete came and took the boys in her arms and said, "You all can come and visit whenever you want, yet you both belong with me. We are family and we had a nice time visiting this home, but as they are all doing better, we can actually leave now."

I watched Margriete not face me, yet I asked, "If that is what you want to do, then I have nothing to say. I assumed this was your home too Margriete and the boys belong in Kasteel Vrederic. I never once even thought my Margriete would be leaving my house alive. Not as long as her heart beats, yet here you are, and I guess you are just Margriete. Not the other half of my soul."

Margriete watched me and said, "I am tired of having to prove myself and justify to anyone who I was or who I am, Jacobus. It's not fair as I always have to live with the memories that even you doubted me. How do I know you believe me or know me for myself? It's not fair Jacobus."

I watched my family members stand in the courtyard and no one said anything as I did insult Margriete over and over again. I tried to prove she was not my Margriete. I guess she was thinking I decided based on looks. Yet it was because I did not want to cheat on her even with her.

Papa came and held her hands and said, "No sweetheart, not in this life. You will not abandon this father. You see I still have my memories. Remember as long as I am well and standing, I shall never let you go. I did that once and I have paid for it, life after life, with karma taking away everything from me. I really don't care what happens but don't take yourself away from me. I know you love this Big Papa of yours. So at least be my daughter now and see me through her eyes."

She hugged Papa and Mama as they were both standing there. I felt like I should spank her buttocks and ask her does she not know my heart? How could she be mine and not see my inside?

Margriete was trying to say something when I saw one of her feet was inside of the courtyard and one outside. At that moment, I watched the lighthouse was shutting down as Theunis and Alexander too were sitting down in pain. I heard Katelijne cry in pain as I saw a lightning bolt was coming out of the lighthouse and was about to strike Margriete. I ran in front of her and pushed her aside.

I told Margriete, "Don't love me, don't remember me, at least don't insult my love and my oath. For you, I did not accept you. What would you have said if I had made love or had an affair with every woman who came prophesying their love for me? The one I lived for and am willing to die for and have kept myself protected under a veil for is now asking why I could not see her through the veil of a different face. Is it my fault you have different eyes, different hair, and a different face? Is it my fault I only wanted you, however and whatever you looked like?"

She sat on the ground next to me and said, "Are you hurt Jacobus? Please don't leave me because then I will finish you with my own hands for leaving me again. This life at least promise me, I will die before you."

I watched her and told her, "No, I am doing fine. I just wonder why the lighthouse was so angry. Also to your request, it's not possible for me to make that kind of a promise as I want to live with you and die with you."

Mama and Papa came and picked up the two boys. Andries and Antonius came and took all of Margriete's belongings. I watched my whole family standing in the courtyard as everyone smiled, laughed, and cried at the same time.

Katelijne came and told Margriete, "Once Big Papa and Big Mama accept you as their daughter, you should never leave this home at least alive. That's my oath, I shall never leave Big Mama and Big Papa or this family as long as my heart still beats. I know I was born to be in this family and this home eternally. I shall only live for this family, for it is my family."

Margriete came and hugged Big Papa and said, "As long as there is breath in my body, I shall never let you go. Not in this life or in any other life. Last life, I was not in my senses and that's why I let you go. I take a vow to never let go of this family ever again."

Antonius took advantage of the moment and said, "Ahem, what about Jacobus? Will you not take an oath to

265

never let him go ever again in holy matrimony again in this life?"

I saw laughter broke out in the courtyard where a fight had broken out only the night before. The lighthouse was back on again. The two boys were busy with Andries as they were talking amongst themselves all day.

That night as I was in the library talking with some of my hospital staff, Antonius came over and said, "Jacobus, the police commissioner is here, and he wants to talk with you. He has a lot of people with him."

I saw a very tense Antonius watching over me as I told him, "Gather up all of the family members. Go and knock upon Aunt Marinda's door three times only. She will answer and know where to come. Let's get this over with."

It felt like a whole courtroom just came to our home. There were attorneys, council members, police, and special agents. There were other personnel including politicians in our home.

I watched Papa and Mama sit very elegantly with Antonius, Andries, Katelijne, Margriete, Uncle Matthias, Bertelmeeus, and Aunt Marinda. They were with the two toddlers who were also in the room.

The head person I am guessing an intelligence agent said, "Everyone can stay but please remove the two boys from here as they should not be involved in these talks."

Aunt Marinda got up and said, "Come on boys, let's go and have some fun and games and let these boring adults be on their own."

Theunis said, "No, I won't leave Jacobus alone! That bald guy is a bad guy. He helped those goons to enter our home. I don't want him hurting my Jacobus."

Luckily no one except our family members understood Theunis's baby words. I watched them leave with Aunt Marinda as then in their place I saw the adult Theunis and Alexander appear.

Mama got a grip on the situation first as she said, "Please have a seat and let's get this over with. As I am Dr. Jacobus Vrederic van Phillip's mother, I will start the conversation and put some rules in place. I don't want my family involved in what should have been a police case that never should have been closed. Therefore, it is your fault all of this has happened. The details of my son Andries and why we thought he should be kept in hiding is our own decision and we will not go into any details on the matter. All the details regarding this were known to the police commissioner. Now you can talk."

They did not say much, only that they wanted to give their appreciation and send their gratitude toward our family.

The guy leading the investigation said, "They found out Aideen had tried to have Katelijne and other girls participating in different beauty contests murdered or have them sold as sex slaves. However, in Katelijne's case it was different because they wanted her dead at any cost. They were worried she might have witnessed more than she was willing to say. Also, because she knew Diana the ten-year-old victim. That's how everything had begun. Antonius and Andries both were at the wrong place at the wrong time. They assumed Andries had the papers or some kind of documents that had the names of all politicians, police officers, and other high-end society members listed as drug dealers, sex traffickers, and just plain being involved in having sex with minors. The ten-year-old girl whom Andries was teaching was going to be sold off that night. Yet as Andries saved Katelijne, he saw the child he was giving free piano lessons in the church and told her to go home. The girl was last seen alive with the Bakkers."

The lead investigator watched the police commissioner for a while and then said, "If Andries were to have lived or if it was known he had lived, he would have been murdered because he was a firsthand witness to the crimes committed against Katelijne and the ten-year-old girl whose name was Diana Maijer. Her posters are still found in all the grocery stores. The crimes were being committed under everyone's noses. There were a few people who had complained including the church gardener who kept on saying he saw Diana at the hotel with the Bakkers and Katelijne who was raped by them there. The fear again was that you probably have the names as she was your student and she had found them and witnessed the goons trying to kill Katelijne. The child asked you to help Katelijne as you probably don't remember Andries. Your brother too was unconscious at the time. So, the wealthy and well-known society members want the paper with their names, so they can have their names erased from it."

The police commissioner looked very unsettled as the higher intelligence service had taken over the case. I wondered what the commissioner knew about Andries. Mama said he knew about how we hid him. Papa also said he knew and he told the commissioner how we had to do this. But why then did he not share it with the others as it felt like they were not all in the same place?

That's when the intelligence officer intentionally said something yet made it look like a slip of a tongue.

He said, "Last year, the commissioner said your son was back. He actually never died. As there were so many ghostly sightings, he said either your son was floating like a ghost or was back."

I wondered as did Papa how he knew last year when Andries only became an adult in the last few weeks. I watched Papa as he then knew what I was wondering and got up.

Papa said, "Strange, I just spoke with the commissioner in the last two days. My family and I had our son hidden in our home for his own safety yet never shared the story with anyone. I did tell him recently as the questions of where he came back from will come into minds. Obviously, he did not return from death. Also, the person who had donated his heart to Katelijne, was buried here as that was his family's last wish. Strange how he knew this a year ago. Also, I do object to the thoughts of our home being haunted by ghosts. Our house is protected by our ancestors."

I saw my family members started giggling as the spirits of Theunis Peters and Alexander van der Bijl were floating above us. All the guests were watching them float as they all were pointing their fingers upward.

Mama said, "What is it? Why are you all pointing to the ceiling? It's an old house. It is what it is. Now tell me how you all knew my son is back from wherever he had gone to while no one else, even I did not know. Only my husband and my sons knew. I was a dead woman living without a life as my son was murdered, my daughter-in-law was almost murdered, my other son was hurt, and the bitch was hiding in my own home which I believe you knew as that's why you knew or thought my son was back. You too were here, right? Oh yes, I forgot to mention this house is not haunted but has psychics who live here and know who is bad and who is good."

That's when from the ceiling fell Andries's old phone that was lost. Griet, our daughter also known as the girl with the lantern, was holding on to it. She was now smiling as she had given the phone to her new mother Katelijne and brother Andries. I saw Theunis just smile as he nodded to me. I knew he wanted me to do something with the note as I watched Katelijne touch her womb.

She said, "Big Bro, I have uploaded the note to all of my social media pages. It's now all over the web in all different countries as proof of people who tried to murder me, my Andries, and Diana, the innocent child who through her death may have saved thousands more.

The intelligence officer only smiled and said, "Jacobus, we also have been following this case for years.

We are finally happy to have all the names of the social elites who hide under their social privileges. I believe Erasmus, you will be hurt to know that your buddy the police commissioner too has found his name at the top of the list. He was not trying to help you, but rather he was trying to conceal the paper in your own home through the Bakkers."

He watched us and said, "We actually had him under surveillance and asked our own officer Bertelmeeus to help you as he was already here. He said he would help you at any cost. The commissioner had him shot when he realized the depth of it. While they were trying to shoot Bertelmeeus, they accidently shot your family members."

I watched everyone leave as the police commissioner was arrested. I could not believe how big this was as we had the names of international criminals. Papa had asked them to erase our names from everything, so no one ever comes after our family.

In the middle of our courtyard in front of the lighthouse, I watched the enchanted moon was out with its full glory. I knew the nightingales were all out singing beautiful harmonious melodies as they called out for one another. As the stars came out, I had in front of my family asked Margriete to be my wedded wife then and there.

I asked my beloved, "In this life and therefore forever in all other lives, be mine and only mine. Take the vow of eternal bliss and be my wife eternally, my twin flame. For you I have risen from ashes and for you I shall forever and ever be only yours. Marry me tonight as we both have learned and every member of this home knows that there is no other time to celebrate than now, the present."

My beloved wife said with one word, "Yes."

I saw her eyes had filled up with tears and her face glowed up with happiness that we both shared eternally. The whole house was decorated with forget-me-nots, tulips, and roses. Margriete asked for a quiet wedding like the one we had after we had received Rietje in our life and I had Margriete back in our previous lifetime.

Mama and Katelijne had decorated the house with Bertelmeeus. Antonius and Papa had a new family portrait made for our home with their own hands. Papa had talked with Margriete in private before our small wedding where my two brothers were both my best men. Mama and Katelijne were bridesmaids.

Katelijne's father had come to officiate the wedding. He had not seen Andries for a while and was confused what was going on in our home. But as a church minister, he said nothing and was happy Katelijne was happily married to her twin flame.

Then I saw the most beautiful bride was walked down the aisle by Papa. I knew he had wanted to do this. As he came down the aisle to give away the bride, he said, "I am blessed to be able to have you as my daughter-in-law. For thousands of days and thousands of nights, I stayed awake wishing to be able to do this one day. I give you away to my son so then I can have you in my home forever and eternally here after as my daughter-in-law. Tonight, my wishes have come true. So, everyone please don't ever give up on your wishes, as some take centuries yet finally do come true."

Margriete wore the blue dress she was carrying with her. I knew everything in this life has a reason for happening. The dress she had that made me think she was a beautiful blue flower that blossomed just for me, now she was wearing the same blue dress to become eternally mine.

Then we saw the famous pianist Andries van Phillip, back on his piano. Everyone was brought to tears as his musical fingers found the musical notes and created magical music. He had been our musician who filled the house with a one-man piano concert.

The pianist was so amazing. I saw both his mothers were crying. Katelijne said, "My heart beats because of you, my son. A child gives back a mother's life, and then is born from her womb. This is the miracle I live with. I heard those amazing musical notes playing on a piano. As I walked toward the musical notes, I found Antonius and you."

Big Mama was crying as she said, "Dear son, may this world always know you don't have to carry a child to be a mother. In a few years after raising the child, he carries you along in his heart as you carry him in yours and the hearts beat for one another."

Andries went to both women and cried on their laps. He kissed them and said, "All of these miracles are only possible in this home, our home, Kasteel Vrederic."

Nightingales were singing with joy all around Kasteel Vrederic. The joy that had erupted in our home was nothing like before.

I watched my newly wedded wife and told her, "I only pray may all of my mistakes be forgiven by our daughter Griet. For I know she will have the world's best father in Antonius and a blessed mother in Katelijne. He will fight destiny and his fate to make right what all of his family members and ancestors have wronged. He taught me to see with my inner heart, not eyes only. I see you and know I am blessed to be able to witness this miracle from within my soul. May all mistakes be forgiven by our daughter Griet as today her parents have become one again and have blessed her to be reborn to Antonius and Katelijne, as the blessed daughter of Kasteel Vrederic. It's true I am only half without you. For with you, I am complete. May this blessed night be remembered by us. Let the stars be our witnesses and the moon be our witness. Let Mother Earth be our witness for after hundreds of years, we the eternal twin flames unite."

TWIN FLAMES HAVE UNITED

Rising phoenixes awaken magnificently,

To unite with their other half,

Yet then again

Without the other half,

They become ashes,

To only rise again.

I too had become ashes,

Without you,

For you,

Because of you.

Yet with hope,

Love,

And faith

As my guide,

I have risen again

Only to

Unite with you,

My beloved,

After hundreds of years,

As you too

Have risen

From the ashes,

To be with your twin flame.

Yet like the nightingales

Calling upon

One another,

We found each other,

As tonight,

Two minds, two bodies,

And two souls,

Found each other,

As we knew like

The rising phoenix,

We have risen

From ashes

To become

One mind,

One body,

One soul,

As tonight,

My eternally beloved,

My evermore beloved,

We the

TWIN FLAMES HAVE UNITED.

CHAPTER TEN:

Blessed Daughter Of Kasteel Vrederic

"Karma comes back at all like a boomerang yet love halts the curses and even karma gives up to the magical charms of pure love. A father, a brother, a son too can break down this curse if only they believe in the magical powers of love."

Antonius van Phillip keeps his vows from the beyond and brings back the forbidden daughter of Kasteel Vrederic as the blessed daughter of Kasteel Vrederic.

FORBIDDEN DAUGHTER OF KASTEEL VREDERIC: VOWS FROM THE BEYOND

Time heals everything. Yet what happens when time becomes the enemy? What about when you have wronged, yet the person you have wronged had limited time and you had unlimited? How do you rectify the wrong? After centuries of pain and sufferings, the guilty mind finds peace only when you know you have rectified the wrong. Reincarnation is a blessing when you remember your wrong and can redeem and awaken with all the memories.

I was lucky as the person I had wronged came back to my house as the girl with the lantern. She is half of the spirits of Kasteel Vrederic. I say half because her twin flame is the other half and in union, they are the spirits of Kasteel Vrederic. Once upon a time, centuries ago, I was blessed to have met Theunis Peters, the father of the lighthouse.

Theunis Peters had brought back to my home the physical body of my then-departed daughter. For his love and sacrifice, I had my daughter Griet van Jacobus back even after her death. We the inhabitants who had wronged a pure soul, waited to right the wrong and more so let the blessed child of Kasteel Vrederic come back to her house through birth. Today as we awaited her arrival, I remembered we are all here because of my daughter Griet and Theunis, her mirror soul. In union, they had kept the family tree going.

Time was our enemy, yet through the door of reincarnation, we befriended even time. We, the family members of Kasteel Vrederic, learned to take life as a journey and enter the door of reincarnation at the end. Today our household was celebrating for today the forbidden daughter of Kasteel Vrederic would once again enter this home as the beloved daughter of Kasteel Vrederic.

There was no knock on the door, but my mother was on her way in. I saw my wife smile as she said, "I love the mornings and Big Mama's visits."

Mama said, "I am coming in, are you two up yet? Fresh coffee! Also get up and get ready! Everyone is ready. Katelijne is having contractions, so I think it's time."

Margriete jumped up and was smiling in joy. She hugged Mama and said, "I should bring in your morning coffee. It's not fair a mother does it and a daughter sleeps in. Tomorrow you sleep late, and I will bring in the morning coffee for both of you. Also, Big Papa's morning papers. Coffee is easy. I just use our coffee maker. I can manage that."

Then suddenly I saw Margriete sit down. She said, "I feel dizzy Big Mama. Somehow, I just feel so nauseous too."

Mama just stared at her and said, "Well, get up and let's get some good food in you as you are going to be a Big Mama today."

Margriete watched me and Mama and said, "I would like to be called Mama Margriete. Because in this house, there is and shall always be one Big Mama, you, and one Big Papa. Jacobus can be Papa Jacobus."

Big Mama only kissed her head and said, "As you all wish."

That's when we heard a crash and knew my brother Antonius was coming. He was seen sooner than expected. He was shaking and was worried, so I held on to him for a while.

I asked him, "What is it Antonius? Why are you shaking? What happened?"

He watched me and said, "Katelijne is not breathing right Jacobus. Like you asked, I checked her vitals every day and every morning. Her oxygen level is like 89 and her temperature is 103. Her blood pressure too is high. I am worried if something is wrong."

I had my cell phone in my hand, so I called the hospital to get the operating room ready. I also arranged an ambulance to come here. Margriete and I both went to Katelijne's room.

I watched the lighthouse and saw everything looked normal. I called Theunis in my mind for help. I saw Margriete the doctor take care of Katelijne.

Margriete smiled and said, "Everything looks good. We will take her in and have the baby today. It seems like your baby wants to be born today. I will make sure the baby and her mother are comfortable during this stage."

The whole gang, my whole family, went into the hospital as my family members own the hospital and are regular visitors. Everyone just walked into the wing with Margriete. I saw Mama, Papa, and all of my family members including the two toddlers, were all walking in the waiting lounge and panicking.

I took them inside to a separate wing for doctors and told them, "Please wait and do not worry. Things happen and that's why we have doctors who can also handle these kinds of things. We need to let the doctors do their work. Katelijne's gynecologists are in there with her. They have asked me to take Antonius out of there. He is panicking and is saying weird things. They think he has gone mental. Actually, he was trying to talk with Griet in front of everyone. He said he knows Griet can hear him. He told her soon she will be home and Griet won't be the forbidden but the beloved daughter of Kasteel Vrederic. He also said in front of the doctors that Theunis was floating in air, so he asked Theunis to leave and wait outside."

Andries broke out in a laughing fit and asked, "Was he like that when I was born?"

Big Papa took him aside and said, "Actually Antonius was really calm and did not say anything at all, when you were born."

Andries laughed out into a fit now and asked, "He fainted, really? During my birth?"

Papa and Mama both went into a laughing fit with Andries. I watched my family members and told them, "I will be going inside as will Margriete. I will be there just to monitor her heart conditions as they will do a C-section. Margriete is only going in as a pediatrician, who will monitor the baby. Nothing to worry about everyone. Just keep Antonius under control as he won't be allowed in there because of the procedures which are totally normal."

After a while, I saw for the first time there was our blessed daughter who came to this world in my own hands. Because the doctor did not have enough expertise in Katelijne's heart condition, I delivered the baby. Margriete then took the baby in her hands and she held the child to her heart and just watched the baby.

Katelijne was sleeping through it. Just before she did go to sleep, she told us, "I am glad you two will be the first ones to hold on to her. Karma is just after all as karma has given your daughter back to you through Antonius and me."

The day passed quicker than we thought it would pass. Every member of our household stayed at the hospital with Katelijne and Griet Vrederic van Phillip all day.

Katelijne had said, "Since my doctors, Jacobus and Margriete, are both live-in doctors and the baby's Papa Jacobus and Mama Margriete, it is better she and I just go home with the family if it is all right with her doctors."

I agreed and told them, "We have the house ready for our patients and believe it is completely all right to come home."

Antonius and Katelijne had come home that night. They did not want the child to stay at the hospital and lose one night of her life not being in her blessed home. We all walked in front of the lighthouse and held our blessed daughter in front of the lighthouse.

Antonius was very emotional and as he held on to his daughter, he said, "Dear beloved daughter of this home, tonight as the moon shines over our home, I welcome you to my ancestral home, your father's home. This is now your home, my beloved daughter."

Antonius gave the baby to Big Papa as Big Papa was crying. He held the blessed daughter to his chest and said, "I am the blessed Opa who can now say my granddaughter is finally home. May my blessings be with you eternally. As you had protected this home, may this home and all her inhabitants protect you eternally."

Then Antonius gave Griet to me as he said, "We have told all of you, with your blessings we want to call her Griet Vrederic van Phillip for she is the blessed daughter of Kasteel Vrederic. Also, the other person who carries Vrederic in his name is her blessed Papa Jacobus."

I finally got her in my arms and as I held on to her, I told her, "Dear Griet, I have searched for you eternally. You had left a letter for me saying if only I was yours, you would never let me go. I am all yours and I promise as I take an honorable godfather's oath, an uncle's oath, and the oath from your Papa Jacobus, I shall never let you go as you are now ours."

After Margriete finished kissing her maybe a thousand times, she said, "May this Mama Margriete's blessings be with you as a protection eternally."

Then Mama came and said, "Like I said, all the children of Kasteel Vrederic belong to Erasmus and me. Also, sweet child do remember you are the soul of this home as this family has given you the title, beloved daughter of Kasteel Vrederic."

On this magical night, we brought back to Kasteel Vrederic the blessed daughter of Kasteel Vrederic. The quest to bring back the daughter of this home had begun centuries ago. Finally, today we were rewarded with the birth of the blessed child.

Not a single member of our household slept on this enchanted night. As a small beloved child slept in her home for the first time, every member of the household wanted to make sure she was doing well. Like a fairy princess, she slept in her crib as all of my family members watched over like her guiding angels.

Aunt Marinda came out of her room and said, "So everyone must want to know what happens to Theunis and Alexander. They have been adopted by me as my boys, yet I give them to you to keep and bring up as my treasured possessions. You all know they will need tender loving care. I know Erasmus you wanted to adopt the boys, but you see these boys are related to the two precious daughters of this home. Until the daughters are of eighteen years of age you will not tell them anything about their past. They will be normal children but will all have some kind of mystical powers from me."

290

She then kissed Griet and she touched Margriete's womb and just watched the lighthouse. Aunt Marinda then said, "They will know more than they will share. They have the power of giving you the one thing you will need Jacobus, as will Andries. He too is very special, and I have made sure he too has returned to be here with the beloved daughter of Kasteel Vrederic. There never was nor will ever be any forbidden daughter of Kasteel Vrederic. Forever all daughters and sons of this home shall be known as the beloved children of Kasteel Vrederic."

That night as we all stayed awake, I wrote a poem for our blessed daughter who has returned, back to her own home.

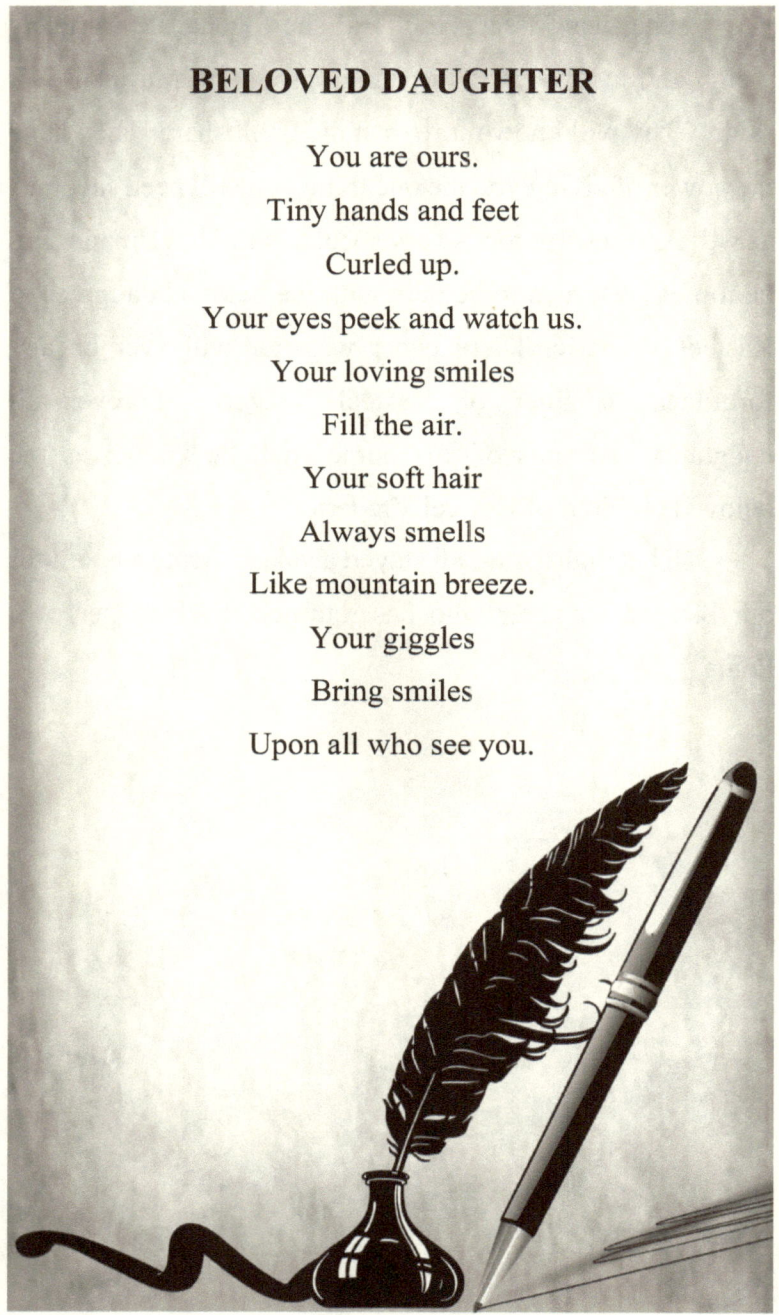

BELOVED DAUGHTER

You are ours.

Tiny hands and feet

Curled up.

Your eyes peek and watch us.

Your loving smiles

Fill the air.

Your soft hair

Always smells

Like mountain breeze.

Your giggles

Bring smiles

Upon all who see you.

Holding you is a blessing.

Sharing you with

The family

Is a joy

As we know you

Are our

Precious gift.

Like a magical

Fountain,

Whoever sees you,

Makes a wish

As everyone knows

Through your love,

All of our wishes

Have come true

For you are

Our,

BELOVED DAUGHTER.

CONCLUSION

Forever And Ever Be Only Mine

"Time the enemy of all humans is impatient and waits for no one yet love never gets tired of waiting as love lives on even beyond time. So, remember everyone, time has lost this battle to love, the immortality serum."

Erasmus van Phillip holds his two beloved granddaughters after finally facing karma with his centuries of penance. He believed they returned to him as they were always his and he shall never let them go.

L ife in Kasteel Vrederic had finally returned to normal. The sun was bright, and the green forest outside had even more deer and birds as her residents. The wild animals have discovered a magical lake in our backyard and all of them had fun drinking the magical water.

We had a very, very, very happy few months as our precious daughter was being brought up in a joint family by loving family members. A very chubby and cute girl. She looked like Papa, Antonius, and me, mixed. Some actually say she looks just like me.

I wonder if she were a boy, she could actually pass on as Dr. Jacobus Vrederic van Phillip. In the last few months as Griet was beginning to crawl, her Mama Margriete had begun to sit more and more. Griet's Mama and Big Mama have to play with her more and more. Yet Griet keeps on coming back to Margriete and wants to be on her lap and sleep on her lap too.

Margriete came in and said, "Jacobus, I need to go to the hospital."

I told her, "Be safe my love. Also, Papa is going to the hospital for story night, so he can go with you."

I was trying to feed the chubby baby girl with her father Antonius. It felt like he had most of the food as she always waited for him to eat before she had anything. The strangest part was this girl only ate from her Papa or Papa Jacobus or her Opa. No one else could feed her.

Margriete screamed now and said, "Jacobus, I need to go now!"

Big Mama and Katelijne came running in as they both screamed and said, "Jacobus, car! Get the van! We need to go to the hospital now!"

I jumped up as Antonius and our adorable baby with messy face were all shocked at Margriete's screams. We knew then Margriete was going to have the baby. If she did not go to the hospital, she would have the baby here.

Margriete said, "I don't want you delivering my baby. Obviously, I can't deliver the baby, so I have to go now."

Mama got the van and I watched Katelijne get all of Margriete's stuff as Papa, Antonius, Andries, and I got in the van with our baby girl and the two toddler boys. We realized Mama does not like driving and Katelijne freezes while driving. Andries offered to drive when we saw there was a man or a mountain running toward the van.

Bertelmeeus said, "I will drive. This great-uncle of Rietje has been waiting for her for so long. I won't let her have to wait for me. I am here for you baby Rietje."

FORBIDDEN DAUGHTER OF KASTEEL VREDERIC: VOWS FROM THE BEYOND

That evening, we brought another daughter of Kasteel Vrederic home with us. As we brought the two girls in front of the lighthouse, I saw Griet extend her hands and touch Rietje.

Papa started to tear up as he said, "They are back with us now. Everyone, the girls are back home with us. Now let's take the girls inside and keep them protected eternally."

Margriete, Katelijne, and Mama walked with the two girls as did Andries, Antonius, and Papa. I saw the two boys and Bertelmeeus follow us inside as we all went into the baby's room.

Antonius carried her in the same breadbasket he had carried Griet in as he had prepared the same basket for both girls. We still get breads in for the babies. He stood in front of the lighthouse as he said, "Rietje Vrederic van Phillip, welcome back to your home."

That's when we saw Aunt Marinda in the living room waiting for us. She kissed both girls and said, "So the babies have arrived. Now you all must figure out a way to time travel one more time. This time you must find the immortality serum. You all, even the babies, will stop aging at the age of thirty, yet Margriete will not and that's why I want you all to figure this out on your own."

We were all ready to have a quiet night at home after the long pregnancy and were not expecting this news. I knew about Margriete aging normally but thought we would figure something out. I watched the two toddler boys come and sit next to a very tired Margriete.

Andries said, "I am not worried as I know what we have to do. We all had traveled through the tunnel of light before and I had traveled through this tunnel after death alone. However, we will travel through the tunnel of light once more with our family to get this miracle completed. I know this journey will be completed when the four miracle children are able to talk and walk on their own. I will lead my family through the tunnel of light once more. We shall all in union travel through this magical tunnel and figure out the eternal truth of the immortality serum. From my last trip, I remember meeting all of you and even the toddler boys and the girls. They were a little older when we did this journey. So, I am guessing we will all be there together to find the answers to our question, all of us together, the inhabitants of Kasteel Vrederic."

Mama stood up and said, "Jacobus, I saw this in my dream and have spoken to Andries, Antonius, Margriete, Katelijne, and your Papa about this. We had decided not to bother you as you would then do things right away and not sit and wait until it's time to go."

I watched my family members and told them, "A life with Margriete, even old Margriete, is better than no Margriete. I would not let age decide or amputate my beloved twin flame, my eternally beloved, from my life. I will fight for us."

Margriete came close to me and said, "Dear husband, as long as you will have me as young or old, I will be yours eternally. For my vows were to be yours in this life and beyond. If life and time do separate us, then let my vows tie us in a bond eternally. I promise Jacobus, I will never let you go."

I held on to my twin flame and told her, "My beloved, this vow that ties us eternally will also save us and let us be together forever. No time zone can separate us as I will bring you back from beyond Earth. While on Earth for one day or a hundred, I will be only yours and shall never let you go."

It was then Kasteel Vrederic saw her first miracle performed by the two baby girls. As they touched one another's hand, there appeared a light from their hands to Margriete's heart. All of it came from the lighthouse on to the baby girls to Margriete. That's when the two toddler boys floated and joined the circle of light and placed Margriete in a circle.

Aunt Marinda said, "The four children have placed Margriete in a circle of light. This will protect her and prevent her from aging until you are able to take the trip and be back. Also, Andries you will meet your twin flame through that journey. Remember not to fall for anyone before that time."

Andries watched Aunt Marinda and said, "There I was planning to elope and now you have to stop me."

He watched his two baby sisters and said, "Okay little sisters, I think I can be busy with overloaded baby cuteness until then."

I knew we must start to plan our trip to the place that holds the immortality serum. I watched my mystical family go back to their normal day's life. As our faith is strong, we would be guided to the place, how to go there, and when by the spirits of Kasteel Vrederic, at the right time.

Margriete came and said, "Dear beloved, don't worry about tomorrow as today I have you and you have me. We have our blessed family and our sacred home Kasteel Vrederic. Our daughter who was called by the society, through our mistakes an illegitimate child, the forbidden daughter of Kasteel Vrederic is now back. Griet is our beloved daughter as is Rietje and their twin flames Theunis and Alexander are all here. We shall find the immortality serum in the next diary. For now, let's enjoy and celebrate our blessed children, the children of Kasteel Vrederic."

I knew we shall find the immortality serum in the next diary. Yet as I end this diary, I have written another poem which I have dedicated to all the children of this world. For remember each and all children born to this world are magical and have a miracle in their own sleeves. All you have to do to find this miracle is to hold on to the children very close to you and listen to their musical heartbeats. The next diary in the *Kasteel Vrederic* series is called *The Immortality Serum: Vows From The Beyond*.

Yet before you all go and read where and how we find the immortality serum, let's go and see what my family and I have been doing each night as we read stories to young children. These stories are filled with magical and supernatural fairytales. This children's book I call *Enchanted Tales: A Kasteel Vrederic Storybook For Children*, is coming to your home for your beloved and magical kids, in the *Kasteel Vrederic* series.

Hold the blessed children close to your heart and believe me as the son of Kasteel Vrederic, I know every single child holds within his or her heart some magical serums. You shall only find these magical serums as each child learns to share their stories with you.

Remember don't be an arrogant and ignorant person like myself. Love your children. For remember as their heartbeats call your name, your heartbeats will also call for them as you only take a look at their faces.

Here is a poem for all of the blessed children of this world.

BLESSED CHILDREN

The sun shines bright,

Only when you laugh.

The pouring rain is

A blessing,

If you need it

To stay calm.

The beautiful

Green grass

Outside spreads

Itself around,

For your tiny feet's

Comfort.

The fruits pour,

Sweet immortality

Serum

As juice

To quench your thirst.

Mother Earth furnishes you

With

Corn, rice, and wheat.

She also provides

You with

All the water you

Need to drink

To help you

Survive,

A beautiful and blessed,

Life on Earth.

For you all are

This Mother Earth's

BLESSED CHILDREN.

INHABITANTS OF FORBIDDEN DAUGHTER OF KASTEEL VREDERIC

Dr. Jacobus Vrederic van Phillip   Medical doctor with multiple specialties, and one-of-a-kind specialist in never-done-before transplant surgeries. Son of Erasmus van Phillip and Anadhi Newhouse van Phillip, cousin of Antonius van Phillip and Andries van Phillip, uncle of reincarnated Andries van Phillip and Griet Vrederic van Phillip, twin flame and husband of Dr. Margriete van Achthoven, and father of Rietje Vrederic van Phillip. Reincarnated form of sixteenth and seventeenth-century Jacobus van Vrederic.

Dr. Margriete van Achthoven   Medical doctor, cardiologist, and pediatric cardiovascular surgeon. Co-owner of Agatha and Marinda's Orphanage. Twin flame and wife of Dr. Jacobus Vrederic van Phillip, and mother of Rietje Vrederic van Phillip. Reincarnated form of sixteenth and seventeenth-century Margriete van Wijck.

Anadhi Newhouse van Phillip Author. Daughter of Dr. Andrew Newhouse and Dr. Gita Shankar Newhouse, granddaughter of Martin Newhouse and Miranda Newhouse, granddaughter of Hari Shankar and Parvati Shankar, twin flame and wife of Erasmus van Phillip, mother of Dr. Jacobus Vrederic van Phillip, aunt and adoptive mother of Antonius van Phillip and Andries van Phillip, grandmother of reincarnated Andries van Phillip, Griet Vrederic van Phillip, and Rietje Vrederic van Phillip. Reincarnated form of sixteenth-century Mahalt.

Erasmus van Phillip World-renowned painter, and twenty-first-century owner of Kasteel Vrederic. Son of Greta van Phillip, descendant of the van Vrederic family, twin flame and husband of Anadhi Newhouse van Phillip, father of Dr. Jacobus Vrederic van Phillip, uncle and adoptive father of Antonius van Phillip and Andries van Phillip, and grandfather of reincarnated Andries van Phillip, Griet Vrederic van Phillip, and Rietje Vrederic van Phillip. Reincarnated form of sixteenth-century Johannes van Vrederic.

Antonius van Phillip   World-renowned painter. Son of Petrus van Phillip and Giada Berlusconi van Phillip, nephew and adopted son of Erasmus van Phillip and Anadhi Newhouse van Phillip, twin brother of Andries van Phillip, cousin and adoptive brother of Dr. Jacobus Vrederic van Phillip, twin flame and husband of Katelijne Snaaijer van Phillip, and father of reincarnated Andries van Phillip and Griet Vrederic van Phillip.

Katelijne Snaaijer van Phillip   Stepdaughter of Ghileyn Snaaijer, twin flame and wife of Antonius van Phillip, and mother of reincarnated Andries van Phillip and Griet Vrederic van Phillip.

Andries van Phillip   Deceased world-renowned pianist, son of Petrus van Phillip and Giada Berlusconi van Phillip, nephew and adopted son of Erasmus van Phillip and Anadhi Newhouse van Phillip, twin brother of Antonius van Phillip, and cousin and adoptive brother of Dr. Jacobus Vrederic van Phillip. Now reincarnated son of Antonius van Phillip and Katelijne Snaaijer van Phillip, grandson of Erasmus van Phillip and Anadhi Newhouse van Phillip, nephew of Dr. Jacobus Vrederic van Phillip and Dr.

Margriete van Achthoven, brother of Griet Vrederic van Phillip, and cousin of Rietje Vrederic van Phillip.

Griet Vrederic van Phillip

Daughter of Antonius van Phillip and Katelijne Snaaijer van Phillip, granddaughter of Erasmus van Phillip and Anadhi Newhouse van Phillip, niece of Dr. Jacobus Vrederic van Phillip and Dr. Margriete Achthoven, sister of Andries van Phillip, and cousin of Rietje Vrederic van Phillip. Reincarnated form of sixteenth-century Griet van Jacobus.

Rietje Vrederic van Phillip

Daughter of Dr. Jacobus Vrederic van Phillip and Dr. Margriete van Achthoven, granddaughter of Erasmus van Phillip and Anadhi Newhouse van Phillip, and cousin of Andries van Phillip and Griet Vrederic van Phillip. Reincarnated form of sixteenth and seventeenth-century Margriete "Rietje" Jacobus Peters.

Matthias van Phillip

Spiritual yogi. Cousin of Erasmus van Phillip and descendant of van Vrederic family.

Petrus van Phillip

Deceased husband of deceased Giada Berlusconi van Phillip, biological father of twins

Antonius van Phillip and Andries van Phillip, cousin of Erasmus van Phillip and Matthias van Phillip, and descendant of van Vrederic family.

Aunt Marinda   Time traveler, spiritual seer, nurse, and herbalist from the sixteenth century in the present day. Co-owner of Agatha and Marinda's Orphanage. Sister of Aunt Agatha, and adoptive guardian of Theunis and Alexander.

Aunt Agatha   Catholic nun. Co-owner of Agatha and Marinda's Orphanage. Sister of Aunt Marinda.

Theunis   Adopted son of Aunt Marinda. Adoptive brother of Alexander. Reincarnated form of sixteenth-century Theunis Peters.

Alexander   Adopted son of Aunt Marinda. Adoptive brother of Theunis. Reincarnated form of sixteenth and seventeenth-century Sir Alexander van der Bijl.

Chef Bert   Famous voluntary chef at the Agatha and Marinda's Orphanage and at the Vrederic Hospital and Clinic, and policeman. Reincarnated form of sixteenth

312

	and seventeenth-century Bertelmeeus van der Berg.
Ghileyn Snaaijer	Protestant preacher. Stepfather of Katelijne Snaaijer van Phillip.
Aideen Bakker	Adopted daughter of Mirrorless Hotel owners Luyt Bakker and Livina Bakker-Beenhouwer.
Luyt Bakker	Owner of Mirrorless Hotel. Husband of Livina Bakker-Beenhouwer, and adoptive father of Aideen Bakker.
Livina Bakker-Beenhouwer	Owner of Mirrorless Hotel. Wife of Luyt Bakker, and adoptive mother of Aideen Bakker.
Ella The Prostitute	Look-alike of sixteenth and seventeenth-century Margriete van Wijck.
Diana Maijer	Ten-year-old victim of unjust human trafficking.
Miranda Newhouse "Grandmother"	Seeker. Dutch-American paternal grandmother of Anadhi Newhouse van Phillip, mother of Dr. Andrew Newhouse, wife of Martin Newhouse, and descendant of sixteenth and seventeenth-century Bertelmeeus van der Berg.

Parvati Shankar "Nani" Indian maternal grandmother of Anadhi Newhouse van Phillip, mother of Dr. Gita Shankar Newhouse, and wife of Hari Shankar.

Greta van Phillip Mother of Erasmus van Phillip and descendant of van Vrederic family.

Griete van Phillip Aunt of Erasmus van Phillip, mother of Matthias van Phillip, and descendant of van Vrederic family.

Grietje van Phillip Aunt of Erasmus van Phillip, mother of Petrus van Phillip, and descendant of van Vrederic family.

Jacobus van Vrederic Sixteenth and seventeenth-century nobleman, diarist of the *I Shall Never Let You Go* diaries, Protestant preacher, and owner of Kasteel Vrederic. Twin flame and husband of Margriete van Wijck, son of Johannes van Vrederic and Mahalt, father of Griet van Jacobus, and grandfather of Margriete "Rietje" Jacobus Peters.

Margriete van Wijck Twin flame and wife of sixteenth and seventeenth-century Jacobus van Vrederic, mother of Griet van Jacobus, and grandmother of Margriete "Rietje" Jacobus Peters of the *I Shall Never Let You Go* diaries.

Mahalt Sixteenth-century twin flame and wife of Johannes van Vrederic, and mother of Jacobus van Vrederic.

Johannes van Vrederic Sixteenth-century nobleman, and original owner of Kasteel Vrederic. Twin flame and husband of Mahalt, father of Jacobus van Vrederic, grandfather of Griet van Jacobus, and great-grandfather of Margriete "Rietje" Jacobus Peters.

Griet van Jacobus Legendary spirit of Kasteel Vrederic, sixteenth-century daughter of Jacobus van Vrederic and Margriete van Wijck, twin flame and wife of Theunis Peters, and mother of Margriete "Rietje" Jacobus Peters.

Margriete "Rietje" Jacobus Peters Sixteenth and seventeenth-century inhabitant and seventeenth-century owner of Kasteel Vrederic. Granddaughter of Jacobus van Vrederic and Margriete van Wick, daughter of Theunis Peters and Griet van Jacobus, twin flame and wife of Sir Alexander van der Bijl, and inheritor and co-diarist of the fifth diary in the *Kasteel Vrederic* series.

Theunis Peters — Legendary spirit of Kasteel Vrederic, sixteenth-century honorable soldier, twin flame and husband of Griet van Jacobus, father of Margriete "Rietje" Jacobus Peters, and son-in-law of Jacobus van Vrederic and Margriete van Wijck.

Sir Alexander van der Bijl — Sixteenth and seventeenth-century inhabitant and seventeenth-century knight. Great-grandnephew of Sir Krijn van der Bijl, and twin flame and husband of Margriete "Rietje" Jacobus Peters.

Bertelmeeus van der Berg — Sixteenth and seventeenth-century caretaker of Kasteel Vrederic. Non-blood related uncle of Jacobus van Vrederic.

Sir Krijn van der Bijl — Sixteenth-century knight. Great-granduncle of Sir Alexander van der Bijl.

GLOSSARY

Get acquainted with some Dutch and Hindi terms, and places in the Netherlands, India, and the United States that were used in this book.

Aloo Naan	Typical Indian dish consisting of a type of Indian bread stuffed with potatoes that is normally baked in a tandoor.
Amsterdam	Capital city of the Netherlands.
Batik	Type of print design originating from Indonesia and popular in Asia made using dye on clothing.
Death	End of life on Earth, when the body and soul separate. More information on death can be found in the book *Eternal Truth: The Tunnel Of Light* by Ann Marie Ruby.
Doctors Without Borders	Non-governmental organization that provides humanitarian and medical assistance internationally.
Dreams	REM (rapid eye movement) cycle is when a sleeping body

can travel through dreams.
Proven scientifically dreams
can occur and people do travel
during their dreams. However,
their bodies do not leave their
places. Major religions have
mainly come through dreams.
More information on dreams
can be found in the book
*Eternal Truth: The Tunnel Of
Light* by Ann Marie Ruby.

Dutch Term refers to both the
language spoken and the
people in the Netherlands.

Gallows A place commonly known
where witches were hung to
their death.

Grim Reaper Mythological personification
of death, also known as the
Angel of Death who takes the
soul to the afterlife.

India Officially the Republic of
India, country located in South
Asia, and the second most
populated country in the
world.

Kaftan A garment that is loose and
ankle-length with long flowy
sleeves, originating from
Mesopotamia and popular

throughout the world for
different uses.

Karma Reaction to a person's actions
throughout his or her life. One
of the core beliefs of Hinduism
and Buddhism.

Kasteel Vrederic Castle Vrederic is the home of
the van Vrederic family in the
Kasteel Vrederic series,
spanning from the sixteenth
century through the present.

Los Angeles City in California, USA.
Second-largest city in the
USA. Famous for the nation's
television and film industry.

Meditation Meditation, also known as
Dhyana, is the concentration
of the mind, body, and soul.
The concept first appeared in
the Vedas in Hinduism and has
since evolved worldwide.

Miracles Unexpected gift that cannot be
explained by science or
medicine. More information
on miracles can be found in
the book *Eternal Truth: The
Tunnel Of Light* by Ann Marie
Ruby.

Naarden City in the province of North
Holland in the Netherlands.

Nani   Maternal grandmother in Hindi.

Oma   Grandmother in Dutch.

Opa   Grandfather in Dutch.

Palak Paneer   Common Indian curry made out of cheese cubes and spinach.

Reincarnation/Rebirth   Belief of a lot of people worldwide such as Buddhism, Hinduism, Jainism, Sikhism, and more. Today science can't disprove reincarnation. Also a lot of people have given proof of their rebirth. More information on reincarnation can be found in the book *Eternal Truth: The Tunnel Of Light* by Ann Marie Ruby.

San Francisco   City and county in California, USA. Current home of Ann Marie Ruby.

Scheveningen   Seaside resort and fishing port on the North Sea in The Hague, the Netherlands.

Seattle   City in Washington State, USA.

Soul Family   People who are in various lifetimes reborn in the same house, neighborhood, or around one another. More information on soul families can be found in the book *Eternal Truth: The Tunnel Of Light* by Ann Marie Ruby.

Spaniards   Members of the Spanish army who fought for the King of Spain.

Stakes   A place where witches were burned to death.

Tennessee   State in USA.

The Hague   Den Haag, political capital of the Netherlands within the province of South Holland.

Tunnel Of Light   Scientifically it is known as the NDE (near-death experience) tunnel. More information on the tunnel of light can be found in the book *Eternal Truth: The Tunnel Of Light* by Ann Marie Ruby.

Twin Flames   Research has shown twin flames can survive as individuals yet are complete in union. More information on twin flames can be found in the book *Eternal Truth: The Tunnel Of Light* by Ann Marie Ruby.

Vince Camuto   American fashion designer.

Witch Hunts   A tribunal, heretical, and shameful time for the world, as innocent women or men were accused of being witches or warlocks, because someone might have just accused the person or the person could have had some special gift.

MESSAGE FROM THE AUTHOR

"Through the journey of life, mistakes committed and admitted are messages left behind for the future inhabitants of this world."

Dear Readers,

 The *Forbidden Daughter Of Kasteel Vrederic: Vows From The Beyond* is a very special book. In this book, I touch upon a topic which is neither really welcomed nor spoken about in our society, the illegitimate children of our world. My question is how could a child be illegitimate if the action committed by the parents were wrong, not the result from their actions?

 Unwed mothers, rape victims, or just unwanted children dropped off at orphanages or just left in trash bins, come upon the news. These news stories barely make any headline news, nor are they printed in newspapers around the globe. No one talks about them as the news gets forgotten, and the child involved in the news grows up as an illegitimate child. Just think, do you ever go back and think whatever happened to the victims of these stories? How do these issues even come and become stories around the world?

 Some strangers might have had a one-night stand. They forgot about the world. They forgot about their one night's mistake and the result of their action. For a few minutes of fun and excitement they will have to live with the regret forever. The individuals were so oblivious to their acts, as both individuals committing this act were intoxicated.

The victim of this one-night stand becomes known to this world as the illegitimate child of this society. Throughout this world, children of one-night stands, children of rape victims, or just unwanted children of this society end up in orphanages or on the roads of so many developing countries or even in western civilizations.

These children too have beautiful eyes they cry and spill tears with. Their little fingers curl up to be comforted by a mother's touch, or a father's strong grip assuring the child everything will be all right. During a thunderstorm, these children try to hide within their parents' arms they never find. If they get sick, no one wants to touch them as everyone whispers around them, "Don't touch them. They might have contagious diseases."

The little hearts beat until they become the little stones that don't feel anything as they just watch all other children who are blessed to have a home where the mothers had kept them. Where their fathers stay awake all night making sure the child is not afraid of the thundering storms of the night.

I have written this book with these children in my heart. What happens when you are called the illegitimate child of the society? It develops a character for you, the character this society that had not been there for you when you needed them but gives you.

In my first book of this series, I wrote about the parents who were married yet life had separated them. However, the society had not known that. Yet it did not stop the society from talking and spreading rumors.

I have brought back the topic as within the pages of my books, I can bring back people from the world of dead. As then I an author can on my own give the forbidden daughter a home, a loving family, and let her know she was and is loved and will always be loved by her family. Life is a journey where mistakes are made, yet as the journey is a one-way road, we can't go back and change our committed mistakes. We try to learn from them and move on. We leave our mistakes as a warning sign for others to be guided by.

In my paranormal books, I actually tried to give justice to the committed mistakes of the inhabitants of Kasteel Vrederic through reincarnation and memories that were their guides. Today you too can be a part of the solution, not the problem. Don't be the critical voices of the society. Don't criticize others for if you had looked into the mirror without knowing it's your own life you see in it, I know you would be criticizing your own reflection too.

Let's accept the children of this world as pure and blessed children. No race, no color, and no religion should keep them apart. Let those cute and blessed hands create a bridge of pure love and acceptance in your heart. Open your inner soul and make this world the blessed home for all children.

How they were born, where they were born, to whom they were born is not the story. For they were just born, and their storylines are yet to be completed through the journey of their life.

In my book, I have Griet Vrederic van Phillip back as the blessed daughter of Kasteel Vrederic, not the forbidden daughter, for I believe the only thing forbidden should be hate. Love is always a blessed journey. Choose love and forgiveness.

Read all the books of the Kasteel Vrederic series, as all of these paranormal romantic family sagas have one thing in common, that is love eventually is and shall always be victorious. All of these books will bring back faith in true love. Love does not mean always happily ever after, as life has death, birth, and sorrows as well as happiness all blanketed into one. Yet we all want to escape to another world where we can all feel like we too belong in this world.

Here everyone feels like family. Here everyone is welcomed. Here you too can feel right at home.

So to forget all of your troubles and feel like you are on a permanent vacation where you can just be in your own home and still be in the Netherlands with the Kasteel Vrederic family members, why don't you all walk into the world of Kasteel Vrederic? Here, yes, you will cry with them. You will laugh with them and always at the end come out feeling it's all going to be just all right.

Come and be a member of this family just by reading all the books in this series. For remember, after reading this series, you too shall believe in the door of miracles, the door of reincarnation, and the door of dreams which shall actually take you to a blessed home everyone knows as Kasteel Vrederic.

Books are miracles from the beyond. Within the pages of my books, I can even change the destinies of the destined as I don't believe in destined to destiny but be my destiny. I don't believe any child of this world is illegitimate as the action was wrong but the children from the wrongfully committed actions are beloved blessings of humanity.

Don't miss my next book, a paranormal, magical, fairytale, supernatural book for children. This book covers stories for children from around the globe, where we will visit all the continents of this globe and meet up with children from around the globe and listen to their stories. We shall unite the world with a book. Come join me and celebrate all children of this globe through this magical book which will be released soon.

BOOK ONE:

Eternally Beloved: I Shall Never Let You Go

This book introduces you to Kasteel Vrederic through the first diary of the famous diarist Jacobus van Vrederic. He walks you through his sad love story and goes through the love story of his daughter Griet van Jacobus and the brave soldier Theunis Peter. Based during the Dutch Eighty Years' War in the sixteenth century.

BOOK TWO:

Evermore Beloved: I Shall Never Let You Go

Here you walk through the amazing love story of Jacobus van Vrederic and his beloved wife Margriete van Wijck, where we get to meet Jacobus's beloved granddaughter, baby Rietje. Based during the witch trials and the Dutch Eighty Years' War in the sixteenth and seventeenth centuries.

BOOK THREE:

Be My Destiny: Vows From The Beyond

This book takes you through reincarnation and the blessed door of dreams. Here infinite twin flames Erasmus van Phillip, a twenty-first-century descendant of Jacobus van Vrederic and the reincarnated father of Jacobus van Vrederic, is reborn again to find and unite with his forever twin flame, Anadhi Newhouse, also the reincarnated mother of Jacobus van Vrederic. Find out how their son reunites them through the twenty-first century and takes them back to Kasteel Vrederic.

BOOK FOUR:

Heart Beats Your Name: Vows From The Beyond

Here you will get introduced to a blind son of the Kasteel Vrederic family, the nephew and adopted son of Erasmus van Phillip and Anadhi Newhouse van Phillip. In this paranormal thriller, you will see how Dr. Jacobus Vrederic van Phillip, the biological son of Erasmus and Anadhi, guides his brother to unite with his pronounced dead wife, while trying to solve her murder mystery. A paranormal book where everyone realizes family members are bound with one another throughout time.

BOOK FIVE:

Entranced Beloved: I Shall Never Let You Go

Twenty-first-century Dr. Jacobus Vrederic van Phillip must return to the seventeenth-century Kasteel Vrederic, as he realizes his beloved granddaughter is missing and must be rescued for the inhabitants of *Vows From The Beyond* to even exist. This can only be done through the miraculous hands of the famous twenty-first-century physician. So here we go, Dr. Jacobus must travel time and go back to the *I Shall Never Let You Go* diaries. Walk back and get reacquainted with the seventeenth-century Kasteel Vrederic family members with Dr. Jacobus as he meets his sixteenth-century self, Jacobus van Vrederic. Margriete "Rietje" Jacobus Peters and Sir Alexander van der Bijl's love story is written and retold by the twenty-first-century famous physician, Dr. Jacobus from the *Vows From The Beyond* diaries.

BOOK SIX:

Forbidden Daughter Of Kasteel Vrederic: Vows From The Beyond

Dr. Jacobus Vrederic van Phillip and Dr. Margriete van Achthoven through the door of reincarnation traveled time yet now must face the wagon of karma. The unborn child asks, "Why am I the forbidden daughter of Kasteel Vrederic?" With the answer, revolves the existence of the Kasteel Vrederic Lover's Lighthouse and the father of the lighthouse. Trying to find an answer to this question, Dr. Jacobus finds out his family is being terrorized by a murderer who hides within Kasteel Vrederic.

-Ann Marie Ruby

ABOUT THE AUTHOR

"Meet Ann Marie Ruby from San Francisco, California.
This is her story."

Ann Marie Ruby was born into a diplomatic family for which she had the privilege of traveling the world. This upbringing made the whole world her one family. She never saw a country as a foreign country yet as a neighbor who was there for her as she would be there for them. After all, isn't that what families do for one another?

Ann Marie became an author as she started to place her chosen words into the pages of her diaries. She knew she must collect all her thoughts and produce them into different diaries. Each diary became her different books.

Ann Marie's life goal is not to just write something but only what she believes in. So all her thoughts and words remained within the pages of her diaries until she realized it was time she must share them with you. Otherwise, she felt selfish and knew that was not her characteristic as she lives for everyone, not just for herself.

INTERNATIONAL #1 BESTSELLING AUTHOR:

Ann Marie became an international number-one bestselling author of nineteen books. Alongside being a full-time author, she loves to write articles on her website where she can have a better connection with all of you. Ann Marie, a dream psychic, became a blogger and a humanitarian only because she believes in you and herself as a complete, honest, and open family.

PERSONAL:

Ann Marie is an American who grew up in Brisbane, Australia. She resided in the Washington, D.C. area, later settled in Seattle, Washington, and currently lives in San Francisco, California. In her spare time when she is not writing books, she loves to meditate, pray, listen to music, cook, and write blog posts.

BESTSELLING:

Ann Marie's books have placed her on top 100 bestselling charts in various countries including the Netherlands, United States, United Kingdom, Canada, and Germany. In 2020, she became a household name as her books began to consistently rank #1 on multiple bestselling charts. *The Netherlands: Land Of My Dreams* and *Everblooming: Through The Twelve Provinces Of The Netherlands*, both became overnight number-one bestsellers in the United States.

In 2020, *The Netherlands: Land Of My Dreams* also became a bestseller in the Netherlands and Canada, consistently becoming #1 on various lists and one of the top selling books on Amazon NL. *Everblooming: Through The Twelve Provinces Of The Netherlands* became #37 on the Netherlands top 100 bestselling Amazon books chart which includes all books from all genres. Ann Marie's other books have also made various top 100 bestselling lists and received multiple accolades including *Eternal Truth: The Tunnel Of Light* which was named as one of eight thought-provoking books by women.

ROMANCE FICTION:

Ann Marie's *Kasteel Vrederic* series was written in a diary fashion. She has always kept a diary herself, so she thought her characters too could keep a diary. All of their diaries became individual books yet collectively, they are a part of a family, the Kasteel Vrederic family.

OTHER BOOKS:

All of Ann Marie's nonfiction and fiction books are available globally. You can take a look at short descriptions about the books at the end of this book.

THE NETHERLANDS:

Ann Marie revealed why many of her books revolve around the Netherlands, sharing that as a dream psychic, she had seen the historical past of a country in her dreams and was later able to place a name to the country. This is described in detail in *Spiritual Lighthouse: The Dream Diaries Of Ann Marie Ruby* and *The Netherlands: Land Of My Dreams* where she also wrote about her plans to eventually move to the Netherlands.

Ann Marie has received letters on behalf of His Majesty King Willem-Alexander and Her Majesty Queen Máxima of the Netherlands after they received her books *The Netherlands: Land Of My Dreams* and *Everblooming: Through The Twelve Provinces Of The Netherlands*. Additionally, Ann Marie has received letters on behalf of His Excellency Mark Rutte, the Prime Minister of the Netherlands for her books.

WRITING:

Ann Marie also is acclaimed globally as one of the top voices in the spiritual space, however, she is recognized for her writing abilities published across many genres namely spirituality, lifestyle, inspirational quotations, poetry, fiction, romance, history, travel, social awareness, and more. Her writing style is hailed by critics and readers alike as making readers feel as though they have made a friend.

FOLLOW THE AUTHOR:

Now as you have found her book, why don't you and Ann Marie become friends? Join her and become a part of her global family. Ann Marie shall always give you books which you will read and then find yourself as a part of her book family.

For more information about Ann Marie Ruby, any one of her books, or to read her blog posts and articles, subscribe to her website, www.annmarieruby.com.

Follow Ann Marie Ruby on Twitter, Facebook, Instagram, and Pinterest:

@TheAnnMarieRuby

BOOKS BY THE AUTHOR

INSPIRATIONAL QUOTATIONS SERIES:

This series includes four books of original quotations and one omnibus edition.

Spiritual Travelers: Life's Journey From The Past To The Present For The Future

Spiritual Messages: From A Bottle

Spiritual Journey: Life's Eternal Blessings

Spiritual Inspirations: Sacred Words Of Wisdom

Omnibus edition contains all four books of original quotations.

Spiritual Ark: The Enchanted Journey Of Timeless Quotations

SPIRITUAL SONGS SERIES:

This series includes two original spiritual prayer books.

SPIRITUAL SONGS: LETTERS FROM MY CHEST

When there was no hope, I found hope within these sacred words of prayers, I but call songs. Within this book, I have for you, 100 very sacred prayers.

SPIRITUAL SONGS II: BLESSINGS FROM A SACRED SOUL

Prayers are but the sacred doors to an individual's enlightenment. This book has 123 prayers for all humans with humanity.

SPIRITUAL LIGHTHOUSE: THE DREAM DIARIES OF ANN MARIE RUBY

Do you believe in dreams? For within each individual dream, there is a hidden message and a miracle interlinked. Learn the spiritual, scientific, religious, and philosophical aspects of dreams. Walk with me as you travel through forty nights, through the pages of my book.

THE WORLD HATE CRISIS: THROUGH THE EYES OF A DREAM PSYCHIC

Humans have walked into an age where humanity now is being questioned as hate crimes have reached a catastrophic amount. Let us in union stop this crisis. Pick up my book and see if you too could join me in this fight.

ETERNAL TRUTH: THE TUNNEL OF LIGHT

Within this book, travel with me through the doors of birth, death, reincarnation, true soulmates and twin flames, dreams, miracles, and the end of time.

THE NETHERLANDS: LAND OF MY DREAMS

Oh the sacred travelers, be like the mystical river and journey through this blessed land through my book. Be the flying bird of wisdom and learn about a land I call, Heaven on Earth.

EVERBLOOMING: THROUGH THE TWELVE PROVINCES OF THE NETHERLANDS

Original poetry and hand-picked tales are bound together in this keepsake book. Come travel with me as I take you through the lives of the Dutch past.

LOVE LETTERS: THE TIMELESS TREASURE

Fifty original timeless treasured love poems are presented with individual illustrations describing each poem.

KASTEEL VREDERIC **SERIES:**

ETERNALLY BELOVED: I SHALL NEVER LET YOU GO

Travel time to the sixteenth century where Jacobus van Vrederic, a beloved lover and father, surmounts time and tide to find the vanished love of his life. On his pursuit, Jacobus discovers secrets that will alter his life evermore. He travels through the Eighty Years' War-ravaged country, the Netherlands as he takes the vow, even if separated by a breath, "Eternally beloved, I shall never let you go."

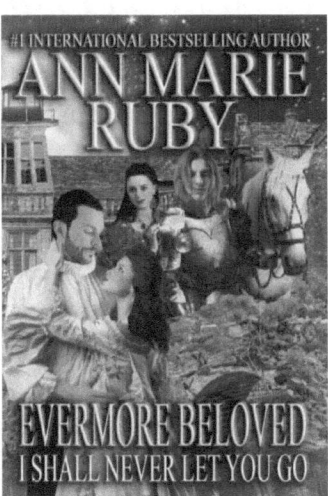

EVERMORE BELOVED: I SHALL NEVER LET YOU GO

Jacobus van Vrederic returns with the devoted spirits of Kasteel Vrederic. A knight and a seer also join him on a quest to find his lost evermore beloved. They journey through a war-ravaged country, the Netherlands, to stop another war which was brewing silently in his land, called the witch hunts. Time was his enemy as he must defeat time and tide to find his evermore beloved wife alive.

BE MY DESTINY: VOWS FROM THE BEYOND

Fighting their biggest enemy destiny, twin flames Erasmus van Phillip and Anadhi Newhouse are reborn over and over again only to lose the battle to destiny. Find out if through the helping hands of sacred spirits of the sixteenth century, these eternal twin flames are finally able to unite in the twenty-first century, as they say, "Reincarnation is a blessing if only you are mine."

HEART BEATS YOUR NAME: VOWS FROM THE BEYOND

While one is sleepless, the other twin flame is sleeping eternally. Now how does Antonius van Phillip awaken his twin flame Katelijne Snaaijer from beyond Earth, and solve a murder mystery, she is the only witness to yet also a victim of? Find out how the musical sound of heartbeats guide him to his sleeping beloved while he solves the mystery sleepless.

ENTRANCED BELOVED: I SHALL NEVER LET YOU GO

The pages of Margriete "Rietje" Jacobus Peters's love story from her diary slowly go missing from the library of Kasteel Vrederic. The twenty-first-century descendants fighting death and time must travel back in time to save their ancestors and their beloved Kasteel Vrederic. Traveling through the tunnel of light, the family of the twenty-first century must save the seventeenth-century twin flames. Rietje and her beloved twin flame Sir Alexander van der Bijl must create another paranormal, magical, historical, romantic diary for the dynasty to even exist.

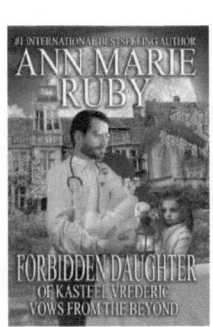

FORBIDDEN DAUGHTER OF KASTEEL VREDERIC: VOWS FROM THE BEYOND

Jacobus Vrederic van Phillip stopped pouring tears and burning himself with memories of passion to become a stone, so he could live with memories and not recreate new ones. The Vrederic family members realize the curse of past life's karma will come and meet them in this life and erase the only child who kept the dynasty going, the child known to all as the forbidden daughter of Kasteel Vrederic. The man who has sacrificed his life for all members of his family and society now must find a way to awaken his sleeping soul, recognize his twin flame, and bring back as the beloved daughter the only child he had rejected. To this world she was known as the forbidden daughter of Kasteel Vrederic.

Coming Soon

THE IMMORTALITY SERUM: VOWS FROM THE BEYOND

THE IMMORTALITY SERUM: VOWS FROM THE BEYOND

The seventh book in this series is coming soon.

Coming Soon

ENCHANTED TALES: A KASTEEL VREDERIC STORYBOOK FOR CHILDREN

ENCHANTED TALES: A KASTEEL VREDERIC STORYBOOK FOR CHILDREN

Kasteel Vrederic's storybook is coming soon.